"BEWARE, AESOP," SNARLED THE SPHINX.

The gladiator spit into the sand, then raised his sword and pointed it at the creature. "Woe be it to you, wretched crow, if you trouble us again!"

"Please, Pelaphus!" I squeaked.

The sphinx smiled playfully, but her eyes glowed with evil madness. The wondrous wings unfurled and beat the wind with such force that the sand streaked our faces and our hair blew straight back. With a few powerful strokes she achieved considerable height and flapped away to the south.

We could see a group of slaves cowering in the distance. The sphinx bore down on them with terrifying swiftness, and the slaves broke into a run. She snatched the fattest one, a simple-minded Judean, and carted him off to devour him, gnawing and tearing at the quivering pieces of flesh

The
FABULIST

JOHN
VORNHOLT

AVON BOOKS • NEW YORK

THE FABULIST is an original publication of Avon Books. This work has never before appeared in book form. This work is a novel. Any similarity to actual persons or events is purely coincidental.

AVON BOOKS
A division of
The Hearst Corporation
1350 Avenue of the Americas
New York, New York 10019

Copyright © 1993 by John Vornholt
Cover illustration by Daniel Horne
Published by arrangement with the author
Library of Congress Catalog Card Number: 93-90333
ISBN: 0-380-77320-1

First AvoNova Printing: October 1993

AVONOVA TRADEMARK REG. U.S. PAT. OFF. AND IN OTHER COUNTRIES, MARCA REGISTRADA, HECHO EN U.S.A.

Printed in the U.S.A.

RA 10 9 8 7 6 5 4 3 2 1

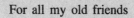

For all my old friends

CONTENTS

FOREWORD

For the past twenty-five hundred years, I've had to watch helplessly as my name has come to signify a harmless old fellow who tells cute fables to children. I myself never felt the need to tack simpering morals onto my fables, and the majority of them were definitely *not* intended for children. The fables haven't really changed much in all these years, and for that I'm grateful; but the time has come to set the record straight about my life, my fables, and the context in which they were created. Don't bother to investigate how this autobiography came to be written. Suffice it to say, I still have friends among the gods.

Given the circumstances of my birth, you'd never have expected I would achieve *anything,* let alone immortality. My mother and father wouldn't even tell me who they were! Of course, that's not unusual in slave families, where parentage is mainly a result of close sleeping quarters. No one rushed to claim a dark-skinned child who was obviously a dwarf mute.

The ancient histories assign the year of my birth to about 600 B.C., and I know of nothing to refute them. I know I was born in Phrygia (which is now a part of Turkey), because nobody would've paid good money to bring me there. The historian Babrius described me as being "pot-bellied, misshapen of head, snub-nosed, swarthy, dwarfish, bandy-legged, short-armed, squint-eyed, liver-lipped—a portentous monstrosity." Well, he clearly exaggerated. My head was not misshapen, it was perfectly fine! But the fact of the matter was, I was not a pretty baby.

Being born mute was the worst indignity. I had to learn to express myself by other means. If I hadn't learned at an early age to dance and clown and make people laugh, I probably wouldn't have been fed. I wasn't much good at picking figs and olives, and that was the only trade I knew before becoming a famous orator. I could've run away from my masters countless times, but I never saw anything in Phrygia which warranted undertaking such drastic action. Not that I didn't thirst after freedom, *I did,* but most freemen I saw fared little better than I. Poverty is just slavery by another name. Besides, how many paying jobs were there for an illiterate dwarf mute?

Few of you living today in the latter part of the twentieth century can have any idea what life was like in 600 B.C. Greece and Asia Minor. Monsters and ghosts ruled both the known and unknown world. Supernatural was natural! It was a *scary* place! Humankind had not totally subdued nature in those days, as they have now. The forces of the earth and the stars took on all sorts of manifestations that no one would think possible today. The ancient gods were meddlesome, vengeful, fickle, and just plain eccentric. They managed to surprise us all the time, and we were ready for them!

Of course, all this divine interference didn't keep men and women from behaving just as greedily, lustfully, and disreputably as they do today. In fact, the human animal has changed very little in the past three thousand years. Nominally, humans are in charge now. About all that means is that the gods support human beliefs instead of challenging them, as they did in my day.

Given the peculiarities of the gods, I don't think you'll find this account hard to believe at all.

CHAPTER 1

The Gods Have
a Sense of Humor

I had never met a god personally until that fateful day in the summer of 565 B.C. The gods were smart to avoid me, because I'm sure I would've done nothing but complain about being a slave, a mute, a dwarf, and so on. As it was, my meeting with the goddess was not entirely by chance.

Agathopous and I had been told to check the northern grove of olive trees, which meant walking half-the-day over thistle-strewn hills, where nothing dwelt but weeds and insects. Normally, I would have enjoyed such an all-day assignment, far from the house and the master and the inevitable beatings. But I found the company of Agathopous to be insufferable. Nothing is worse than a boastful slave.

"I tell you, Aesop," he said, swatting a gnat from his narrow brow, "I was born for greater things. It's not enough to be the most valuable slave in Phrygia. By rights, I should be your master!"

I looked at him, trying to appear interested. In reality, I was remembering the many times when Agathopous had blamed me for something he had done, like just the other night when he ate the master's figs and placed the blame on me. Unable to defend myself vocally, I shoved my finger down my throat and vomited up my meager dinner of cracked barley, then I motioned to Agathopous to do the same. For once, he got the beating instead of me.

And now I had to listen to this infernal idiot's bragging. "Did you see that new slave, the fair Hittite?" he smirked.

How could I have missed her? She arrived buck naked except for a leather thong about her neck. The master had promptly taken her into the house. I nodded and made an appreciative grunting sound.

"She will be mine before the week is over!" he announced.

Sure, I thought, and I will become a famous orator before the week is over. Perhaps Zeus or Apollo heard that remark and, being in a particularly humorous mood, caused the lovely priestess of Isis to daydream at that moment and wander off the path.

Agathopous cooperated too. He spotted a cluster of palms, yawned, and stretched his arms imperiously. "Proceed on to the grove, Aesop. I will check this cluster of palms for dates."

We both knew there were no dates in these palm trees, but they did create an inviting bed of shade and soft grass. I salaamed and trotted ahead, glad to be rid of Agathopous.

Soon, I was skipping along, practicing silly dance steps to amuse the master and maybe the fair Hittite slave. I was also thinking about what to have for lunch. In my pack were a chunk of bread, a sack of cured olives, and a full wineskin. But I didn't think that would be enough. I hated to eat uncured olives off the tree, but I knew of a patch of wild asparagus just east of the olive grove. I headed straight there, thinking how well the asparagus would complement my lunch.

At first, I thought she was a crane or some other great white bird caught in a hunter's snare. I left the path and picked my way cautiously down the rock-strewn hillside, squinting into the noonday sun. I was soon shocked to see that what I thought were huge flapping wings were in reality arms clad in flowing white sleeves. When I heard her weakened cry, I really began to hurry, so much so that I tripped over a vine, tumbled the rest of the way, and landed in a heap at her feet.

"Dear me!" she shrieked. She tried to back up, but her delicate white gown was snarled in a tangle of thickets. She succeeded in doing nothing more than showing me the delicious curve of her bare thighs.

The sun glinted so brightly off the gown that I had to shield my eyes. In thirty-odd years of life, I had never seen anyone clad so glamorously, like something divine. That's exactly what she looked like, a goddess! Her youthful face was framed by golden curls, her eyes gleamed with purity and light, and her lips cooed each lilting syllable. Before I knew it, I was genuflecting, bowing, crossing myself, and doing whatever else I could think of to keep her from striking me down dead.

"Please, please," she begged. "I mean you no harm. I am Demma, priestess of Isis." She fluttered her eyelids beseechingly.

I've always pictured myself as gallant, though I've never had much call to prove it. I stood up and bowed graciously, pointing to my mouth and shaking my head.

"You are mute!" she said incredulously. "But you do understand me, is that correct?"

I nodded and did a cartwheel for her.

The priestess Demma laughed, and I knew I had won her over. "I am so terribly lost, and now this ..." She pointed to her entangled gown.

I crawled forward and touched the hem of her dress. She gasped and recoiled slightly, but I forgave her. After all, I wasn't the most handsome of saviors. Carefully, I disengaged each thorn and thistle from the luxurious gown. Even touching such fine cloth was a treat; I tried not to imagine what was underneath it.

"I was on my way to Hattusa," she remarked, watching me, "where the goddess Isis is held in great esteem. Egyptian and Greek gods are both revered in this land, are they not?"

I nodded. My master worshiped Assyrian gods, but I didn't want to tell her that.

"I don't know what I was thinking," the priestess sighed, "but all of a sudden, I was off the road, wandering among these thistles. Must be the sun, wouldn't you say?"

I freed the final thorn and bowed obediently.

"I see you have a pack there," she smiled. "There wouldn't be any food in it, would there be?"

I had the wineskin out immediately. In my experience, priestesses all love wine. She liked my olives and my bread, too. But it was worth it. We sat by a small stream in the shade of the olive trees, and I watched this heavenly creature eat my food. I was beginning to think she might pass the entire day with me, but she stood and stretched her arms wearily. "I must continue on, my friend, if you will only point the way to the road."

Point the way? I *danced* the way, swooping and bobbing about, portraying every nearby hill and rock in my inspired dance. Demma laughed and applauded several times, much to my gratification. I mimed unspoken instructions, and she seemed to understand every one.

"My lovely friend," she beamed, "you are truly blessed with the power of communication, though you cannot speak. I am forever in your debt. Now why don't you lie down and take a short nap? You must be exhausted after such a strenuous explanation."

She was right. Immediately, I curled up in a ball and listened to the sweet gurgling of the stream, the humming of the cicadas, and the song of the blackbirds in the trees. I was asleep yet still hearing. Had I known then what I know now, I would have suspected the doings of the gods.

The girl's voice took on a deeper, more colorful timbre. "Oh, dearest Isis, crown of the world, she of many names, have pity on this poor slave who suffers so. Repay him for the great kindness he has shown me, your humble servant. He is in desperate need of talents, good looks, and natural charm, but he is in the greatest need of a voice. Oh, Isis, ruler of light, I pray thee, show favor to this poor wretch."

The cries and sounds of the olive grove multiplied in harmony, as if the nymph Echo had supplied her imitative voice to the chorus. Though asleep, I could see Apollo's finger reach down from the sun in swirling golden lights. On this sunlit avenue, the chariot of Isis bore down from the sky, the radiant goddess at the reins. Beside her, nine more beautiful goddesses materialized one after another, like the columns of a rainbow. They gathered around my immobile body, and I was helpless to do or say anything.

"He isn't very pretty," remarked a goddess in a flowing blue robe. She bent over me and poked me with a scroll.

"I wish to thank the nine Muses for coming," said Demma, "but we're not rewarding this man because of his beauty."

"Demma is correct," Isis agreed, her voice thundering and very godlike. "He may be ill-favored in appearance, but he rises above all others in piety. Because of the kindness he offered my servant, I grant to Aesop a voice and bestow upon that voice most excellent speech!"

Calliope, the muse of epic poetry, sniffed with disdain. "A voice won't do him much good if he has nothing to say. I bestow upon Aesop the gift of storytelling."

"A voice which only speaks is boring," said Euterpe, brandishing her flute. "As the muse of music, I grant Aesop the ability to sing like a harp!"

Thalia, muse of comedy, frowned. "I grant him the talent to make others laugh."

A muse clad in red swirled her cape over my head. "As Terpsichore, muse of the dance, I increase his athletic prowess!"

"He will go down in history and be remembered always!" proclaimed Clio, muse of history.

Melpomene, muse of tragedy, shook her head and clicked her tongue. "I grant him the ability to see through men into the darkest part of their souls."

Erato, muse of love, smiled. "I give Aesop the power to see into the souls of women and know what pleasures them."

"Let him read the stars as he would a book!" proclaimed Urania, muse of astronomy.

Isis, the Muses, and the priestess Demma all turned to face the solemn Polyhymnia, muse of sacred hymns. She shrugged. "What is left for me to grant Aesop? I could, of course, make him the most handsome man on earth."

"By Ra, don't do *that!*" screeched Isis. "With his talents, we would all then fall hopelessly in love with him! His loathsome appearance will be his greatest asset, allowing all men and women to love and accept him, despite his great gifts."

"Then I grant him the gift of reason," said Polyhymnia. "In all times and places, Aesop will act logically and cause others to think."

A low grumble of thunder punctuated her pronouncement and stilled the chirping of the birds.

"That would be our master, Apollo," whispered the muse Terpsichore, bowing with both reverence and fright. "Aesop, your true fate lies in his hands."

"I hope we made him smart enough to realize that," Isis remarked. She extended her hand to Demma. "I have to get back to Mount Helicon. Come, daughter, and I'll drop you off along the way."

Effortlessly, Isis lifted her servant into the golden chariot and reined the four translucent stallions, who snorted, reared up, and stamped the ground. Their mighty hooves thundered with all the sound of a summer storm, and the sky blurred with a sparkling drizzle of sun-kissed rain. I stirred and blinked, trying to open my eyes, but the drug of dreaming still imprisoned them. When I awoke, the divine apparitions were gone, if they were ever there, and warm chunks of rain were striking my cheeks.

I stretched my arms, enjoying the refreshing rain. I knew it would end in an instant, because the sun was still blazing over my head. "What an odd dream," I remarked to myself. I immediately whirled around, having just heard a voice I had never heard before. But no one was there, not even the beautiful priestess. I leaped to my feet, calling, "Priestess! Priestess! Where are you?"

The mysterious voice pounded in my ears, echoing back my very thoughts. I thought it must be sorcery! Where did that mellifluous sound come from? The voice of a god perhaps? I whirled around so many times, I began to get dizzy, and I screamed at the top of my newfound larynx as I stumbled and fell. In that patch of thistles I sat, cursing and laughing at the same time. "I can *speak!*" I shrieked.

I did a somersault, landed on my feet, and proclaimed: "By the Muses, blessed Isis, Apollo, and all the beautiful gods on Mount Helicon, the *dream is true!* I can speak! Oh, thank you, thank you, thank you!"

I kissed the ground and ran splashing through the stream, howling and laughing and babbling. Even babbling felt wonderful! I wanted to gather a crowd at once, tell a few jokes, sing a couple of songs, and hold them enthralled with my oratorical skills. But there was no one present except a few gnats and dragonflies. I drew the little buggers around me.

"Listen, you lowliest of creatures, you have the immense privilege of being the *first* to hear Aesop speak! Before, I was like the gnat who landed on a bull's horn. After sitting there all day, the gnat decided to leave and asked the bull's permission. The bull said, 'Why, I had no idea you were even there, and I certainly won't notice if you leave.'

"I will no longer be an insignificant speck in the world. From now on, I am *Aesop!* I don't know what that means exactly, but I do know one thing: I'm not going to keep my mouth shut!"

Still chatting with the gnats, I skipped back along the path toward the palm grove where I had left my associate, Agathopous. I had so much to tell Agathopous! For one thing, I was ready to escape the bonds of slavery this very afternoon and journey to parts unknown, maybe even Greece itself. I felt certain I could talk Agathopous and myself into reasonable employment. Of course, Agathopous didn't have much imagination, so I would have to couch this potentially dangerous plan in terms he wouldn't fully understand.

The problem brought to mind a story, which I relayed to the gnats, about a dying farmer who wanted to teach his lazy sons how to farm. "Boys," he told them, "a treasure is buried in one of my fields." After he died, the sons took plow and spade and dug up the whole farm. They never found any treasure, but they were rewarded with greatly improved crops.

My plan had to be postponed when I saw Zenas and Agathopous headed my way. Zenas was the overseer, a barrel-chested freeman who liked nothing more than to beat lazy slaves who were caught sleeping under palm trees. I could tell from Agathopous's downcast shoulders and Zenas's swagger that he had administered a stern lesson to my fellow slave. I fought the impulse to cry out and proceeded to lumber toward them.

"Aesop!" grumbled Zenas, "I suppose you've been sleeping too. I warn you, if those olive trees aren't pruned, I'll prune your backside with a cactus spine!"

I replied, "A rooster stood on a rooftop and made nasty threats to a wolf who happened to be passing below. The wolf said to him, 'It is not you who are making those remarks, it is only your position.' "

Zenas blinked at me and made a good imitation of a fish. Agathopous threw himself on the ground and beseeched the protection of Baal and whatever other gods he could think of.

"Get up, Agathopous," I said, "before you injure yourself."

"It is *I* who give the orders!" Zenas sputtered. "And you . . . *you* shouldn't be speaking!"

"I shouldn't be a slave either, but there you are."

"And you called me a rooster!" Zenas cried. The overseer scuffled off, tripping over his own pudgy feet. "The master will hear of this impertinence!"

A new idea began brewing in my brain. Why should I escape and become a hunted slave, roaming around the wilderness, lions and griffins chasing after me? The best way to see the world is to have others pay for it.

I clapped my hands and exclaimed, "Look at the possibilities!"

Agathopous shook his finger at me. "Aesop, you're bewitched! A spell has overtaken you! *The gods are angry!*"

"Nonsense," I replied. "The gods have a sense of humor."

The master was a stern man, a big man, and not a very bright man. To his credit, he never tried to do very much, being content to let a motley mixture of slaves and freemen tend his vast estates. As far as we could tell, his lands extended just about as far as a person could walk in a day, because we never saw any neighbors. We were *it* as far as the local population went. The master was also gone a lot in conjunction with various honorary political posts, and we never saw all that much of him. I, least of all, because I was kept dirty and unwashed and not allowed in the house as a general rule.

Tonight was an exception. The master condescended to see me right after dinner. Whenever I entered his house, I was always amazed at the small size of it. With porticoes, columns, and balconies galore, all in the most garish Greek tradition, the place looked like a sumptuous palace from the outside. Inside, it was a regular Assyrian house with baked clay walls and dusty throw rugs. Zenas himself marched me in and deposited me before the master's dinner table.

The master, who had never cared much for my appearance, grimaced slightly as he pushed his plate aside. With a linen napkin, he carefully massaged his lips. "So, Aesop, Zenas tells me you have started talking. What is this about?"

I shrugged. "Nothing special, sir. I have decided to speak my mind, nothing more."

"And speak his mind, he does!" snapped Zenas. "He called me a *rooster!*"

The master nodded sagely. "I salute your newfound interest in speaking, Aesop, but you have to remember your position in life. You are a slave and a very ugly one besides."

"Sir," I replied, pacing importantly. "I likewise have an observation to make. You are a poor excuse for a master, and the slaves have no respect for you."

"What!" he roared. Zenas started toward me with the whip, but the master held his hand out to stop him. "You are wrong, Aesop, my slaves love and revere me!"

I put a finger into the air and paused for dramatic effect. "A sculptor's slave once loaded a statue onto the back of an ass to take it into town. As the statue was that of a famous king, many people bowed along the way. After several miles, the ass began to think that the people were bowing to him, and he stopped and would go no farther. The driver thumped him with his stick and scowled, 'You really are a fool if you think people would bow to an ass like you.'"

Zenas laughed out loud, and the master glared at him.

"Shall I beat him now?" Zenas gulped.

"What good would it do?" shrugged the master. "He was never a very good field hand, but he was amusing in a pathetic way. Now he's simply insolent. Take him to the market and sell him for whatever you can get." The master narrowed his eyes at me. "You'd best speak civilly while you're on the block, Aesop, or you'll get that beating after all."

"I intend to," I smiled.

But speaking civilly was not really one of my talents. When you don't have a chance to speak at all for over thirty years, speaking civilly is not a high priority. I tried. Zenas took me to a village called Faba, which was really nothing more than a crossroads between two trade routes, one headed south to Arabia and the other headed west to the Aegean Sea. Across the Aegean Sea lay Greece.

This plan was working well as far as I was concerned. Already I was seeing more of the world than I'd ever seen in my life. Even the tattered tarps and tents of Faba were exotic, a labyrinth of shadowy alleys which could change in a moment with the shifting of a few poles. I could see that Zenas was edgy, but I couldn't understand what a freeman had to be edgy about. We sat on a rickety wooden platform in what may well have been the center of the town. I didn't know, because I was lost.

"Slave . . . slave for sale," Zenas cried weakly to an occasional passerby.

"Slave for sale!" I crowed.

Zenas rapped me in the stomach and hissed, "Be quiet, Aesop! They'll believe *you* to be the seller and me the *slave!*"

"Oh!" I said. "Are slave-traders that unscrupulous?"

"I plan on taking no chances," the overseer whispered.

I assumed, at this point, that we would sit on this wooden block until we starved to death. Then a brutish Ammorite who made *me* look quite handsome stepped directly in front of us. He put his hands on his cloak, revealing a curved Turkish sword about four feet in length. Specks of blood coated the entire length of the blade.

"Which one of you is the slave?" he snarled.

"He is!" Zenas and I both announced.

Zenas smacked me across the head and held up my arm, rattling my bronze slave bracelet, which by now had turned a deep hue of green. "Here is the slave, sir! A fine specimen he is, and priced to sell!"

The Ammorite grabbed my chin and yanked my head around. "A fine specimen he *isn't,* and I'll decide about the price. What is it?"

Zenas sighed, "What will you pay?"

"I will pay sixty shekels!" a voice behind us announced.

We all turned around to see a quite chubby man with the simple robes and demeanor of a priest. He smiled benevolently, but his hand rested on the hilt of a double-edged broadsword, which looked as if it would need two men to carry it. He strode across the wooden platform, shaking a bag of gold. "Have we a deal?"

Zenas glanced at the Ammorite, as did I. The ugly man's hand slipped around the hilt of his long crescent blade. "I need this slave, stranger, and I don't wish to bid or barter."

"Neither do I," said the chubby man. "So what is your answer? Is that price enough?"

"Certainly!" I answered. "More than fair!"

Zenas shoved me halfheartedly, but he was already edging away. I stepped up on the platform. "Dear People of Faba, is sixty shekels not enough for a slave of my appearance? I submit that no one would pay more! Therefore, I declare myself sold to this friendly traveler . . ."

The friendly traveler had drawn his huge blade in response to what I saw were six Ammorites surrounding our tiny podium. My new owner sidled up to me, grabbed me by the collar, and hissed, "Can you handle a blade?"

"I can wrestle," I replied.

"If I part one from his blade, you take him. I am Pelaphus, by the way."

"Enchanted," I gulped. "I am Aesop."

The Ammorite leader drew his sword with a snap,

screamed like a wounded camel, and charged. The others swarmed at his side, whooping like an enraged flock of sea gulls. Instantly, Pelaphus brought the great sword swooping through the air, taking the Ammorite's head clean away at the shoulders and knocking another one's sword high into the air. Of the two, the head traveled much the farther, hitting a fat Arab woman in the groin. She and other casual viewers screamed with terror and delight, and the fight really commenced.

Pelaphus leaped from the platform and landed in a crouch. Then he did the most remarkable thing I had ever seen. Advancing crablike, he proceeded to slash at the legs of the attacking Ammorites. Their blows fell harmlessly into the air, while his severed legs at the knees with practiced precision. One by one, the hapless Ammorites dropped, screaming and clutching their missing appendages. Many of them would live, I thought to myself, but they would crawl instead of walk. I noticed one shrinking back, the one without a sword, and I leaped. I landed on his back, and we tumbled to the dust. I had never attacked another human being, but how good it felt! Best of all, I was acting on orders from my master!

The Ammorite and I struggled, but his interest was more in escaping than fighting. I held him as long as I could, but abject fear made him fairly strong. As soon as he got to his feet, Pelaphus took his head off with one slash. I rolled away to avoid the falling body, and Pelaphus picked me up.

"Well done!" he said. "You appear to be able-bodied." He turned to the amazed throng. "Listen! I am buying able-bodied male slaves all day today at the price of sixty shekels per. Bring them to this spot!"

Then Pelaphus motioned sadly to the fallen and groaning Ammorites. "And tend to these men. I will pay all expenses."

Zenas crept forward with his hand held out, and Pelaphus deposited a stack of coins in the shuddering palm. Without even counting, the overseer dashed away, and Pelaphus laughed. "Aesop," he said to me, "you are the first slave I have ever owned. What exactly am I to do?"

"Make me the overseer," I smiled.

CHAPTER 2

The World is Full of Monsters

I hope someday that someone *does* invent a time machine, so we can see that every bizarre thing from another era isn't just mythology. In 600 B.C., if I had told people that someday humans would fly around the globe and carry the sound from hordes of musicians in their shirt pockets, they would have mumbled and crossed themselves. Only gods do that, they would have said. Similarly, if I say to a modern man that I was almost eaten by a sphinx, he would think I had overindulged in pharmaceuticals.

I don't know why. Both are plausible, considering the forces in effect at the time. I don't know where transistor radios come from, nor do I know where sphinxes come from, but they are both all too frequent in their respective time periods.

Pelaphus made me into his overseer, but he gave me few responsibilities. This wasn't because the jolly swordsman had no faith in my abilities; he was simply so full of energy and cooperative spirit that he insisted upon doing everything himself. For example, I could have easily overseen the buying of the slaves for the caravan. For sixty shekels apiece, we were buying able-bodied male slaves who could walk and carry a pack. Nothing too complicated about that. We didn't receive many specimens who were worth much more than sixty shekels, and we turned away all the enterprising fathers who tried to foist their daughters upon us. So the buying of the slaves went smoothly until we had twenty or so.

The evening before our departure from Faba, Pelaphus took me into his confidence. "Aesop," he said, pulling me aside. "You're probably wondering why we're buying slaves instead of pack animals."

"They eat less?" I asked.

"Good point," Pelaphus nodded, "but that's not it. I have a cargo of precious dye, indigo from Persia, and it must arrive in the port of Ephesus by the next moon. The dye is like wine; it cannot stand much tossing about. Men travel smoother than camels, and I don't need a herd of foul-tempered camels spitting in my face."

I winked knowingly. "Also, a large party of men, even slaves, will be more likely to scare off bandits than a party of two. You could, however, be risking the fate of the hen and the snake's eggs."

Pelaphus blinked with confusion. "Hen and snake's eggs?"

"Yes," I shrugged. "A hen once took in some snake's eggs, thinking they looked as harmless as her own, and she kept them warm and hatched them. Of course, as soon as they were big enough, they ate her and her brood."

Pelaphus nodded sagely. "Yes, I see what you mean. Twenty slaves on the open desert does entail some risk. But able-bodied slaves happen to fetch high prices at Ephesus, or so I've heard."

I shuddered, both with delight and fear. To me, the existence of the world's great oceans had been little more than rumor. The most water I had ever seen at one time was a heavy rainfall, and that was rare enough in Phrygia. However, much as I longed to acquaint myself with the sea, the prospect of being sold into service as a galley slave sent shivers through my spinal cord. The life expectancy of a galley slave was approximately six months.

"I am so grateful, Pelaphus," I gushed, "I would be happy to remain in your service forever!"

"Nonsense," scoffed Pelaphus. "You're worried about being sold as an oarsman to a slave galley, and you would much prefer to be a freeman than to be in my service or anyone else's."

A *freeman*, I thought in awe. What must that be like, to be as free as Pelaphus, as free as a hawk, free to roam the face of the earth like a cloud roams the sky? I couldn't imagine such freedom, but I knew I would strive all the rest of my life to get it. After all, a few short days before, I couldn't have imagined being able to speak. If my voice and mind could be freed, maybe the gods would see fit to do the same for my miserable earthly shell.

"What must a slave do to achieve freedom?" I asked Pelaphus.

The chubby warrior scratched the middle of his three chins. "I achieved it by learning to kill other men."

"*You* were a slave?" I gasped.

"A soldier first," said Pelaphus. "I was captured in battle, then enslaved by the Assyrians. They were impressed when I strangled two of their torturers with their own leather thongs. I was sent into gladiator training and have since earned my living by administering death. The dye we carry is payment for squashing a rebellion. If you think freemen are truly free, then I pity you, Aesop."

"I would like to try it and develop my own opinion," I replied.

The big man laughed. "I hope you'll have a chance one day. In the meantime, if you'll help me see my cargo safely to Ephesus, I will promise not to sell you into the bowels of a galley."

"Agreed!" I said, extending my hand. In true gladiator fashion, Pelaphus gripped my forearm and held it like the hilt of a sword, until I returned the grip with all my strength.

That night, I dreamed of freedom.

* * *

I didn't care for the idea of roping the slaves together by their slave collars and bracelets, but we had a caravan to keep intact. At least half the slaves looked as if they would run away at the first opportunity, and the other half looked like they would kill us and then run away. As the overseer, I identified more with Pelaphus than with my fellow slaves, but, wanting to set a good example, I had Pelaphus tie me up along with the rest of them. Having been a slave all my life, I was very familiar with the habits of slaves. One thing slaves don't like is to have another slave bossing over them. A freeman they can do nothing about; a slave they can beat and kick at the earliest opportunity.

Pelaphus outfitted us royally, as far as I could tell, though I had no idea what were the length and hazards of our journey. I was merely babbling over with excitement to be going anywhere. My only fear was the horrible galley ships anchored in the port of Ephesus. True, I had Pelaphus's word that he would not sell me as a galley slave, but that word was hardly a public document; and Pelaphus had to survive the journey to make it stick.

The luggage included everything from jars of the precious dye to a locked chest, reed mats, mysterious equipment, and baskets and jars full of food. My first thought when I saw all of it was that Pelaphus had bought everything for sale in Faba. I wasn't too far wrong.

"Aesop!" proclaimed Pelaphus on the morning of our departure. "You, as premier slave, have the choice of the lightest pack. Please take your pick."

I glanced around the stocks, spread across a canvas tarp, which would also have to be rolled up and carried. A jar of dye would undoubtedly be the lightest duty and would carry with it special treatment and prestige. I glanced at Pelaphus, and his smile told me that he approved of my taking a jar of the deep purple dye. On the other hand, another slave's misplaced foot might cause a disastrous fall, resulting in any number of severe beatings. I strolled over to the largest pack of all, a giant basket containing all the bread for the trip, which must have been sixty loaves.

"How about this?" I asked, indicating the bread basket.

Pelaphus roared with laughter and was soon joined by several of my fellow slaves. "You can't be serious?" he gaped. "I was going to assign three or four men to carry that basket!"

"I'll carry it alone," I said.

"What a complete fool!" crowed a skinny Ethiopian. "And he claims to be the wisest of all of us!"

"He claimed to me he would carry the lightest load!" another guffawed.

Pelaphus looked pained and concerned for my sanity. "Reconsider, Aesop," he begged. "I can have any two or three of these beggars carry it."

"I'll not be deterred!" I said. "Please have someone lift it upon my shoulders."

"I know!" screamed one simpleton. "He's worried about not getting enough to eat! He has designs on that bread!"

Now everyone, including Pelaphus, broke into laughter. He pointed to a knot of five or six slaves. "If Aesop insists upon being stubborn, help him up with the basket."

I was surrounded by happily chattering slaves, and I marveled at the fact that everyone, even a slave, enjoys the beginning of a trip. When they lowered the weight of the basket upon my back, my knees buckled, and I staggered several feet before I was caught by another cadre of slaves. It took practically all twenty of them to right me and send me lumbering in a generally western direction. Every slave was laughing as he picked up a pack, which must have made Pelaphus happy. I didn't mind being the object of their derision. What they didn't realize was that with each loaf eaten, the basket would become progressively lighter. I reached up, grabbed a loaf myself, and began the process of lightening my load.

* * *

The desert was alternately as searing as a Turkish rotisserie and as freezing as the grip of Hades, god of the Underworld. About eight days into our journey, deep into a wilderness of unrelenting thistles, I had reason to think I might soon be meeting Hades in his kingdom of the dead.

We were staggering along a dry riverbed in the Phrygian lowlands. The cracked earth made for slightly better footing and easier headway than the parched grassland. I don't know what time of day it was, but the sun was at a raging broil in the sky. The sky was as drained and lifeless as the land under it, bone white with no clouds and hardly a speck of color. The whole landscape was as sparse and bleak as a clean table without food.

I first saw the thing as a black speck off in the sky, and I thought it was a bird, probably a vulture. If we hadn't been carting so much food and drink, I would've been afraid. As it was, I was sure our hardy band of twenty-two men could fend off any number of vultures. But then I noticed that this flying thing was several miles away, which made it very large. And it was obviously coming toward us, its broad wings flapping with effortless grace, every movement slow and deliberate. The thing seemed suspended in the sky, like a child's kite, but it was ominous in its size and blackness. One by one, we slaves stopped to gape at this slowly approaching apparition. I took the opportunity to set down my basket.

"What's the delay, Aesop?" asked Pelaphus, returning from relieving himself in a thicket.

"Up there," I said, pointing. "Some kind of monstrous bird is approaching."

Pelaphus peered into the sky, his jaw slackened, and he staggered backward. "Run for cover! Everyone!"

That was easier said then done. First of all, there was no cover, save for a few scraggly bushes; secondly, we were all roped together by our slave collars. One group of screaming slaves leaped for the thickets, while several more set out at a dead run. The rest of us were yanked rudely off our feet, and the entire caravan degenerated into a sprawling web of wailing humanity. Pelaphus drew his sword and began slashing at the ropes which bound us. Meanwhile, the black specter in the white sky drew ever closer, its mammoth wings alternately slapping the wind and gliding with the currents. The thing was in no hurry, I thought. It knew we had no place to go.

With their shackles unbound, some of the slaves were running for freedom, not cover. "Stop!" roared Pelaphus "Stop, I say!"

I tugged at his sleeve. "They'll return when they realize they have no food or drink. Meanwhile, what is this thing coming toward us?"

Pelaphus squinted into the sun, his teeth clenching. "I saw such a thing in Thebes once. It's a frightful monster, constructed from the gods' pure hatefulness. Only keeping our wits about us will save us."

"Why is that?" I asked.

Pelaphus pointed toward the flying beast, which had swooped into a gradual dive straight toward us. "Do you see the four legs, dangling like the paws of a lion?"

Yes, I nodded.

"Her claws are twice as long as any lion's, and they can part a man in two at the waist, faster than he can draw a breath. I have seen it. But the *face!* The face is the most hideous, because it is so familiar and pleasant."

"What is the face?" I asked, shuddering.

Intoned Pelaphus, "The face of a *woman!*"

"A sphinx!" I gasped, staring wildly into the sky. The sound of the great flapping wings was now loud, beating the wind. Had I not heard the stories of the sphinx, I would still have thought the creature was a giant bird, a bird which happened to be carrying a woman in one great talon and a lion in the other. For this is what the sphinx looked like, an unholy abomination wrought from the wicked imagination of a god. "What is it going to do to us?" I murmured.

The big man sighed, and I could see the sword flexing in his massive grip. "The sphinx was sent by Hera to rid the world of stupid men. It will ask a riddle, and if we do not answer it, it will eat us."

"Right," I nodded. I watched Pelaphus crush some sand with the tip of his blade. "Master, I will try to answer the riddle. If I speak your name, it means I have failed. Then you are to kill it."

"Agreed!" spit Pelaphus. At that moment, I knew that Pelaphus hated the gods and their predetermination over mortals. He had obviously had some dealings with them.

The sphinx giggled as she landed, a high, tinkling laugh which sounded slightly demented. Her face was indeed bland, the face of a young peasant woman, shorn of conceit and vanity. But her eyes blazed with an insane purpose, and the huge wings and lion's body didn't do much for her appearance.

"Hello, mortals!" she chirped. She nodded toward Pelaphus, whose sword was leveled waist-high. "Surely, you know the folly of that, Pelaphus. Was it not your troop at Thebes of whom I ate the entire number?"

I saw Pelaphus blanch, the ire rising in his eyes. "You ungodly abomination! Slithering pet of the gods! Why don't you return to the slime pits of Hades, from which you sprang!"

I nudged Pelaphus softly. "Master, why don't we try to reason with her first? She may leave us in peace."

The sphinx smiled. "It is you whom I seek, Aesop. Olympus is abuzz with the foolishness of Isis. I came to see for myself—and at the behest of Apollo, to whom the Muses are subservient—if you are indeed such a blessed mortal. I see one thing for a fact: you *are* as ugly as anything living, including myself!"

I bristled a bit at this insult, because *nothing* could be as ugly as a bird with a lion's body and the face of a shrewish wife. "Truly," I said, bowing, "the fabled magnificence of the sphinx pales beside the extraordinary presence of the original!"

The sphinx scratched the ground with a claw as long as a dagger. "Your tongue is indeed fluent, ugly slave. But can you answer my riddle and save the lives of yourself and these other wretches?"

"Before you ask that riddle, oh Mighty Sphinx," I said, scraping the ground as I advanced a bit closer to the beast. "Consider that you are in a rut."

"A rut?" the sphinx asked.

"Yes," I answered. "You always ask a riddle, testing only the riddle-answering prowess of your subjects. If you were to listen to one of my humble fables, you would perhaps learn a great deal more about both me and life."

"Life?" asked the Sphinx. "I am a monster. What do I have to learn of life?"

"An eagle was once chasing a rabbit," I said, "and the rabbit, in his desperation, ran to the house of a tiny tumblebug. The tumblebug begged the eagle not to eat the rabbit, saying the rabbit was his houseguest. But the eagle scorned the tumblebug, scooped up the rabbit, and ate him on the spot before the horrified eyes of the tumblebug. That day, the lowly tumblebug declared war on the eagle and all her offspring.

"Whenever the eagle left her nest to search for food, the tumblebug would fly up to her nest, roll her eggs onto the ground, and smash them. The eagle was distraught, having no idea how her eggs came to be destroyed each time. So she flew to the throne of Zeus, protector of all eagles. 'Zeus,' she said, 'allow me to lay my eggs in your lap, so that they might be protected.'

"Zeus complied, and the eagle contentedly laid her eggs in the god's lap. The tumblebug, knowing his usual scheme wouldn't work, covered himself in steer manure and flew straightaway into Zeus's lap. The god, stunned at the chunk of manure in his lap, leaped up, dropped the eggs onto the ground, and smashed them all."

The sphinx nodded slowly, and I was relieved to see a slight smile cross her face. "I suppose I am the eagle," she observed, "and you miserable mortals are the tumblebugs? Yes, by force of cunning, a tumblebug may prevail, but I believe it will be a long time before the gods fail me, as Zeus did the eagle. You must still answer my riddle."

I cleared my throat. "Ask it!"

The sphinx flapped her wings and expanded her sinewy hair-covered chest. "There is a temple, and in it is but one column. Atop the column are twelve cities, and each of these is roofed with thirty beams. About each beam run two women. Of what am I speaking?"

I breathed a huge sigh of relief. I thought the sphinx would ask something tough. Pelaphus and the remaining slaves stared at me with frank terror. "You speak of a calendar," I said. "The temple is the universe, for it embraces all things. The column is the year, the cities upon it are the twelve months, and the thirty beams are the thirty days of the month. The two women moving about them are night and day, for one follows the other."

The sphinx bowed, a difficult maneuver for a creature with an awkward body. "Everything said about you is true, Aesop. I will report to Apollo that you are a testimony to his greatness. But beware, Aesop . . ."

"Yes?"

The sphinx smiled malevolently. "You are protected by Apollo while you remain a slave, for Apollo is a benevolent god. But, should you become a freeman, his protection is withdrawn. You will be on your own, Aesop."

"I intend to give the great god Apollo an offering!" I declared proudly, hoping the sun god was listening.

"Words are weaker than actions," said the sphinx, revving her wings to fly. Before taking off, she glared at Pelaphus. "Pelaphus, it is proper for you to make a sacrifice to *me.*"

Pelaphus managed a smile which was altogether too defiant for my taste. "You want something to eat, don't you, you hoary scavenger?"

"Yes," snarled the sphinx.

"And why not?" I said magnanimously. "I believe we must be able to share some of our foodstuffs with the sphinx! Perhaps she would care for some mangoes . . ."

"She deserves nothing!" snapped Pelaphus. "We answered her ridiculous riddle! Now she should take her horrid aspect to the mirrored depths of the river Styx!"

The sphinx erupted with a guttural growl quite out of keeping with the serene face. "Sacrifice to me, Pelaphus! It is my *due!*"

"Please, Pelaphus!" I squeaked.

The gladiator spit into the sand, then raised his sword and pointed it at the creature. "You may have the slave who has run the farthest. But woe be to you, wretched crow, if you trouble us again!"

The sphinx smiled playfully, but her eyes glowed with evil madness. "Farewell, Pelaphus and Aesop." The wondrous wings unfurled and beat the wind with such force that the sand streaked our faces and our hair blew straight back.

Pelaphus watched her every instant, his sword angled upward, poised for a thrust. But the sphinx achieved considerable height and distance with a few powerful strokes and flapped away to the south. We could see a group of slaves cowering in the distance. The sphinx bore down on them with terrifying swiftness, and the slaves broke into a run. Even at a distance, their cries were nightmarish. She snatched the fattest one, a simpleminded Judean, and carted him off into the sky, roaring and tearing at his arms and legs, trailing pieces of flesh across the desolate plain.

After seeing their fellow escapee being carted off by the sphinx, the other runaways returned quickly to the main group. But the damage had already been done. Pelaphus stared morosely at eight or nine broken jars of the deep indigo dye, a result of the melee attendant upon the arrival of the sphinx. Only three jars remained intact; the powdery contents of the other jars mingled with the sand, creating an interesting hue of mauve.

"If I had five good archers," Pelaphus seethed, "I would bring that four-legged whore crashing out of the sky! Never again would I submit to her idiotic riddles!"

"I'm sorry," I sighed, feeling somewhat at fault. After all, the horrid creature had been seeking me when she made her startling appearance.

Pelaphus breathed deeply for a moment, his rage subsiding. "It's not wholly your fault, Aesop," he admitted. "I, like you, have dealt frequently with gods, not always to my advantage. I have served many kings and queens, some of whom warred with gods. I have served gods, all of whom war with each other. Sometimes, I believe every action in life creates an enemy."

"Still," I sighed, "it was my presence here . . ."

"In fact, you saved me an even worse fight," Pelaphus interrupted. "Had you not answered the riddle, all of the jars would've been broken and most of the slaves eaten. But I, for one, would have gone down with my blade in that monster's throat. As it is, we are not delayed in the slightest, and I still have all my slaves, save that one poor wretch."

"I am to remain a slave then?" I asked, hope fading from my voice. I don't know why, but I had expected that being the center of all this attention would in some way warrant a change of my occupational status.

"It is Apollo's wish that you remain a slave," remarked Pelaphus. "Or didn't you hear the sphinx?"

"She only said I would lose Apollo's protection. If such attention involves monsters like the sphinx, I may be willing to forgo it."

"I like you, Aesop," said Pelaphus, punching me in the stomach. I couldn't stand up straight for a month.

* * *

Pelaphus was true to his word. He didn't sell me to a slave galley in Ephesus. Of course, that left him with the rather interesting problem of exactly to *whom* he should sell me. He had unloaded the other slaves to the first dealer he met, by simply asking one hundred shekels for each. The slave dealer was willing to pay that for some but not for all. I saw him cast a disparaging glance at me, for instance. But Pelaphus stood firm, saying he was selling the whole lot or none. "Less Aesop," he said, patting me on the shoulder."

The slave dealer blinked. "The ugly one—I do not have to pay one hundred?"

Pelaphus nodded. "He is not for sale, not to you, at any rate."

"Fine," the dealer nodded, snapping his fingers. A minion brought forth a tiny chest and opened it. The chest contained emeralds, jewels, and gold of every description. Pelaphus took a few of the baubles but demanded the bulk of payment in shekels, the most familiar coin of the realm.

"You're setting me *free!*" I chirped happily as Pelaphus led me away from the dingy slave market. We were still half a mile from the shore itself, but I could smell the alien scent of the open sea, fresh yet reeking of life. The smell reminded me of a vegetable patch.

"Calm down," said Pelaphus. "I'm not going to sell you to a galley, but you are to remain a slave."

"Why?" I gasped. "I will gladly be your servant and work for the lowliest of wages. Please, Pelaphus, grant me my freedom! What money could you possibly be out? I will fetch next to nothing!"

Pelaphus stopped, smiled, and put his big hand on my shoulder. "Aesop, you may think me a brave man. I am. But I'm not a fool, at least not always. Apollo wants you to be a slave. *I* will not be the one to disobey his edict— enough gods are mad at me already. Perhaps your next master will set you free. At any rate, Aesop, slave or not, I imagine you will have an interesting life."

"But how can you sell me in this town?" I blubbered. "You know what will become of me!"

"That is a problem," Pelaphus agreed. "Still, there must be another class of slave in this town."

There was. Prostitutes and actors.

CHAPTER 3

The Loss of a Friend

After selling the slaves, Pelaphus and I continued to explore Ephesus. We followed our noses toward the sweetly decaying smell of the sea and the waterfront. Ephesus itself was little more than one clay hovel piled upon another, but it had a vibrancy and purpose I have since discovered in every port city I have known. As gateway to the mysteries and adventures of the sea, a port city is like a giant *bon voyage* party, rampant with excitement and yearning. Pelaphus purchased each of us a leg of lamb from a curbside rotisserie, and we gnawed our bones as we walked.

The street broadened and dipped toward an incredible blue expanse. My first thought was that the sky had changed colors, but then I saw the beautiful ships, with their snapping banners and garish hulls, sitting firmly in the center of the blue. I stopped and sucked my breath. Pelaphus stopped and laughed.

"Never seen the ocean, Aesop?" he asked teasingly.

"So this is why we have no water in Phrygia!" I gasped. "It is all lying here!"

"This is only a part of it," said Pelaphus. "No one knows how much water there is in the sea. Past the Pillars of Heracles, the sea is endless."

"Endless?" I marveled.

"So they say. Those who sail too far west never return. Even a few miles offshore, the sea can turn wicked and send an entire crew of men into the cold grasp of Poseidon." The big warrior shivered, and I could tell that the sea was perhaps the only thing he feared.

At the moment, the sea looked delightfully restful. The huge ships bobbed gracefully in their moorings, while the flags and banners waved rhythmically, beckoning us to come on board. I knew nothing of the sea, but I knew of the ferocious strength of the wind, the way it could uproot palm trees and turn a peaceful desert into a choking blanket of sand.

"Once there was a shipwrecked man," I said to Pelaphus, "and he cursed and derided the sea for its fury. So the sea appeared to him in the form of a woman, saying, 'Please, dear friend, blame me not. I am, by natural disposition, just as calm and benign as you see me now. Blame the wind for your troubles. It is the wind which appears suddenly, whipping me and turning me into a wild monster.' "

Pelaphus smiled. "I'm always blaming the thing I see, not the agent behind it."

"That's why you should keep me around," I remarked. "I'll help to point out your shortcomings!"

"Thanks, Aesop, but I am already well aware of them."

A shriek arose from somewhere behind us, and Pelaphus and I whirled around. Everyone on the crowded waterfront did likewise. But before we could determine the source of the weird cry, a burst of hearty male laughter erupted behind us, accompanied by a lascivious female cackle. We smiled dumbly at one another, cajoled into good humor despite our confusion. Suddenly, two short muscular men, naked except for the briefest loincloths, burst from a side street. They immediately formed a human springboard, and a third man bounded into their hands and was tossed effortlessly over our heads. He landed in a wondrous somersault and bounded onto his feet, flashing us a broad grin.

As the other tumblers joined him in a series of complicated somersaults, a pair of jugglers rushed into the crowd,
their oblong clubs blurring between them. Like the rest of
the audience, we backed up against a wall and just
watched.

"Citizens of Ephesus!" boomed a great male voice, "who
but the Kashmir Circus could bring you such wondrous
sights as these? Death-defying tumblers, nimble-fingered
jugglers, and the Sultan's breathtaking harem?"

A dozen or so scantily clad women suddenly materialized and swished among us, tickling the men's noses with
their loosely flowing veils. Though I was still mystified,
Pelaphus apparently wasn't; the hale-hearted warrior
reached out and scooped up one of the maidens in his
massive arms. By the way she giggled and squealed, I
knew the attention was not altogether unwelcome, but she
fended him off with a good-natured slap and wriggled out
of his arms. With a wink, she continued to circulate among
the other leering males.

The owner of the booming voice strode into the center
of the thoroughfare. His thin elderly appearance belied his
stentorian vocal cords. "The Kashmir Circus has pitched
its tents on the northern hill overlooking fair Ephesus! We
shall be in this city a scant four days, until our ship sails
for Greece! So, please, hurry to visit the Garden of Delights, the Palace of Wonderment, the Kashmir Circus!"

Pelaphus banged me on the shoulder. "Now we know
how we are to spend the evening!" he grinned.

The tents of the circus turned out to be fairly elaborate.
The Palace of Wonderment was a huge circular tent with
iridescent purple-and-green stripes and exaggerated aw-
nings. The Garden of Delights was, as far as I could tell,
a labyrinth of smaller tents, each one made from luxuriant
satin and decorated in strange color combinations, like orange and silver. Pelaphus was obviously torn between
which to visit first, the Palace or the Garden, but we got

swept up in a surge of eager customers headed for the larger tent, where flute music and drums beckoned us.

Inching our way in, we soon became enthralled with a troupe of dancing girls, who were swaying in dogged unison to the lilting music. The girls were in no way good dancers; *I* was probably more graceful. But they certainly held our interest. We stepped over toes and bungled our way to a pair of seats, never taking our eyes from the swooping and bowing women. I saw the girl whom Pelaphus had swept up in his arms. Pelaphus saw her too. He licked his lips hungrily as he watched her gown billow open and shut with her clumsy movements.

The dance ended to tumultuous applause, and the dancers scampered off, to be replaced by the fragile announcer with the rotund voice. "Members of the Sultan's Harem are appearing in private performance in the Garden of Delights!" he intoned, to even greater applause.

A thunderous drumroll sounded, accompanied by shrieking acrobats who poured into the center of the tent and began hurling each other onto one another's shoulders. Meanwhile, Pelaphus and I were accosted by a one-eyed midget, who squinted at us accusingly and held open an embroidered purse. Pelaphus fed a couple of coins into the purse, and the midget scurried off. "I'll return soon," Pelaphus said, jabbing me in the arm. Before I could protest, he ducked into the crowd and vanished.

I resumed my seat and continued watching the show. I laughed a few times at the antics of a succession of acrobats, jugglers, and clowns, but the audience around me constantly changed. I became increasingly uneasy, certain I was overstaying my welcome. No one had to explain to me now that the Garden of Delights was the real attraction, and the Palace of Wonder was merely a waiting room. The midget circulated constantly and began casting baleful glances at me. I, in turn, did my best to camouflage my slave bracelet.

Now a troupe of dancing males came on, none of whom

were wearing enough to squelch a sneeze. The midget studied me frankly, wondering perhaps if this was what I was waiting for. For a few moments, I watched the men, all of whom were lithe and young and moved with studied sinuosity. I coughed slightly and removed myself from my seat, treading over several toes on my way to the exit. The midget looked relieved.

Out in the night air, the smell of the sea was overpowering, and so was the prospect of freedom. Here I was, unobserved and unencumbered. I could easily slip off into the darkness. But my loyalty to Pelaphus was strong, nearly as strong as my abject fear of what lay out there in the darkness. I had seen enough since my encounter with Isis to know that the world was a substantially more dangerous and unpredictable place than I had imagined. The fact that Apollo had somehow taken an interest in my life filled me more with dread than relief.

I wandered over to the entrance to the Garden of Delights, hoping to find Pelaphus. But a giant, a foot taller than Pelaphus and perhaps a foot broader at the shoulders, barred the doorway. "No slaves," he said simply, fingering my slave bracelet.

I smiled at the giant, whose massive chest and determined jaw bore the scars of several encounters with sharp blades. He himself possessed a gleaming golden collar about his neck. "I'm looking for my master. He's been in there for some time. Perhaps you've seen him, a big man in simple robes and . . ."

"Sit by the dock and wait," the guard muttered.

But I was not about to go unaccompanied to the dock, where one of the slave galleys might decide at the last moment they were shorthanded. "What might I do to gain admittance?" I asked.

The guard curled his lip. "You may not gain admittance under any circumstance."

"You know," I remarked, "it's not always such a terrible thing to be refused admittance to a place. One day, a dog and a pig were bickering over which was the more favored of animals in the eyes of the gods. The dog bragged, 'I accompany man wherever he goes, while you are not allowed to enter a single religious shrine, and any man who has eaten pork is also outcast from the temple.' To which the pig replied, 'The gods decree this because they love me so. It pains them terribly to see me sacrificed or eaten.' "

I saw the beginnings of a smile etched across the giant's face, but he refused to give in. Behind him, however, a hearty laugh erupted. The elderly announcer of the circus stepped from the folds of the tent.

"That is a very fitting story," he observed. "All manner of indignities are taking place behind these canvas walls, and you are spared them all."

"You are the master of the circus!" I exclaimed. "I'm enjoying your show immensely!"

The man bowed. "Thank you. And you are Aesop. Your master told me of you."

"He did?" I answered with astonishment.

"Yes. And he said you were not only a remarkable raconteur but an acrobat as well."

I believed I blushed. "Well, I have some talent in that regard."

"Please demonstrate," the man smiled, holding out a hand.

I looked around. The ground appeared soft and sandy, no harder than the soil of Phrygia, where I had clowned and cavorted for my supper for thirty years. "Very well," I said. I took off at a running start and did a cartwheel, which blended smoothly into a hand flip and a somersault. The actions seemed easier than ever, and I reprised them, ending with a handstand and a backflip.

Even the gigantic guard applauded, along with his master. I don't know why, but the sight of someone ugly and misshapen flying through the air always elicits a warm response.

"Wonderful!" the announcer exclaimed. "You're a born performer!" He turned to the towering guard. "Rango, take Aesop to the dormitory tent. See that he is fed and given a bed."

I protested, "But my master, Pelaphus . . ."

"Wrong," smiled the announcer with a hint of cold authority. "I am your master. I have just purchased you from Pelaphus." He snapped his fingers, and I felt the giant's steely grip on my shoulder.

I smiled up at Rango. "Onward to the dormitory tent."

Rango brought me a plate of food, and the dinner was quite sumptuous for that of a slave: fresh asparagus and fruit and a grilled fish of some sort. I had never eaten fish before, and I was amazed at its delicate taste and consistency. I was forced to eat alone, however, as all the other performers were busy shucking shekels from the citizenry of Ephesus. Alone with my thoughts, I couldn't help feeling somewhat betrayed by Pelaphus. On the other hand, he had kept his word not to sell me to a galley ship. I suppose I should've felt proud to possess talents which were marketable. Nevertheless, the transaction appeared to have been a bit callous.

"Aesop?" called a voice just outside the tent. I thought I recognized it.

"Here!" I responded.

Pelaphus entered the tent, looking both chastened and exhausted. I could well imagine how he had spent the money he had received for me.

"Hello, Pelaphus," I said with little enthusiasm.

He knelt beside me and touched my shoulder. "I didn't think Hesiod would accept my offer so quickly."

"Hesiod?" I asked.

"The man who runs this place. He is a poet of some note."

I nodded solemnly.

"I'm sorry, Aesop," he said. "I shall miss you."

"And I you," I said, softening.

"We might have had many adventures together," the warrior sighed. "But I abhor the idea of owning a slave."

I sat up. "Then *free* me! It's not too late! Say you will buy me back, and then you can free me!"

Pelaphus shook his head with honest regret. "I cannot afford to anger Apollo. Never tell anyone about Apollo's wish that you remain a slave. I'm sure someone will free you at some point."

"But I wish to be free *now!*" I moaned.

"Poor Aesop," Pelaphus smiled. "The gods have blessed you with talents divine but so very little patience." He stood up and extended his hand in the now familiar gladiator style. "I will look for you in my travels, and you look for me."

I stood and returned the mighty clasp. "When we meet again, Pelaphus, it will be as freemen."

"I believe it," the warrior smiled, his chubby face beaming.

Pelaphus loosened his grasp and strode out of the tent and into the night. Thus it was that I lost my first true friend.

CHAPTER 4

The Apes Who Built a City

The first thing I discovered about being an actor was that the hours are totally reversed. Instead of sleeping nights and working days, nights are reserved for work and days for leisure. This suited me fine, and I adjusted immediately. My first few days in the circus, I had so much to learn that I hardly had time for sleep, anyway. Rango trained me in the swift raising and lowering of the tents; the jugglers gave me some preliminary instruction, as well as a battered set of juggling clubs; the clowns taught me some basic routines and pratfalls; and Lollo, the one-eyed midget, showed me how to shame the audience into giving more money.

My first performance came as part of the troupe which assailed the townspeople on the street and drummed up interest in our attractions. Hesiod himself instructed me. "Keep tumbling, keep smiling, and keep quiet," he said. I acquitted myself well in the street, but in the actual show I was relegated to soliciting money with Lollo, the reasoning being that the customers felt sorry for deformed specimens such as ourselves and would give more. I somewhat resented being a beggar, but the job afforded me the opportunity to watch the shows and learn from the more seasoned performers. Miraculously, the "four days" we were to spend in Ephesus before "catching our ship" stretched into four weeks. I looked diligently for Pelaphus but never saw him.

The second and most important thing I discovered was that actors observe a caste system every bit as stringent as that of a king's court. The common workers, such as myself, were expected to do and excel at everything, from performing to mending costumes to pounding tent stakes. The featured jugglers, acrobats, and musicians were like nobility, never called upon to do more than their nightly stints in the arena. They zealously guarded this privilege and refused to touch any props or work not directly related to their occupations.

By far, the most privileged among us were the dancer/ prostitutes. They were treated like royalty, with attention accorded to every whim, complaint, or desire. Should they desire asses' milk to drink or bathe in, we would scour the countryside for it. Should they sneeze and wish to see a physician, one would be fetched immediately, even if we had to hire a local charlatan to portray a physician. Should they doubt either their beauty or ability, a soothsayer would be summoned to assure them of a long and fruitful life. Whenever a ship called from a distant land, they demanded and received a new supply of silks, perfumes, and body paints. Needless to say, we common folk were not allowed to speak to these godly creatures unless commanded to.

I didn't really begrudge the dancers their extra privileges, because I realized, as did everyone, that they accounted for the bulk of our profits. I realized, too, that the work they performed behind their tent flaps was both arduous and dangerous. More than once, I heard screaming over the flutes and drums of the show we performed in the main tent. Each time, I ignored it, as did all of us except Rango, who often reappeared later with a new gash in his chest. One night, one of the male dancers simply disappeared. The bedding in his tent was so bloody, we had to burn it.

I kept an amazingly civil tongue in my head during this period. Mainly, I was too fascinated by this remarkable society to risk leaving it. Also, for the first time in my life, I was enjoying good food. I must have gained twenty pounds in one month. Only a regimen of vigorous exercise kept me from looking more grotesque than I already did. Nevertheless, I did develop a dangerous infatuation.

Her name was Hippolyte, after the queen of the Amazons and daughter of Ares, god of war. She was the largest woman I have ever seen, standing taller than any of the men in our company save Rango. Her hair flowed in ringlets to her waist and was the color of the sky at sunset. I had no idea what she did to make it that color and didn't care. When she danced, she was no more graceful than the rest, but her size gave her a queenly grandeur. She was special, and she knew it.

I longed deeply for Hippolyte and often dreamed of her during my morning snooze. As must be evident to you, dear reader, I had never held a woman in my arms, at least not long enough to accomplish anything. At dawn one day, when our work was finished, I confided my longing to the midget Lollo.

The little beggar wheezed a laugh. "Aesop, you dream big, I'll give you that much."

"But what am I to do?" I wailed.

"You cannot risk approaching her now," he cautioned. "If she is insulted, as I think she well might be, she will report your actions to Hesiod. If you were a freeman, he would simply toss you out. As a slave, he would probably have Rango whip you, then he would sell you to a slave galley."

I shuddered. That was a fate I wished to avoid at any cost.

"On the other hand," the midget continued, "if you were to wait until we were aboard ship, he would have no place to sell you, and he might even chalk it up to the boredom of sea travel."

"Are we really to board a ship?" I asked. "I thought that was merely a tale to account for our presence here in Ephesus."

"The ship is already chartered," Lollo replied. "We remain as long as business is good, and it has already started dropping off. Hesiod has a burning desire to return to Greece, where he is known as a poet instead of a pimp."

I nodded, my resolve now as hardened as my loins. As soon as we were safely aboard that ship, I would profess my love to the extraordinary Hippolyte.

Three days later, I stepped off land for the first time in my life. I can't express to you the thrill I felt when I left the quay at Ephesus and felt the soggy wood of the ship under my feet. The deck was swaying ever so subtly, reminding me that the sea was a shifting, transient being. I had ridden donkeys, of course, and they also swayed and rocked. But the good, sturdy ground was always a few feet away—even a fall brought immediate safety. But the sea is unsafe, unpredictable, and unsound. That, I suppose, explains man's enchantment with it.

Before casting off, Hesiod ordered the entire company below, fearing we might fall off or get in the crew's way. But I had been below earlier and found the cramped, noisy confines not to my liking. Rango had pointed out a piece of rotting canvas strung between two poles and pronounced it my "bed." I don't know what the thing was, but it certainly wasn't a bed. I sneaked onto the upper deck immediately, desiring to observe ship-sailing first-hand.

I had no fear of this ship, as it was entirely wind-driven. Slave galleys, I had heard, were used mainly for warfare, where swift power must be available at all times. If slaves died now and then, it was no disaster, as slave ports such as Ephesus were common. The wind, however, was another matter. The wind came and went, often coming and going the wrong way. For the first days of our journey, I sat on deck every moment, watching the clever machinations of the crew as they tried to fool the fickle wind into pushing their vessel in the right direction. They would swivel the sails this way and that, ball them up tightly when the wind became unfavorable, then unfurl them frantically when the wind shifted again. We often sailed in odd zigzags, making the most of southerly winds, which seemed to be the most common. All I knew was that we were headed west to Greece. I often wondered how the captain and crew knew which way that was.

"Aesop!" called Lollo one day, as the sky opened up with a pleasant drizzle. "Why don't you come below? Are you mad?"

"Didn't you ever hear about the group of apes who built a city?" I asked.

"No," said Lollo. "But I am certain you will tell me." The midget crept up the ladder and sat beside me.

"The apes began to envy man, wishing they could live in cities as he did. So a group of them built a city with great walls and gates, as they had observed in the cities of men. Finally, they grew so enamored of their handiwork that they left the trees, went into the city, and bolted the gates. When a group of hunters came by, they threw a net over the city and captured all the apes."

Lollo nodded sagely. "You are certainly right. We have no business on this ship." He spit at it. "Since yesterday, half the company is desperately ill, and the other half are nursing them and cleaning up the mess."

"How is Hippolyte?" I asked.

"The worst of the lot," the midget replied, clicking his tongue. "I've never seen her sick a day, and now she lies in her hammock as if dying. She's so pathetic."

Pathetic was a word I never thought would describe Hippolyte. I knew immediately this was a good time to approach her. I stood up, stretched, and sighed, "I think I shall go comfort her."

Lollo's single good eye twinkled. "She is below, in a cabin unto herself, at the rear of the vessel."

I bade my little friend good-bye and made for the lower decks.

The stench was horrific. I had not been below, even to eat, preferring to live like the crew, eating and sleeping with the lull of the wind. Now I realized the great truth of ships: no matter how large they are, they are always too small. This one was a pathetic vessel for the transportation of anything living. The bowels of it were like a dank sewer, seeping with mildew, fungus, and sweat. Acrobats who were used to flying through the air, laughing at gravity, were suddenly sentenced to Hades and a world of putrid wooden cages and stifling heat. The noise was enough to send an alley cat crawling. It occurred to me that, for once, I was living better than my master, whom I had not seen since we departed. I marveled at the insanity of our leader, Hesiod, who was killing his company in order to claim the dubious rank of poet.

Somewhere, somebody was wailing, and another one was retching, and I hurried through the narrow confusing corridors. Had I been the master, I would have ordered everyone up on the deck at once, to breath fresh air and watch the rocking which was making them so ill. Only by seeing the waves splash against the hull could they get in tune with the sea's motion. Here below, they were victims of an unnatural bombardment which they could neither see nor understand. I reached the last cabin, a triangular shelf sandwiched between the stern and the rudder. I heard her mournful wails from inside and, without knocking, barged in.

She paid me no attention whatsoever, the majestic Hippolyte. Her fiery red hair was damp and clinging, her eyes were glazed, and her gown was soiled. Under the best of circumstances, a person writhing in pain can hardly be called alluring. Still, Hippolyte was more woman than ten other similar creatures combined. Her legs were as smooth as a goat's udder and as shapely as Hestia's spindle. Her bosom was heroic, and her face angelic. I don't know what else to say except that I was totally in love with this awesome creation of Aphrodite's art.

"Rise!" I shouted. "Up on deck immediately!"

She cast a glazed eye at me. "Why? Can't you see, I am ill?"

"Unless you wish to remain that way, you will rise and go above immediately. Doctor's orders!"

"What doctor?" she asked. "You are no doctor. You're a midget from the circus. An acrobat."

I smiled. I was flattered to be identified as an acrobat, instead of a slave. I had thought this marvelous creature had taken no notice of me whatsoever; now I discovered that she had not only noticed me, but had observed my prowess as a tumbler! I let the bit about being a midget pass.

"Hippolyte, I am merely relaying orders. I know not the doctor's name or purpose, only that I am to assist you in going above, where you will feel better."

"Really?" she asked, with a spark of hope in her otherwise nauseated expression. "I will feel better if I go up on deck? But I have been told that the sea is rough and horrid, tossing us about, and that we will fall overboard, or be cursed by the crew!"

"Nonsense!" I scoffed with a regal wave. "I have just come from above, and the sea is utterly tranquil. The sunshine is stunning, and the air is as sweet and fresh as the breath of Aphrodite. Furthermore, I can't imagine any crew of healthy men ever cursing you."

Hippolyte managed a smile and propped herself up on a sturdy elbow. "I can hardly go into public looking like this. Please hand me my comb and a dressing gown. In my trunk."

I reached into my beloved's trunk, thrilling at the touch of silky gowns, ivory hairpins, and vials of scented oils. I was ready to spend the rest of my life as her faithful servant. I could well imagine myself, massaging the oil into those firm buttocks, draping a tunic over those heroic breasts, braiding flowers into her hair with my trembling fingers. I bit my lip, allowing a small whimper to escape.

"Yes?" Hippolyte asked.

"Nothing," I murmured. "Is the blue dress all right?"

I waited patiently in the stench-filled corridor, trying to breathe through my mouth, as Hippolyte the sick transformed herself into Hippolyte the lovely. I have never ceased to marvel at the chameleon qualities of beautiful women, who can appear plain one moment and ravishing the next, as if by sheer force of will. This sorcery must spring from a deep understanding of men and their perception of beauty. Other women can appreciate this transformation but are seldom fooled by it, as men invariably are. Needless to say, the woman who stooped to pass through the low doorway a moment later bore no resemblance to the woman who had lain stricken in bed minutes before. A dab of rouge, a string of pearls, a hint of myrrh, and a gown and matching scarf of iridescent sapphire blended to create their magical illusion. No goddess could look more gorgeous.

"Let's go up quickly," she said, "before I throw up."

When we reached the upper deck, the wind was blowing fiercely, and the drizzle had turned into a howling gale. My heart sank, for this was not the picture I had painted for my beloved Hippolyte. She seemed not to mind and strode forcefully to the railing. Gripping a line from the mast with one hand and a water barrel with the other, she leaned over the railing and relieved herself. When she looked back up, she tried to smile, then doubled over and retched strongly. Her hand flailed for a rope to grip and instead lighted upon a battening pin, which sprang loose in her hand. The fumbling ox then teetered backward, and the barrel rolled after her. She grabbed a rope, yanked on it, and the foresail broke right off its mast and flapped down on top of her. With the next rock of the boat, she was gone! I honestly never saw her go over the rail—I suppose I saw it coming and flinched.

I was distraught! My first impulse was to leap in after my beloved, who was nowhere in sight. The sail had snagged on something and was flapping against the side of the hull, but Hippolyte had vanished under waves high enough actually to be the fingers of Poseidon.

I turned around and saw Lollo staring at me. "You're in trouble now!" he rasped.

Indeed I was. Nobody believed me when I said I had nothing to do with Hippolyte's accident. I freely admitted that I had spoken to her and escorted her above, which was enough to damn me in Hesiod's eyes. I really didn't know what was happening, I was in such a heartbroken daze. I only knew that I spent two nights in chains, stuck in a pantry. I was not complaining, mind you, as I expected far worse treatment. The pantry and chains suited my mood, which was decidedly downcast over the loss of Hippolyte.

Suddenly, in the middle of night or day—I couldn't tell—I heard scurrying footsteps and an excited voice:

"We're docking! Land! Land! We're going ashore!"

CHAPTER 5

Samos

My pantry door was finally opened, and Rango dragged me out. I writhed in his grasp, my comatose joints screaming with pain. Hesiod, nearby, smiled at my discomfort.

"Aesop," he snarled, "I should flay you alive for disobeying my orders. I should beat you until your shade chases that of Hippolyte into the Underworld!"

"Agreed," I cringed. "Were I able to decree such a punishment, I would. My grief is every ounce as great as yours, for I loved Hippolyte more than any man has loved a woman. As much as grief overcomes our reason, however, we must strive to be practical. A dead slave is worth nothing."

Rango cuffed me on the ear, adding to my collection of welts. Hesiod shook his fist at me. "I had planned to kill you, for that is what you deserve! As it happens, we have landed on the island of Samos, and the crew says domestic slaves are in great demand here. The philosopher Xanthus keeps his school on this island, and the flower of Greek manhood is in attendance. Much as I would like to feed your body to the gulls, I have need for ready cash."

"A splendid decision!" I crowed.

Rango rapped me again. "I will see that he is bathed and made presentable," said the giant.

"Take him ashore with the others," snapped Hesiod, striding away with a swirl of his cape.

I must say, I had grown very hateful of Rango during this period. His glee in administering punishment was altogether too sadistic, and he never missed a chance to inflict some indignity upon me now that I was totally under his care. For example, he stuck me in a big bucket of salt water and scrubbed me until my skin blistered. He laughed and said I looked healthy. Then he shoved me into a crisp choir robe that was three sizes too big and hauled me out on deck. I worried that I would blow away, but the wind was gentle for a change.

That was my first impression of the island of Samos: gentle. The land had a gentle, weathered texture. The rocks of the shore were smooth, and the waves washed over them rather than beat them. The trees and plants danced in the soothing breeze, and the sun glowed brightly but not hotly, bathed as it was in a diffused shade of clouds. In the center of the island, near the mountains, I could see the rain streaking through darker versions of the same clouds, but here, on the wharf, all was calm and gentle. The buildings I could see were unremarkable, modest baked brick with enough columns and porticoes to signify Greece. But the buildings were painted in such pleasant pastel colors that they rivaled the work of the sun and rocks.

I, however, could not enjoy this idyllic setting for long, as Rango shoved me down the gangplank. On the wharf, chained to a post, were two other slaves. Their downcast expressions were unmistakable. Only a man who is about to be sold like a sow or a used wheelbarrow can appreciate the horrendous absurdity of it. Here you are, surrounded by men and women and even dogs and cats, and they are walking around free, and you are chained to a post with fewer rights than the fly buzzing in your ear. No matter how ugly or dim-witted you are, you are bound to spy someone with whom you could easily change places and become a freeman, in a world of choice and opportunity. Instead, they are free, and you are tied to a post.

I knew the other two men and had, in fact, no idea they were slaves like me. One was a very good musician who played lyre and harp, and the other was one of the dancers, a muscular lad who had no talent, but dewy sunken eyes and a beautifully chiseled jaw. I had no idea what their crimes were. Hesiod could well have been selling them just to raise money.

Without a word, Rango gathered us by our shackles and dragged us to a quaint marketplace in the center of the village. There, we were met by a slim man with large teeth and hooded eyes. "I'm Mykino, the agent," he smiled, casting an appraising eye at the handsome young dancer.

Rango nodded to him and prodded us. "These are the slaves of Master Hesiod."

Mykino twisted his beard in his fingers as he studied the musician. He plucked at his eyebrow as he studied me. "The dancer will fetch a premium price, three thousand denarii or more. We will sell him as a tutor, skilled in the arts. What arts, it won't matter with *his* looks. The musician is fine as he is—musicians are always in great demand among these playboys." He scowled at me. "But what am I to do with this deformed ape?"

"Do what you can," said Rango, walking off.

"Sir," I replied, "by exhibiting me alongside these handsome specimens, you exhibit your business acumen."

"What?" Mykino asked, glowering at me. Obviously, he was accustomed to dealing with slaves who were so embarrassed by the whole ordeal they could hardly speak, let alone offer him business advice.

I shrugged. "By displaying them alongside me, you make them appear all the more attractive. I salute your enterprise!"

Mykino blinked and tugged his beard. "Yes, well . . . I know my business!"

"You certainly do," I nodded, "and here are three young ladies now who are quite taken with your wares."

He turned to see the same sight I had: a perfect lady in a shimmering robe, who, if not quite young, was still of a delectable countenance. With her were two honestly young and giddy ladies, who snickered and pointed at the handsome dancer and cocky musician, both of whom jutted their chins, flexed their muscles, and appeared ready to burst their chests.

"I am reminded of a story about some bullfrogs who envied the oxen for their size," I remarked. "They puffed themselves up so much trying to match the oxen, they exploded."

Mykino hissed at me through a clenched smile, "Quit your babbling and bow!"

The beautiful woman and her giggling comrades watched us from a respectful distance. "Lady Xanthus," cooed the slave trader, bowing, "I am honored to encounter your presence in the marketplace today."

"In such a frightfully boring place, what else am I to do?" she sniffed. "Do you have slaves for sale today?"

"Indeed I do!" said the slave dealer. "I have three, uh, *two* fabulous young slaves for sale. The tall one with the striking features is a tutor, well versed in mathematics and the classics. The sensitive one is a musician, skilled with the lyre as well as the harp."

One of the maidens could contain herself no more. She burst forward, literally heaving with excitement. "Lady Xanthus, methinks the one on the right is very comely!"

The other girl darted forward, her hand gripping her bodice. "Lady Xanthus, the one on the left is surely created in the image of Apollo himself. Look at his biceps!"

"Now, girls," sighed the Lady Xanthus, "I will not stand for such naked aspirations." Both maids tittered and blushed. Lady Xanthus chuckled as she slyly verified their claims for herself.

"Such a noble household!" gushed Mykino. "I would be

honored to place a slave in the house of Professor Xanthus."

The fairer young maiden—I was finally able to tell them apart—grabbed her mistress's sleeve. "Lady Xanthus, the house is full of nothing but maidservants. Don't you think having a manservant about would be . . . useful?"

"Oh, yes!" squealed the other girl. "Prevail upon your husband to purchase one of the slaves. Please!"

Lady Xanthus smoothed back an errant tuft of hair. "You know my husband prefers maidservants. However, a manservant *would* be useful. To help me out of my bath, to rub me down with oils and powders, to prepare my dressing gown, as you do my husband's." She gasped slightly and added, "We could use his brawn as well . . . to repair the portico of the house."

"Exactly, m'lady," panted the dark-haired girl, "so useful!"

"Master Xanthus could use him to tend the horses," interjected the other maiden. "Tell him that!"

Lady Xanthus sighed, "All that will interest Professor Xanthus is the price. And what is the price, merchant?"

"A mere three thousand denarii, for either the tutor or the musician. Both are extremely skilled in the household arts. To show my gratitude at placing one or both slaves in your noble household, I will throw in the ugly one free of charge!"

"By the gods, no," tittered Lady Xanthus. "It would hardly be a noble household with that monstrosity about. My husband is coming to the village later today with a few of his students. I shall have him speak with you."

"Thank you so much, m'lady," said Mykino, bowing graciously. "Good day to you."

"Good day." The women moved off, pausing to glance over their shoulders every few steps. Their laughter chimed throughout the marketplace.

The slave dealer clapped his hands together. "I think

I've made a sale!" He glared at me. "Though you nearly lost it for me."

"How so?" I asked.

"She didn't want you, even for free."

"That's because she realizes my true worth."

Now the two young slaves laughed. "They'll buy one," said the tutor/dancer/prostitute. "But it won't be you."

"We'll see," I smiled.

I can only surmise at the conversation which took place later that morning, in the boudoir of Lady Xanthus and her noted husband.

"Back so soon from that hovel of a village?" Xanthus intoned, combing his white locks. He sounded and looked every bit the noble Greek patrician, slim and tall, his bearing as immaculate as his dress. Not having been born with money and prestige but wishing to be near them, he had started at a young age tutoring the wealthy. After amassing enough well-heeled students, he needed a permanent school; his major stroke of brilliance had been to locate that school on Samos, an idyllic isle, free from crime and vice and far enough away from Greece to keep the lads at bay from their parents for years at a time.

"I don't suppose there was much of interest in the village," he yawned.

"On the contrary," replied Lady Xanthus. "There are some new slaves for sale."

Xanthus perked up considerably. "Are they pretty?"

Lady Xanthus scoffed, "A great philosopher like you, interested in mere surface beauty? I would have thought you'd have higher things on your mind."

"Ugly, eh? So be it. We have enough maidservants as it is."

"Exactly as I hoped you would say," beamed Lady Xanthus. "For these slaves are of the male gender."

"Then they're expensive," Xanthus growled. "I'm not wasting any more money on frivolities. We are running a school here, not a charity for every brigand who lands on our island."

"For a wise man," said Lady Xanthus, "you are exceedingly stupid. Would it not make better sense to purchase a strong, young slave to help with the chores than to hire laborers from the village? I'll wager we would save money in the long run."

"That's a wager I could not hope to win," Xanthus replied. "If these slaves are cheap, they are probably diseased."

The lady exploded, "Sometimes you talk as if we are destitute! Perhaps if we are in such need, we should divest ourselves of a few of the prettier female slaves. They would bring high prices!"

Xanthus was enough of a philosopher to realize his side of the argument was somewhat tenuous. "I will look at them."

"Thank you, dear," she cooed.

All morning and into the afternoon, we waited for Professor Xanthus. That silly slave dealer refused to speak to any other buyers, so certain was he that he could make a sale to the island's foremost citizen. Though the weather was quite pleasant and the village itself was congenial enough, no one likes to be tied to a post for the better part of the day. I admit my mood was quite surly by the time the great philosopher arrived, tailed by an entourage of fresh-scrubbed students.

My fellow slaves, the musician and the dancer, began to preen at once. I was not impressed by the strutting schoolteacher whose manner was so imperious. His students alternated between imitating his aloof style and giggling like the schoolboys they were.

The slave dealer bowed so low I thought his nose would scrape the ground. "We are honored by your presence, Professor Xanthus. You are shopping for a slave today?"

"Yes," sniffed Xanthus. "I feel it might be cheaper than

hiring laborers from the village. Of course," he smiled, "that depends upon you, Mykino."

"See how clever the professor is," said one adoring student. "He puts the merchant at a disadvantage."

Added another, "I hope you'll not be taking the homely one, Professor."

"Goodness no!" chuckled Xanthus. "My fields already have a scarecrow!"

Everyone laughed, including the other two slaves. I said nothing. I had already made up my mind I wanted no part of this household.

"What is it these slaves of yours do?" asked Xanthus.

"Ask them yourself," said Mykino. "They are extremely well educated. But do not, I pray you, speak to the unsightly one."

"Why not?" asked a student.

"It will only bring you grief," the merchant intoned, rolling his eyes.

"Very well," said Xanthus, turning to the handsome dancer. "What do you know how to do?"

"Everything!" the lad replied.

I laughed out loud.

"Why do you laugh?" asked Xanthus, narrowing his eyes at me.

"Please don't speak to him," begged Mykino. "It only encourages him!"

"I'm not interested in him, anyway," shrugged Xanthus. He turned to the musician. "What do you do?"

"Everything," he answered.

I guffawed even louder.

"By the gods, the ugly fellow is easily amused!" laughed a student. "Why can't we talk to him?"

The slave dealer became frantic. "Please, the others are excellent specimens. The slave to whom you just spoke is primarily a musician. And the other—this will interest you, Professor Xanthus—he is primarily a tutor."

"How much for the tutor?" asked Xanthus.

"I had planned to ask much more," said Mykino, "but for you, Professor, only three thousand."

"And the musician?"

"The same."

"Bah!" waved Xanthus. "They are both too expensive. I could hire a workman for twenty years for that amount. And I wouldn't have to feed him!"

"How much for the hunchback?" asked a student.

"Uh, that is negotiable."

"Let us interview him as well," insisted another student.

"Please, Professor!" another pleaded.

The scholar nodded. "Very well. We shall ask him the same question." From his imposing height, Xanthus looked me in the eyes. "What do you know how to do?"

"Nothing," I replied.

Xanthus looked dumbfounded. "Nothing?"

I shrugged. "How can I know anything, when these two know everything?"

"An able retort!" crowed a student.

"That is why he laughed!" said another. "How can one man know everything?"

"Where were you born?" Xanthus asked me.

"My mother's belly," I answered.

"No, I mean, what place were you born?"

"My mother never told me, but I think it was the kitchen."

The students roared with laughter. "You have always taught us to be specific, Professor Xanthus," said one. "This fellow obviously thinks as you do."

Xanthus studied me a bit more closely now. "What nationality are you?"

"Phrygian," I answered.

Xanthus looked pleased. "Ah, then you are Greek. Do you think I should buy you?"

"What is this?" I asked indignantly. "You do not yet own me, yet you are already seeking my advice. Pay the man, and I will be glad to advise you if you need it."

The students tried to hide their mirth. "What a marvel!" said one. "A slave, advising the philosopher Xanthus."

"Buy him, Professor!" another insisted. "We shall all chip in. We want to ask him more questions!"

Several students murmured their assent, but Xanthus looked undecided. "The Lady Xanthus would skin me alive if I brought home this misshapen bag of bones." He thought for a moment. "On the other hand, she was not too specific about *which* of the slaves I should buy. It might serve a purpose. How much is he, Mykino? Be reasonable, I pray you."

The slave dealer was obviously in shock. "Aesop? I thought I would have to pay to be rid of him. His owner expects to get sixty. Pay me seventy-five, and he's yours."

"Sold!" proclaimed Xanthus, reaching for his money pouch. "That is more the price I had in mind."

As Xanthus paid the slave dealer, I marveled at the valuable lesson I had learned: Being rude to the great and noble is often an asset.

I could well imagine Lady Xanthus and her maidservants had foreseen an altogether different outcome, as they gathered, giggling, around the lady's dressing table.

"Tell me again how beautiful they are," swooned the youngest maiden, who hadn't been fortunate enough to accompany her mistress to the village.

"The images of gods!" another answered. "The musician has the most beautiful hands and fingers in the world. I would trill like a *lyre* at his touch!"

"What's this?" protested another. "I thought you preferred the brawny one. The tutor."

"The brawn in his arm is unimportant. I perceived that the musician had greater brawn *elsewhere!*"

The girls giggled, and Lady Xanthus delicately wiped a smile from her face with her handkerchief. "You are all incorrigible. What makes you think you will have the new slave all to yourselves?"

"He is intended to be the husband of one of us, isn't he?" asked a maiden with alarm.

"Me!" cried another. "I am the eldest!"

"I saw him in my dreams!" a third protested.

"We should all have a chance!" said the fourth.

"Hush, hush!" snapped Lady Xanthus, banging her hairbrush on the table. "If you appear this eager when the young man arrives, he will have *all* of you and marry *none* of you. Any man will come to the bait and nibble, but you must be especially clever if he is to take the bait and entrap himself."

"How did you marry Professor Xanthus, m'lady?" asked the youngest maiden.

Lady Xanthus smiled. "He was preparing to open his school, and many of his greatest clients had told him he was a fool. But he had a purpose in his eyes, and he was not a fool. I could see it. I also knew that no man wants to go into the unknown alone. Every man longs for company of one type or another. Xanthus was tutoring my brother when I met him, and I told him I believed in his idea of a school. We were married on the day we boarded the boat to leave Athens."

"How romantic," sighed a maidservant.

They heard footsteps on the portico.

"The master has returned!" shrieked another. The girls flew out of the room, leaving Lady Xanthus enough time to apply another dab of rouge.

According to my instructions, Xanthus went in first, while I remained on the porch, observing from the shadow of a column. In the front foyer, the four maidservants stood in a perfect row, as if receiving royalty. They looked crestfallen to see the master alone. Lady Xanthus strode purposefully from her bedroom, crossed the courtyard, and swept into the receiving room. She looked angry to see the master alone.

"You are by yourself?" she asked accusingly.

"Yes," he nodded. "I sent the students to their studies."

"And the slave?"

"Uh, yes. I did buy a slave."

The maidservants could barely conceal their excitement. Lady Xanthus fanned herself. "Let us see our latest acquisition."

Xanthus cleared his throat. "You see, it is a point in his training never to enter a house without first securing the mistress's approval."

"I think I shall approve of him. Call him in."

Xanthus nodded. "It is also a point in his training that, once bidden to enter his master's house, he will never leave his master's service as long as he lives."

"We'll give him no call to leave," Lady Xanthus said with some assurance.

"Very well," Xanthus replied. "Aesop!" he called.

"Aesop," whispered one of the girls. "What a cute name."

As soon as I entered, of course, their expressions changed somewhat for the worse. Lady Xanthus glared at me, but she saved her most withering stare for her husband. "I see your cruel and evil purpose, Xanthus. You wish to divorce me and take up with another woman, but you haven't the courage to come out and say so. Instead, knowing how fastidious I am, you bring this *monstrosity* into my house! You wish to make my life unbearable, so that I will leave of my own accord. Very well, Xanthus. Return to me my dowry, and I will be gone on the next ship!"

"Where's his tail?" one of the girls whispered.

Xanthus was utterly at a loss for words, and he turned to me waving his hands frantically. "Help me out, you ugly jackal! You who had all the answers before!"

"Help you?" I asked. "You are doing fine. A bit more of this, and you will be rid of this evil shrew."

"He leaps out to admit it!" Lady Xanthus shrieked. "Oh, Xanthus, this is the foulest of schemes. But I congratulate you, for it is working admirably!"

She ran out of the room, sobbing. The maidservants glared at us and followed their mistress out. Xanthus grabbed my arm and hauled me outside before any more ill will could assail us. For several moments, we heard drawers slamming and pottery smashing, as every woman in the house dramatized her loathing upon the kitchen utensils. Xanthus hid me carefully out of sight behind a gardener's shed.

"We had best take a walk in the garden until this blows over," he smiled, marveling at the ruckus he had caused. He then forced his smile into a frown. "You ought not to have spoken to my wife like that."

But I was paying him no attention. I have been awed my entire life by growing things, but I had never seen such abundance as Xanthus's garden. Intricate rows and hedges ordered the garden into separate plots, each of which sprouted a lush array of vegetation, much of it looking delightfully edible. I saw fat squash and tomatoes, obscene cucumbers, and a dozen varieties of pea pods bursting at their seams. As I drew closer, I saw that the hedges were actually dense berry bushes, flowering with the juicy morsels. I grabbed a handful and ate them.

"Don't do that!" Xanthus hissed nervously. "The gardener will see you!"

"Is this not your garden?" I asked.

"Of course, it's mine," said the philosopher. "The gardener tends my vineyards and grounds for free, in exchange for the vegetables I allow him to grow here. It is an equitable arrangement except for one thing."

"Which is?"

"He is very stingy, and I must beg him for fruit and vegetables if I want any. Or pay him, which I detest even more."

"Call your gardener," I said. "Today you will neither pay nor beg, for the gardener will give us the vegetables of his own accord."

"You don't know him," Xanthus remarked skeptically.

"Call him, and you'll see."

Xanthus shrugged and with his seasoned orator's voice bellowed, "Liguris!"

"Hey, hey!" a weary voice sounded. "What is it now? What is it?"

A stocky man, baked brown as a bean, rounded a hedge. He shook his hoe at us. "You'll not get any free vegetables from me today, Master Xanthus. I need all I have for the market."

Xanthus peered helplessly at me. "See?"

I bowed to the man. "Kind gardener, we are of course willing to offer a trade. In exchange for a selection of your remarkable produce, I will answer any questions under the sun which you put to me. And I will answer it to your satisfaction, or you need pay us nothing."

The grizzled brown man scratched his chin. "You hardly look like a man of letters."

"Appearances can be deceiving," I remarked. "I have a fable for that, but I'll tell it another time. Ask me your question. You risk nothing unless I answer it to your complete satisfaction."

Liguris became excited. "Well, there is one matter which has plagued me in all my years as a gardener. But I doubt if any man has the answer.'"

"What is it?"

The little man crooked a finger, drawing me closer. "Why is it, when I put my plants in the ground, hoe them, water them, and tend them exceedingly well, the weeds, to which I have given no attention, always sprout first?"

Xanthus clapped his hands gleefully. "A worthy conundrum if ever I heard one! How do you answer, Aesop?"

"It's simple," I shrugged. "The Earth is like a woman. When a woman comes to a second marriage with children from her first, she must also care for the children of her new husband. She is the natural mother to her own offspring but a stepmother to those of her husband. Is it not natural for her to lavish more attention and nourishment upon her own children than those foisted upon her?

"The Earth is the same. She is the natural mother of the weeds and things which grow spontaneously, but she's a stepmother to the gardener's plants. Therefore, the Earth nourishes and tends for her own, and the weeds flourish better than the stepchildren you have planted."

The gardener was crying. "I was a stepchild," he sniffed. "Now I understand perfectly. I will no longer trouble myself but thank the blessed gods that the Earth tends my plants as well as she does. Oh, thank you, Professor Xanthus, for bringing me this wise man. Henceforth, I will place a basket of vegetables at your door each day."

"Thank you," Xanthus stammered.

"Think nothing of it!" the gardener waved, rushing off. "I must return to my stepchildren!"

Xanthus turned toward me, frank admiration on his face. "Aesop, in one fell swoop, you have made two men exceedingly happy! How did you know he would respond so generously?"

"The art of gentle persuasion," I said. "It always works."

Xanthus quizzically repeated, "Gentle persuasion?"

I pointed to the sky. "I learned it from the elements, the Sun and the Wind. The Sun and the Wind were arguing one day, over whose power was the greatest. They spied a man walking below, and they made a bet, awarding the argument to the one who could cause the man to lose his clothing. The Wind went first and blew as hard as he could, but the more be blew, the tighter the man held his robes. The Sun shone gently on the man, becoming warmer and warmer until the man happily removed his clothes and went for a swim."

"Ah, yes!" Xanthus laughed, clasping me warmly on the back. "Have you ever lectured to a class before, Aesop?"

"No," I answered quite truthfully. "I have never been in a class before."

"All the better." Xanthus smiled, directing me toward a small amphitheater, where students were already finding seats. "You will be quite refreshing to my afternoon philosophy class. Yes, I believe I have made an astute purchase in the market today."

CHAPTER 6

Our First Dinner Party

I spent the rest of the day at the head of Xanthus's class, where I fielded numerous questions put to me by intent students. Xanthus assigned his fastest scribes to record these exchanges, while the noted philosopher circled the back of the amphitheater muttering to himself. I didn't mind—I was happy not to be tilling a field or pulling an oar. The questions were of such profundity as "Why does a pig squeal when other animals do not?"; "What is the sure way to wealth?"; and "How can a wretched dwarf be so smart?"

"As to the pig, the answer is very simple," I replied. "The cow, the sheep, and the goat do not squeal when their masters come to fetch them, because they know that man keeps them for their milk and wool. The pig, on the other hand, squeals in terror at the sight of his master, because he knows he has nothing to offer but his flesh."

As soon as the murmurs died down, I tackled the next question. "To give you an indication how wealth is achieved, let me relate a story concerning Plutus, god of wealth. When Hercules was elevated to divinity, Zeus arranged a reception for him on Mount Olympus, so that he could meet his fellow gods in a congenial atmosphere. Hercules welcomed each god at the door and bowed courteously, but when Plutus entered, Hercules turned his back on the god of wealth and refused to speak. Zeus took the hero aside and demanded to know why he had treated Plutus in such a rude manner. Scowled Hercules, 'When I was among men, I saw him associating for the most part with scoundrels.' "

Surprised laughter sounded, and when it faded, I answered the third question. "How am I, so small of stature, possessed of such wisdom? The answer again lies with the gods. After Zeus had fashioned men, he ordered Hermes to pour some sense into them. Trying to be fair, Hermes measured out equal portions of good sense and poured that amount into each man and woman. Of course, the result was that each person of small stature became filled with wisdom, while larger persons were left somewhat lacking."

The students hooted their approval, while some glanced guiltily back at their tall professor, prowling the rear of the assembly. "Thank you, Aesop," he smiled. "May I point out that wisdom has left you no more than a slave? How do you account for that?"

For that, I had no ready fable. "I was born a slave, and Apollo wishes for me to remain a slave," I said somberly. "But I intend to gain my freedom before my life is over."

"Not until you repay the seventy-five denarii I put out for you!" Xanthus threatened, eliciting a gale of snide laughter from his students.

The professor waved his hand, and the folds of his gown billowed regally. "We do not wish to exhaust all of Aesop's wisdom in one afternoon. Therefore, class is dismissed!"

The young men bolted from the amphitheater like a herd of gazelles, although a few remained behind to bombard me with more questions. "What does Apollo look like?" one asked.

"Tomorrow, tomorrow!" Xanthus snapped, leading me away. "Aesop isn't going anywhere."

* * *

Unfortunately, he was right. My circumstances had changed once again, but my status hadn't. I was still wearing a slave bracelet. Samos was a distinct improvement over Phrygia or Ephesus, but I had to weigh that against the prospect of living with a mistress who hated me. Should Xanthus take ill or be away on a journey, Lady Xanthus could have me put to death, have my eyes gouged out, flail me with hot pokers, or merely sell me to the first barbarian who passed by. A slave's life is fraught with such hazards. How tenuous is the life of a slave? Imagine all the horrid things a child might do to one of his toys, even an especially prized toy, and realize that such a fate might befall your person. It's amazing slaves are as well adjusted as they are.

I needn't have worried my first night, however. Lady Xanthus greeted us at the door and appeared to have taken a conciliatory attitude toward both her husband and me. But she avoided meeting my eyes with hers, and whenever she did, I could see her despising me for not being the muscular masseur she had envisioned.

"You should have seen the marvelous way Aesop spoke to my class!" exclaimed Xanthus, patting me on the back. He avoided the hunch and patted me on my good shoulder. "And he convinced the gardener to give us fresh vegetables every day!"

Lady Xanthus curled her lip at me. "How resourceful. Dear husband," she begged, "I was looking over the list of scholars you have invited for dinner tomorrow night, and I am mystified as to what we should serve such a noble gathering."

Xanthus frowned. "I promised them the finest thing imaginable."

"Perhaps," smiled Lady Xanthus, "if Aesop is so clever, he could choose and prepare the dinner for tomorrow night."

Xanthus clapped his hands. "Yes, I'll wager he could! Do that, Aesop. Go to the market in the morning and buy the best and finest thing imaginable. Don't tell me what you have chosen—surprise me!"

I nodded. "And how many will there be?"

"Six. All of them men," said Lady Xanthus, taking Xanthus's arm and leading him away. "Now go to the kitchen and ask one of the girls to feed you."

I had a lonely meal of a few bread crusts, some dried figs, and goat's milk. None of the serving wenches would deign to speak to me, which was just as well, for I was busy planning the menu for the next night's festivities. I resolved to make it a more interesting affair than the meal of that night. Since no one told me differently, I curled up on a cot in the kitchen, desiring to be close to the pantry.

The next morning, Xanthus himself gave me a small pouch of coins. This was the first time in my life I had ever been entrusted with money, and I tried not to show how excited I was. What I needed for dinner was relatively inexpensive, and I spent the rest of the money on a new pair of sandals and a sumptuous meal. Word of my arrival in Xanthus's house had spread among the merchants, and they accorded me the utmost courtesy, as well as charging me top dollar.

I refused to allow anyone to enter the kitchen while I prepared the meal. I let the maidservants set the table and instructed them to keep the wine flowing during the course of the dinner, but I asked them to let me serve the food. Each course, I knew, would require a bit of explanation.

The scholars came, and a jovial sort they were. Apparently, Xanthus was famous for his wine cellar, and they set right in to test its merits. Xanthus led them all the way, and the six men were quite on their way to inebriation when I served the first course.

"Ah, here is the first course!" cried Xanthus, clapping his hands.

"Boiled tongue!" cried a fat scholar.

A thin scholar with no hair curled his lip. "That is an odd first course."

"As long as the wine is good, the dinner is good!" cried the merriest of the merrymakers. He drained his goblet with a slurping noise, as if to reinforce his point.

"My tongue has always appreciated the tongue of others!" exclaimed the youngest scholar, taking a huge mouthful.

"The tongue is excellent!" the oldest scholar smiled graciously.

"Yes, it's very delicious, Aesop," said Xanthus, smacking his lips. "But it's not too substantial—bring us the second dish as well, so that we may have more to choose from."

I bowed. "As you wish, Master."

"He's a good cook, even if he's not too pretty!" laughed the jolly one.

I returned quickly and set a plate before each man.

"*Roast* tongue!" sneered the skinny scholar.

"By Zeus's beard, what is this, Aesop?" exclaimed Xanthus.

I replied, "Roast tongue with salt and pepper."

Xanthus shook with exasperation. "Aesop, tongue is a proper first course but not a first *and* second course. Please bring us the main dish."

One of the servant girls swept in with more wine, keeping the complaints to a minimum. I caught her winking at me, as I shuffled out.

As I returned, I heard the young scholar saying, "You are a wonderful actor, Xanthus, pretending you know nothing of these various tongues."

"I swear!" cried Xanthus.

"No need to excuse yourself," said the kindly older man. "This is a superb dinner. The first tongue was a bit bland, but this second one is as sharp and biting as a tongue should be."

"Marvelous!" cried the fat man, as I set his plate down. "Now we are served *pickled* tongue!"

"Aesop!" moaned Xanthus.

The jovial scholar laughed heartily. *"All* of our tongues will be pickled if we drink much more of this wine!"

"Exactly!" exclaimed the fat scholar. "The philosopher Xanthus has collapsed the entire art of conversation into one dinner! First the tongue is bland and nondescript, then it is sharp and spicy, and now it is inebriated!" He raised his glass in salute. *"Stupendous!"*

The guests applauded enthusiastically, and Xanthus glanced uneasily at me. "Perhaps Aesop could elaborate. Why did you . . . *we* choose the tongue?"

I cleared my throat. "My master told me to buy the finest and best thing imaginable. And what is finer than the tongue? With it, all communication, commerce, theater, philosophy, and law are conducted. By means of the tongue, man is lifted from the realm of common animals."

"True," agreed the thin bald man. "But what would you have served had your master instructed you to buy the foulest, most worthless thing imaginable?"

I shrugged. "Why, the same of course—tongue."

"How so?" wondered the older scholar.

I replied, "Is not the tongue the cause of all evil which man commits against his fellow man? Thanks to the tongue and its misuse, we have war, strife, hatred, jealousy, and marital disharmony. The tongue is deceitful, spiteful, harmful, and foul! What is worse than the tongue?"

"Nothing, by Zeus!" clapped the fat man. "All that you say, Aesop, has the stamp of wisdom! Come, have a drink with us!"

The others applauded his idea. Even Xanthus looked agreeable. I snapped my fingers at one of the maidservants, got myself a goblet, and sat down. "Now let us begin some serious conversation!" I enthused.

Oh, I know we were all drunk—I no less than the others. Still, that was no excuse for what happened later that evening. I should have seen where my master was headed with his drunken discourse on the power of the mind. They were all espousing one sort of bumble-brained philosophy or another at some point in the evening. What I failed to see was how skillfully the older philosopher, Lacrimus, was goading Xanthus from one ridiculous conclusion to another.

"That has always been the basis of your teaching," he said calmly to Xanthus. "But I don't believe a man can do *anything.*"

"Of course he can!" Xanthus insisted. *"I* can do anything if I put my mind to it!"

I think I cleared my throat at that point.

Xanthus hiccuped and banged his hand on the table. "You name something, and I'll do it!"

Smiled the kindly scholar, "Can you drink the sea dry?"

Xanthus nodded forcefully, his chin hammering the table. "If it exists, it can be done!"

The scholar leaned forward. "I'll wager my house and properties against your house and properties that you cannot drink the sea dry."

"Done!" cried Xanthus. "Lacrimus, here is my ring to seal the bet."

As I looked on in horror, Xanthus handed his ring to the elder scholar, who smiled gratefully. The others looked on either in astonishment or confusion.

"Master Xanthus . . ." I finally sputtered.

But he was staggering to his feet. "Be quiet, Aesop. I'm going to bed."

The other wagerer stood. "We shall return at one o'clock to see you drink the sea dry."

The fat scholar struggled to his feet and hiccuped, "Nice party, Xanthus!"

CHAPTER 7

Treachery and Sorcery

Lady Xanthus was furious the next day. As I could have surmised, the maidservants had spied on the diners all evening and reported every detail to her. She screamed and yelled at Xanthus before he was even awake, and he went back to sleep as soon as she left the room. Amidst great wailing and recriminating stares at me, the lady and the maidservants stalked out of the house. I had no idea where they were going, and my head was not equipped for much thinking that particular morning.

"Aesop! Aesop!" Xanthus moaned softly from his bed.

I padded into the room. "Yes, Master Xanthus?"

"Bring me something cool to drink. And bring me something cool to put my head in." He lay back, groaning.

"Yes, Master."

When I returned, he felt around his pillows and blankets and grumbled, "Where is my ring? I seem to have lost it."

I nodded solemnly. "That you did, Master."

"And where is my wife? I seem to have lost her too."

"Quite possibly," I agreed.

He blinked his eyes at me. "What exactly happened last night?"

"You bet everything you own that you could drink the sea dry. To seal the bet, you gave Lacrimus your ring."

He grabbed his temples and wailed, "I am ruined!"

"Without doubt," I agreed. "Your wife was so upset to discover the wager, she left this morning. But one of the maidservants will return and tell me where she has gone."

"How do you know this?"

"I know women," I admitted.

"But the wager!" he screeched. "When am I to perform this insane miracle?"

"They are coming at one o'clock today," I answered.

He sunk to his knees. "Oh, Aesop, you must save me! My wife I am capable of dealing with . . . I think. But how am I to win a bet to drink the sea dry?"

I let him sob for a few moments, then replied, "I have given the matter some thought, and, although I cannot make it possible for you to win the bet, I believe I can get you out of it."

"By the gods, how?" he gasped.

"First, I have a request," I said diplomatically.

"Say it," grimaced Xanthus.

"Grant me my freedom."

"But you are the best slave I've ever owned!"

"If you lose that bet, I'll belong to Lacrimus," I reminded him.

Xanthus sighed. "Very well. Extricate me from the wager, and I shall free you."

I smiled. "After you have eaten, I will coach you in what to say to Lacrimus and the others when they arrive."

Arrive they did, as close to noonday as was seemly. All had broad smiles on their faces, especially the old fox, Lacrimus. I began to realize that Xanthus's success had spawned more than a little jealousy and that these so-called friends were really a pack of jackals, waiting for the lion to stumble.

"Good afternoon, Professor Xanthus," said Lacrimus with a low bow. "You appear none the worse for wear."

The others chuckled. Xanthus merely looked bored. "As

my slave once illustrated with a fable," he sighed, "appearances can be deceiving."

"Are you ready to drink the sea dry?" the fat scholar asked, bursting with laughter.

Haughtily, Xanthus replied, "Laugh if you like—I am ready to do my part."

The thin bald scholar looked incredulous. "You can't be serious?"

"Xanthus, my old friend," said Lacrimus magnanimously, "if you turn over to me the majority of your property, I am prepared to be lenient and leave you the school with which to earn a livelihood."

At that point, I put a jug of seawater and a large goblet in front of Xanthus. "Here is the seawater, Master."

"Thank you, Aesop," said Xanthus, rubbing his hands. "We are ready to begin."

The young scholar bowed. "Professor, I salute your sense of humor in the face of adversity."

"You carry this charade too far," scowled the skinny one. "Admit you cannot drink the sea dry."

Xanthus smiled agreeably. "My memories of last night are a bit cloudy. What are the terms of the bet?"

"You are to drink the sea dry?" laughed two or three of them at once.

"That and only that?" asked the philosopher.

"Only that," smiled Lacrimus.

Xanthus nodded solemnly. "Very well. Across the entire earth, there are many rivers and streams which empty into the sea. Since the terms of the bet are to drink the sea dry and only the sea, you must first stop the rivers and streams from flowing into the sea. After you have done that, I will proceed."

"But we can't do that!" roared Lacrimus.

The philosopher shrugged. "I am not obligated to drink the rivers and streams dry as well."

"By the Muses, he is right!" shrieked an amazed scholar. "The bet is disallowed!"

"Xanthus has triumphed!" screamed another. They all gathered around him, kissing his hand and fawning.

Lacrimus was truly repentant. He knelt before Xanthus and bowed. "Master Xanthus, I underestimated you. You are truly the greatest philosopher of all time. Here is your ring. I beg your forgiveness."

"By rights, I should have your fortune for not fulfilling your part of the wager," scowled Xanthus. "But I'll let it pass this time. Arise and trouble me no more with such simple problems."

Reverently, the scholars arose and backed out. "Hail Xanthus!" several of them muttered.

When they were gone, Xanthus turned to me and cackled, "What a pack of dolts!"

"We got the best of them!" I agreed.

Xanthus rose and shook my hand. "Thank you, Aesop, for your help."

"My freedom will be thanks enough."

"Yes," said Xanthus, walking away, "I must give some thought as to when that will take place."

"When?" I squeaked. "I thought it would be now!"

Xanthus cocked his head and kept on walking. "I don't believe there was any specific mention of time in our agreement. I said I shall free you, and so I shall. Someday. Until then, Aesop, you have learned an important lesson—never take anything for granted."

I watched the departing figure with shock and utter dismay. And I stalked out the rear door of the house.

In my anger, I wandered high up into the hills, far from Xanthus's household. By the time I stopped to catch a breath in a chest that was still heaving with anger, I could no longer see the complex of buildings, the amphitheater, or even the seaport beyond. I could no longer see the sea. All I could see was a patchwork of rocky hills and wind-ragged trees. I didn't realize I had been climbing and climbing, but I had; and now I was lost in a land I scarcely knew.

I'd like to say I didn't become afraid, but I did. How was I to know that Samos didn't have bandits or wolves or *griffins* prowling her rugged hills? Certainly, no one lived here, not with the lush land near the sea. I began scanning the horizon for landmarks, but I couldn't tell one rock from another. I also feared that Xanthus would think that in my anger, I had chosen to escape, and he would come after me with dogs and nets. Many a slave-driven galley called in the port of Samos, and that would be a fitting end for an escaped and captured slave.

Then again, I thought to myself, perhaps I had run away, albeit unwittingly. I had every reason to run away from an ungrateful and dishonest owner like that! Of course, a tribunal wouldn't see it that way. Maybe, I thought, the other side of the island held refuge or escape! I wasn't known in this place, and in a different city on the other side of the island, I might pass for a juggler and tumbler, as I now practiced both those noble trades. My pulse quickened with the delirious joy of freedom.

Then my eyes caught the gleam of my copper-colored slave bracelet. It was welded in place, fit tightly, and had sharp edges—some masters spent more for the bracelets and collars than for the slaves who wore them. The bracelet was as much a part of me as my hunched back or lopsided nose, but I knew it was more of a detriment than either of those. It branded me as somebody's property.

Just as I was about to sit on a rock, in abject despair, the wind turned, and a dark mass of clouds swirled overhead. I was not so accustomed to island life to know that a storm could attack instantly, as it did that afternoon in those craggy hills. A drop the size of a pomegranate hit me in the face and rolled down my neck. The rain felt quite wonderful, soothing, and I stood there for some moments before I began getting cold and thought about shelter.

The hillside was not mountainous enough to possess actual caves, big enough to shelter a man. But I don't know
if I would have had the courage to enter a strange cave
anyway; griffins and sphinxes were still large in my
thoughts. No, I was definitely looking for a house, hut, or
lean-to, something built by a man, whom I have always
trusted more than the elemental forces of the earth.

I was clinging to a slippery rock wall, expecting it to
lead me somewhere, when miraculously it did! I came to
some scraggly vineyard, ill and unkempt, though there
were grapes growing on the vine. This was a good sign,
because it meant that they probably had wine. But I had to
remind myself that I was an escaped slave and shouldn't
be thinking along the lines of meeting people. I decided to
look for a gardener's shed or barn and hope it wasn't too
leaky.

Nevertheless, I was drawn irresistibly to some puffs of
smoke I saw fighting their way through the rain. A tiny
thatched house was the only building I saw, and the only
thing inviting about it was the smoke curling from a tiny
cookhouse in the rear. I should have ducked under the
vines or made myself a lean-to, but the idea of a fire,
warmth, and food conquered my resolve to keep myself
hidden. I was a slave who was lost, it was as simple as
that. And if they didn't like it, or me, or I didn't like them,
I was prepared to run.

As soon as I stepped gingerly through the gate, the rain
let up. I could have run then and there, but instead I froze
in my tracks, just looking at the door of the cottage, expecting it to open. The door promptly did open, and a
plain but not unattractive woman in a well-worn tunic
stepped out and glared at me.

"Do you want something?" she asked.

"No!" I said, shaking my head and tumbling backward.
I pointed dumbly at the sky, but of course the rain had
stopped and the clouds were blowing away.

"Yes, it rained," she nodded. "That doesn't give you

permission to trespass. Had you walked into my house, I would've turned you into a pile of cinders!"

"Well," I said, waving, "I can always be leaving now." I moved through the gate, ready to run.

"Wait!" she called suddenly. "You are Xanthus's slave!"

That, like so many things this woman did, caught me dead in my tracks. I whirled to face her. "How did you know that?"

"Your bracelet," she said, pointing and walking toward me. I now saw that she had a very beautiful and very strange necklace draped across her nicely rounded bosom. The necklace was strung of gems, dried pods, animal teeth, and lizards' heads. Except for the lizard's heads, it was quite beautiful; when the sun struck it, the jewels and crystals glowed majestically.

"Your bracelet marks you," she said again, shaking me from my reveries. "You are the slave of whom I heard . . . Aesop!"

"Who did you hear it from?" I asked, not imagining that many people had passed this way since my arrival. Maybe this unusual woman was a friend of Lady Xanthus.

"The birds," she shrugged. "The squirrels and the lizards. They've told me much about your arrival in the household of Master Xanthus." She spit out his name, and I instantly warmed to her.

"I share your distaste for Xanthus," I agreed. "He is disgusting, vile, and odious, and that's why I have run away! Perhaps you could shelter me here for a night . . ."

"Aesop!" she screeched, sending me rocking back on my heels. "Do you know what they'd do to me if they caught me harboring a slave? They hate me enough as it is!" She smiled wickedly. "Of course, they fear me too."

When she smiled with that evil glint, I thought the woman was quite beautiful, though she was my equal or more in age.

"You know my name well enough," I said. "What is yours?"

"Netha," she replied, offering me her hand. No woman had ever offered me her hand before, and I didn't think at first that she was serious. But she held it out there until I gingerly took it in my own and kissed it. This was a singularly impressive moment for me, and I felt real kinship for this woman, Netha. But I was still an escaped slave with pressing problems, and she had already said she wouldn't help me.

"It's a pleasure to meet you," I said, drifting back out the gate.

"Go home, Aesop," she said. "Xanthus will not be mad. He has been frantic, wondering what has become of you, thinking that one of his friends has stolen you. Between you and his wife, I'm not sure which one he misses more."

I gaped at her with amazement. "How do you know all that?"

"Ask anyone about Netha," she smiled mysteriously. "And follow that path to the right of the house. It leads to town, and I'm sure you can find your way from there." She waved pleasantly, but it was a wave of dismissal.

I stumbled out and found the path with very little problem. It was not a wide path but a well-worn one, indicating that few people came here together, but many people came often by themselves. My first unpleasant thought was that Netha was a whore. That would explain why some people didn't like her and even how she came to know so much. But this rough hillside at the center of the island seemed an unlikely place for a whore to conduct business. Men might go around the corner for that sort of thing, but not climb halfway up a mountain. She was certain about her notoriety, there was no doubt about that. What had she meant about talking to birds and lizards, whose little heads adorned her neck? What about reducing me to a cinder? If these claims were to be taken at face value . . . Netha was a sorceress!

At the port, it didn't take me long to verify that Netha was Samos's resident sorceress, though no one I spoke to claimed to have met her personally. The innkeeper said she was a creature of great legend, and he doubted she existed. Nevertheless, priests and emissaries from around the world sometimes called in port specifically to visit Netha, and they rarely returned looking disappointed. Sobered, yes, but not disappointed. Once or twice, adventurers had gone up there to kill her—either they didn't find her, or they never returned. Anyone who did go to see Netha, he winked, would not likely tell people about it. I certainly didn't tell anyone that *I* had seen her.

A carpenter told me that wicked people went to see her all the time, but she killed good people on sight. A barmaid told me that her grandmother had visited Netha a generation ago to cure her infertility. A goatherd insisted that Netha was dead. A one-legged beggar told me that Netha was hard to find, unless you made it very clear you were seeking her by saying so aloud every step of the way. The well-worn path had a means of vanishing, he said.

With night falling, I dashed home, my mind awhirl with all these possibilities. What had seemed a hospitable and common woman now turned out to be a mysterious and powerful witch, and I considered myself very lucky, indeed, that I wasn't a pile of cinders.

Xanthus nearly turned me into a pile of cinders with his heated wrath. "Where have you been? What have you been doing? What are you going to do about Lady Xanthus?"

"What am *I* going to do about Lady Xanthus?" I asked with disdain. "Give thanks that she's gone! The way you cheated me out of my freedom, I owe you nothing."

"Please, Aesop, please!" he begged me, dropping to his knees. "I shall not rest as long as you are a slave, I swear it! Forget your grievance and help me win my lady back—I beg you!"

The pathetic lovesick fool actually prodded my heart. "You won't rest a day?

"I won't rest a day!" he reiterated.

"Very well," I sighed. "I will see that she returns, but first you must hear a fable."

"Anything!" he shrieked.

"This is the story of the lion who fell in love with a maiden. A farmer had a beautiful daughter, so beautiful that a lion fell in love with her at first sight. He moped around until he could stand it no longer, and he asked the farmer for the maiden's hand in wedlock. The farmer was, of course, loath to give his daughter in marriage to a beast, but he was too afraid of the lion to say so. Yet the farmer was smart, and he said to the lion, 'Of course, I am proud to have my daughter marry the King of the Beasts! But she is frightened of your claws and your teeth and would prefer that you have them removed before the wedding.' The lion was so foolishly in love that he had all his claws and every tooth removed to the root. When he returned to the farmer's house for the wedding, the farmer easily beat him to death with a club."

Xanthus gulped. "You think I am being foolish?"

"I *know* it!" I replied. "But that is the cost of love.

"When will you win my lady back?" he asked meekly.

I wandered off to the kitchen in search of a bite of food. "We must wait until tomorrow, when a maidservant returns."

The next day was sheer bliss, what with Lady Xanthus and all the maidservants gone and Xanthus in such a state of depression that he could hardly talk. I busied myself teaching Xanthus's classes, though I admit I did little more than regale them with fables. That's what they wanted to hear, and I have never failed to please an audience if I could. Often, my mind turned uncomfortably to thoughts of Netha, the mysterious sorceress of the hills. Not that thinking of Netha was uncomfortable, but the idea that I could be as stricken by love as poor Xanthus—that was disturbing.

I did not blame him, however, for taking some time off from his classes. The afternoon philosophy class, in particular, was afflicted with an extreme case of snobbery and class consciousness. One pampered ingrate insisted that he should not have to sit through a lecture administered by a slave, when he could just as easily be chasing barmaids. I took this as a cue, of course.

"Many years ago," I began, "when animals spoke the same language as men, a mouse mistakenly ran across the body of a sleeping lion. The lion reached up, seized the mouse, and was about to devour him, when the mouse said, 'Oh, please, master lion, do not eat me! I am but a pitiful mouthful, and if you spare my life, I will return your kindness someday.' The lion laughed at such a silly notion, but he was in a good mood and decided to let the mouse go. Only a few days later, some hunters built a trap with a net, into which the lion plunged. No matter how much he struggled, the net held him fast. The lion had all but given up hope, when the tiny mouse heard his groans and came to his rescue. The mouse quickly gnawed through the net and set the lion free, saying as he left, 'You see, even the lowliest of creatures can be of aid to the mightiest.' "

I don't wish to brag, but the class was completely won over by this tale and demanded more. They also wanted explanations of the fable-weaving process. "How many fables do you know?" one asked.

"An unlimited number," I replied, "because I make them up as I go along."

Another asked, "Why do you always tell fables about animals?"

I chuckled. "The human race is very vain and doesn't like to hear about its own shortcomings. People listen better when they think the story is about animals."

"Surely, Aesop, you must know one with people in it!" the student insisted.

"Well," I shrugged, "there is the tale of the middle-aged

man and his two mistresses. One of the mistresses was elderly and the other young. As the elderly mistress was ashamed to be seen with a younger man, she plucked the black hairs from his head at every opportunity. But the younger mistress was equally sensitive about being seen with an older man, so she pulled out his gray hairs at every chance. Between the two of them, the man quickly found himself bald!"

Gales of laughter greeted this conclusion, and someone shouted, "'Tis folly to try to please everyone!"

I nodded, catching sight of a distraught man waving his hands at me from the rear of the amphitheater. "True," I replied, "but we are constantly asked to do so anyway." I made my way down from the podium. "If you'll excuse me, I must confer with our master."

The students turned and acknowledged Xanthus with respectful greetings, but he completely ignored them and ushered me away. "She's back!" he whispered.

"Your wife?"

"No!" he hissed. "The maid—Mineva!" He looked accusingly at me. "You said you could get Lady Xanthus to return when one of her maids returned."

"So I did," I nodded. "And have you forgotten your promise?"

"No, of course not," scoffed Xanthus. "I have already prepared legal documents concerning your freedom. Now, please, *help me, Aesop!*"

"Where is Mineva?" I asked.

"In the kitchen," he sighed. His angular shoulders sloped forward, making him look like a fallen leaf that was curling in the sun.

Mineva was the one I thought would return. Of the four handmaidens, she was by far the most intelligent and capable, the one most likely to be sent on such a sensitive mission. Mineva was not the prettiest of the maidservants, but she was young and fair and had a saucy manner.

"You're history," she said to me, selecting a fig from a huge basket of food she had collected.

"Don't worry about me," I said. "I don't plan upon staying around here much longer. Tell me where your mistress has hidden herself."

"Why should I?" she asked saucily.

"Because you wish to see me gone and yourselves back in this house. Our aims are the same, Mineva, believe me. Tell me where she is so that I might tell her how miserable Xanthus is."

She chuckled. "Yes, I've seen him! Pathetic!"

I joined her laughter. "I'd be happy to leave him a day or two in that condition!"

When Mineva finished laughing, she whispered in my ear, "The Lady Xanthus is staying in the house of her cousin Patria, on the River Road."

"It must be crowded in that little house," I remarked. "You are going to stay and keep us company, aren't you, Mineva?"

She hesitated. "Well, I did tell Lady Xanthus that I would return with news."

"I'll go there tomorrow," I promised, "and I'll take the basket of food with me. Stay the night, please. It cheers up the professor to have you back."

"Do you think so?" she asked, fluffing her hair.

"Yes, I do. Wouldn't you rather spend the night in your own bed? You won't have any duties to perform here."

"Well," she mused, stretching her arms luxuriantly. "Perhaps I will. Do you know, Aesop—you aren't so hideous."

"Thank you, Mineva. You are quite beautiful."

She blushed and bobbed me playfully on the nose. "I wish *you* were."

Somehow, I was able to convince Xanthus that one day more before his wife returned wouldn't make any difference. Matters of a delicate nature throve best in the clear light of morning, I told him. I related the story of the goose who laid golden eggs, equating Xanthus with the stupid farmer. After our talk, the sun was setting, a warm drizzle drenched the island, and Xanthus felt better. I could only feel better when I was freed.

The next day, I took my good time in finding Patria's house. I first went into town, dined, and watched a few ships embark, wondering what I would do with myself once I was free. Should I return to Phrygia? What for? Better I should journey the world: Greece, Egypt, Carthage. I waited in town until I saw the other three maidservants doing their shopping. I picked up a length of twine and carried it with me, to back up the story I was about to use.

I can well imagine what took place in Patria's house as I approached. "Someone's coming!" said Patria.

"Who?" asked Lady Xanthus, straightening her gown.

"Your husband's ugly slave."

"Curse him!" shrieked Lady Xanthus. "He mustn't see me here!" She ducked through a curtain.

I rapped on the door, and Patria answered it. She was a well-bred woman with a balding head. "What do you want?" she asked suspiciously.

I smiled dumbly. "I am looking for some geese to buy for a wedding. Do you have any?"

"What wedding?" she asked. "Who is getting married?"

"Xanthus the philosopher." I heard a jar break in the rear of the house.

"Xanthus?" asked Patria.

"Yes," I nodded, "his wife left him some time ago, and now he is getting married to one of the maidservants. Mineva, I think her name is."

"Mineva!" shrieked a voice from the back.

"What was that?" I queried.

"A parrot!" snapped Patria. "It repeats everything one says."

"Not quite everything," I pointed out. "Mineva was only the last thing I said, and . . ."

"Get out of here!" she hissed.

"The goose," I reminded her.

"I have no goose! Now go away!"

I went away, though I heard a voice wailing from within, "I knew I couldn't trust that girl!"

"Yes, yes?" asked Xanthus eagerly. "What did she say? When will she return?"

I hung my head, the portrait of sorrow. "I am sorry, Master. I have terrible news."

He grabbed my shirt. "She is harmed! She is dead!"

"Worse," I muttered. "She is leaving for Greece tomorrow with a caravan of young male slaves."

"Young male slaves!" Xanthus gaped. "I must stop her! Where is she?"

"At the house of her cousin, Patria."

Never, before or since, have I seen Xanthus move so rapidly and with such slight regard for decorum. He ran out of the house in his bare feet and returned from his mad dash cut and bruised. But he returned with his wife at his side, and they were the picture of marital bliss. I am told they met on the path and fell deliriously into each other's arms, maintaining that undignified pose for the better part of an hour. I don't doubt it for an instant, for I have never seen two people so dependent upon one another yet so determined not to show it. That night, they had no choice but to be in love.

The next morning, Xanthus threw open the shutters and proclaimed, "Aesop, we must have a banquet in honor of our reconciliation!"

I cleared my throat. "May I remind you, Master Xanthus, of the terms of our agreement?"

"Agreement?" he asked quizzically.

"You said you would not rest a day while I am a slave."

"Ah, yes," the philosopher nodded sagely. "I have already attended to it, putting a writ in my will saying you are to be freed the instant I die."

The instant he died was nearly the next instant. I reached up for the philosopher's throat, but Xanthus mistook my actions for an embrace and hugged me warmly. It's very difficult to strangle a man who is hugging you with joy, so I let him live. But I knew, then and there, that no one ever willingly frees a slave. Slavery is so unnatural that the only way for both slave and master to adjust is to treat the whole matter as if it were the most natural thing in the world to own another human being.

CHAPTER 8

The Simple Life

A few days later, I was still feeling bridled by slavery, as well as a bit bored, so I took a long walk into the craggy hills at the center of the island. On my mind was the idea that, if humanity couldn't free me, perhaps sorcery could. Plus, I had a strong curiosity about Netha, an apparently simple woman who grew grapes, talked with lizards, and was called a sorceress. She had seemed neither mad nor dangerous, though either was a possibility; despite my usual caution in such matters, I was intrigued.

What had the beggar said? Speak her name aloud every step of the way, and look for the path. That was the gist of it. Paths were hard to come by in this desolate landscape, but there was certainly no one around to mind if I spoke her name now and then. "Netha," I said. "I am seeking Netha."

The path didn't magically appear—by that, I mean it didn't spring into view with a flash or a thunderbolt. But a path did become apparent in the scraggly underbrush, a simple path, such as that worn by goats and wild boar. Before I was fully aware of it, I was walking along the path, already feeling a warm contentment. What a startlingly beautiful day it was! I felt as if I was on an adventure, a hike around the world! Normally, I was very aware of the physical restrictions of the island and my slave bracelet, but today I felt I could walk around the world.

I was in such a happy mood that I was forgetting about my mission, and I was surprised when I rounded the rock wall and saw the little hut, with its crooked chimney and curling smoke. The grapevines were gone, replaced by a field of unruly marjoram and other herbs, most of which were unknown to me. I had the distinct impression that this was not the same house as before; perhaps it was the same house, but it definitely wasn't the same place. I was nervous as I strode toward the house, but I kept thinking about my mission. "Netha, I need your help," I said aloud.

The wind shifted, and the smoke from the chimney curled around me. The smoke was sweet smelling, not fiery and sooty like a normal heating fire. I thought maybe she was cooking something extraordinarily tasty—the smoke had that kind of sticky attraction. I followed it to the door of her house and walked right in.

I was engulfed in incense. The whole house was a furnace of cloying, intoxicating smoke. I nearly fainted, but I managed to land on an animal fur and maintain my senses, though what senses I had were too busy processing the enormous varieties of smells bombarding my nose, mouth, and chest. I sat up and peered through the incense until I saw her slight body slicing through the fog.

"Just sleep now," she said, stroking my head. "You are tired from your long walk, and I have business to attend to."

I don't know how she did it, but she put me to sleep like a lullaby and cradle. I dreamed of the Muses, dancing in the sky the day they showered me with gifts. My voice was now my most precious possession, and I wondered how I ever existed without it. Someday, maybe I would feel the same way about my freedom. These pleasant thoughts entertained me until she gently stroked my shoulder.

"Wake up, Aesop," she cooed. I blinked awake immediately.

I gazed into unearthly green eyes, the color of the sea when seen from a mountaintop. The face was plain yet oddly alluring, as if the plainness was a disguise and not the real personality, which was much more fiery and direct. At times, she seemed like an earth mother, nurturing and reassuring, and I felt like curling up in her bosom and going back to sleep. But I was much too curious to miss anything now.

"Netha!" I exclaimed. I looked around and saw that the smoke was gone, though its heady fragrance lingered. "Why were you burning so much incense?"

She smiled, "I had difficult work to do."

I was suddenly parched and smacked my lips. "Do you have anything to drink?"

"Of course," she nodded. "What kind of hostess would I be? Will you have wine, water, or goat's milk?"

"Wine!" I answered, scrambling to my feet.

She returned in a blink with a hand-carved marble goblet brimming with rosy wine. Even the wine smelled riper and more intoxicating than anything I had ever smelled before. All my senses seemed drunken, and trying to get drunker.

"So, you're a sorceress," I remarked with studied indifference. "I've never met a sorceress."

She shrugged modestly. "I know some things. You are quite a special person yourself."

"A *slave!?*" I gaped. "How could a slave be anything but the lowest of creatures?"

"Quit feeling sorry for yourself, Aesop!" she scoffed. "You've been blessed by the gods with a magnificent array of talents that even the gods envy!"

As usual, I was stunned by her omnipotent knowledge. But I had a point I was trying to make. "These talents which the gods so envy are being wasted upon a stupid philosopher and his petty wife!"

"So you say," she replied, "but look at the influence you are having upon his students, some of the greatest minds of Greece. And don't underestimate Samos. This little island is strategically located, ripe for conquest."

"Conquest?" I asked. "What has that to do with me? I'm already a slave, and one more conqueror won't make any difference."

"We'll see," she smiled mysteriously. "I might be of some help to you yet. First, I have to test you, to make sure you are the person you purport to be. I must ask you a question."

I sipped my wine. "Ask what you wish."

"Why is it?" she began, "that when we defecate, we usually stop to look at our own droppings?"

I spit out a bit of my wine, letting it dribble down my chin. I looked at this proper woman and saw that she was perfectly serious. She wanted to know.

"A long time ago," I answered, "there was a certain king's son who had a very loose way of living, which resulted in loose bowels. He would sit for such a long time relieving himself—that one day he passed his own wits! Ever since that day, when humans relieve themselves, they stop to look down in fear that they, too, have passed their own wits."

She laughed, then nodded sagely. "Yes, I believe that is the one and true answer. You may come to visit me whenever you wish. But do not hurry—take your time along the path. Sometimes I must come from great distances."

"Then you'll help me?" I beamed.

"I shall try, but I think you are better off and safer as a slave."

"Why?" I asked.

"Apollo," she shrugged. "You are protected by him as long as you are a slave."

"Suppose I don't want to be a slave?" I bristled. "Isis and the Muses freed my tongue but left my appearance as you see it. That is enough balance in my life, and I see no reason why I must remain a slave too!"

"Apollo wishes it," Netha whispered.

I shook my finger at her. "Apollo, my supposed benefactor, once sent a sphinx to eat me if I couldn't answer a riddle. The gods are always testing me. Perhaps *you* would've turned into a sphinx if I hadn't answered *your* question!"

She reared up angrily, and I instantly regretted my candor. Plus, I wondered if what I had said was actually true? There was much more to Netha than what she presented, though I couldn't fault her for having her secrets, not in her profession.

"I won't kill you!" she spit. "But you should remember that I could in an instant!" She flicked her wrist, and an explosion sounded in my ear. I huddled up in pain, covering my aching eardrum—I thought surely lightning had struck the house! But when I looked up, everything was as before, with Netha smiling pleasantly at me. I scrambled to my feet and made cautiously for the door.

"Bide your time, Aesop," she said. "There is much to recommend a simple life."

But life in the Xanthus household was seldom that. I was involved in one battle or another with Lady Xanthus, while Xanthus came to rely upon me more and more to teach his classes and address his friends. I didn't mind this work, but it was very difficult for me to be applauded at the podium—then be treated like a scourge at the hearth! I felt I was conducting two lives, one of which was not to my liking. To give you an indication of the kind of battles royal I waged with Lady Xanthus, let me relate the following story.

One afternoon, while I accompanied Lady Xanthus and a handmaiden to the town on a shopping spree, we happened to pass a large and loping dog who took an instant dislike to me. He began barking and yapping and straining at his chain. I admit, I cowered with fear—for I'm a small person, and this was a big dog.

Lady Xanthus stopped to observe this with amusement. "Our household needs a good watchdog," she remarked.

"No!" I squeaked. "It would eat us out of house and home!"

But we had already attracted the attention of the dog's owner, a burly woman who looked like a dockworker. "This here dog's not for sale."

When a person goes out of her way to tell you something is not for sale, it most certainly is.

"I am Lady Xanthus," said my mistress imperially. "My husband is in need of a dog such as yours."

The woman bowed with surprising grace. "Lady Xanthus, I might make an exception for your noble household."

Lady Xanthus acknowledged her bow with a nod of her head. "A dog like that might be worth fifty denarii,"

"Eighty denarii," smiled the woman. This was, of course, five more denarii than Xanthus paid for me.

"It looks vicious, m'lady!" I observed.

"Nonsense!" she scoffed. "It looks sturdy and healthy. Fifty-five."

"Seventy-five," the woman answered. "This dog has been in my family for years. My children will be heartbroken."

"Years!" I crowed. "The dog is old and infirm!"

They both ignored me. "Sixty," said Lady Xanthus, "and that is sufficient."

And it was. "His name is Samson," said the woman, as she bent to untie the dog. My life passed before my eyes, and only the presence of several slave galleys in the port kept me from running away. As soon as the sale was concluded, Lady Xanthus handed the dog's chain to me. This rather mystified the beast, who thought he would have to be restrained from eating me; instead, the coast was clear. The loping mongrel, which could have been saddled and ridden, licked his chops and studied me, obviously wondering which of my ill-fitted parts was the juiciest.

As fortune would have it, at that instant a vendor selling roasted sausages came by with a pushcart, and I singed my hand snatching a sausage off the grill. I tossed it immediately to Samson, who consumed the morsel in two large gulps. Lady Xanthus gasped, followed by her maidservant, then the vendor.

"Why on earth did you do that?" the lady shrieked.

"You told me to take care of Samson," I reminded her, "and he looked hungry." Samson smiled down at me, and I reached up to pet his head.

The vendor beat me for some time, unmolested by Lady Xanthus, and my hand hurt for weeks. But it was worth it. Samson, though never taking me into his confidence, never molested me after that. Before the day was out, I learned of at least one activity we both had in common: we loved to steal food! In fact, Samson was far better at stealing than I. He was so tall at the shoulders that he could snatch scraps off any table or counter with a minimum of movement. He was as deft as a pickpocket, and he could swallow a leg of lamb or cut of brisket whole in half a blink. I have seen him purloin a custard pie from the baker's stand, a whole plucked chicken from the fowler, and half a goat from the butcher.

Of course, I was inevitably blamed for most of the missing food. Xanthus and the other servants soon realized what a thief they had accepted into the house, but Lady Xanthus preferred to blame me for everything; Samson just provided more opportunities. I never forgave Lady Xanthus for buying him to torment me.

One night, some departing students were to be honored by a dinner at Xanthus's house. Knowing the prodigious appetites of young men, Xanthus had us buy several cuts of beef, including two ribs which were to be eaten cold. These were cooked and put on the dinner table in advance to make room in the kitchen for other dishes. As I set the tasty morsels on the table, I saw Samson's cocked ear jutting slightly around the corner of the doorway, and I knew the ribs were in imminent danger. Xanthus and Lady Xanthus strolled through the room at that moment.

"Master Xanthus," I said, "only a diligent watch will keep these ribs from that mangy cur."

"Yes, indeed," Xanthus agreed, nodding somberly. "You had better stay here and watch, Aesop."

"Nonsense!" snapped Lady Xanthus. "Aesop is only trying to avoid other duties. I shall lie on the sofa and keep an eye on the plates."

"If you fall asleep," I warned, "Samson will be at them instantaneously!"

Lady Xanthus glared at me, then batted her eyes at her husband. "Xanthus knows—I have eyes in my behind."

Xanthus chuckled. "Yes, she does—never misses a thing! Go ahead, my dear, and rest until dinner. I must work on my speech."

Xanthus lumbered off, and Lady Xanthus sauntered regally to the sofa and reclined. She gave me a nod. "You are relieved of this duty, Aesop. Go and polish the silver." She wrinkled her nose. "And take a bath before you serve us tonight."

I bowed and slipped out, muttering a few choice Phrygian curses. I didn't return to the dining room until I had no choice, which was just minutes before the guests were to arrive. The first thing I saw was, as expected, the ribs were gone from their platters, cleanly and without a trace. Lady Xanthus was asleep and snoring, her back to the plundered place settings. I suddenly got a very strong urge to see the eyes in Lady Xanthus's behind.

Knowing that my lady never wore underclothing, I lifted her gown all the way to her waist. She shifted slightly and moaned, but her movements only further accentuated her delectable hindquarters. For a moment, I somewhat envied Xanthus—but the idea of being married to such a shrew gave me a sudden shiver. Nevertheless, her naked buttocks were a very pleasing sight.

Ten or so handsome young men arrived a few minutes later. I saw no reason to disturb Xanthus from his speech-writing, so I showed the young men into the dining room, instructing them not to disturb the lady of the house, who was sleeping. I watched their dumbstruck faces turn into smiles and heard their incredulous gasps segue into laughter before I slipped out the kitchen doorway.

"What is going on?" one of the maidservants snapped.

"Nothing!" I sputtered, unable to control my laughter.

I dashed outside, but I didn't run far, not wishing to miss the accompanying excitement. Upon seeing her lady's buttocks exposed in such a lascivious manner, the maid-servant shrieked, bringing Xanthus from his study. Within moments, I heard him bellow, "Aesop!"

I put on the most perfect blank face I had and shuffled into the dining room. By now, all the students were certain I had been at the bottom of this delightful diversion, and several of them smiled gratefully at me. The Lady Xanthus could barely stand to look at me, or anyone else, she was so embarrassed.

Xanthus shook with his anger. "Aesop, are you responsible for baring my lady's, uh, loins?"

I coughed. "When I saw she was asleep, I had to do something to activate the eyes in her behind."

Several students guffawed but quickly stifled their mirth under Xanthus's glare. "Out of consideration for my guests, I won't beat you this time, Aesop. But should you ever degrade Lady Xanthus again, I shall have no choice."

The lady in question bristled. "Xanthus, you mean you won't strip him and beat him for this?"

But Xanthus's attention had moved on to other topics. He looked at the table and wailed, *"What happened to my ribs?"*

CHAPTER 9

Netha

Despite several well-founded qualms, I longed to see Netha again. She fascinated me more than any woman I had ever known, including my beloved but tragically lost Hippolyte. So I left the house early one morning, ostensibly on a mission to gather wild herbs. Once again, I looked for the mysterious path in the bramblebush, all the while calling aloud, "Netha! Netha!"

I found the path, as narrow and clear as if worn by a thousand goats; but instead of Netha's house, I found the actual woman! She was strolling along the path toward me, her hair let down and a loose pale gown flowing off her shoulders. I recalled now only having seen her in a hooded garment, and I was amazed at the golden halo of hair which crowned her simple features. She smiled at me as she strode forward, not rushing and not particularly surprised to see me. She had a small basket with her, and she stooped to pick yellow flowers from a scraggly bush.

"Hello, Netha," I said, grinning with pleasure.

"Hello, Aesop," she said, stooping again to study another weed. "I believe we are on the same mission."

"Really?" Had she been seeking *my* help?

"Yes," nodded Netha. "We are both seeking herbs."

I blinked at her, wondering again at her remarkable information network. Of course, I knew if I asked her who her spies were, she would say she had been told by a bird or a toad. I was somewhat relieved on this particular morning to see that her lizard-head necklace was missing.

I shrugged sheepishly. "I really wanted to see you."

"Why?" she blinked. "Are you that unhappy? Does not your master treat you as friend and equal? Are you not revered here on this island for your wit and wisdom? You are almost as great a legend as I, and someday you will be greater."

It was my turn to blink. I had never considered myself fortunate before, but Netha could almost persuade me to believe it. At any rate, I didn't wish to argue the point; even before setting out that morning, I had decided not to keep harping about my slavery. My sole mission was simply to find Netha and get to know her. "I only want to talk to you," I replied.

"Why?" she asked.

I surprised myself by answering, "Because I love you."

Mirthfully she scoffed, "Now why should you be in love with a madwoman who lives all alone in the hills?"

"Because I'm a fool, I suppose," I answered. "What about you, why should you want to see me again?"

"Who says I wanted to see you?" she snapped, feigning displeasure. "I only said you could come see me anytime you wish."

"And so I have!" I exclaimed, clapping my hands. "I have the entire day free—what is there to do in these lonely hills?"

"The gathering of herbs does not interest you?" she asked girlishly.

I smiled with all the debonair charm a hunchback dwarf could muster. "You, dear lady, interest me. The gulls can have the rest of this oasis in the ocean."

"But Samos is an enchanted place," she whispered. "Perhaps you do not know of the Fertility Rock?"

No, but it certainly sounded like a place I wanted to see. "Take me there," I said.

She reached out and enveloped my stubby fingers in her delicate hand. A coolness and power surged through her flesh and into mine, and I felt like we shared a common destiny as well as the present. "Come with me," she whispered.

Transported we were, as if on a magic breeze which lasted no longer than a blink. For when I blinked again, we were on a tall peak, surrounded by towering evergreens. The breeze at this height was cool, so unlike the warm trade winds of the island. I could swear there was no place like this on Samos, but I hardly cared if we were on Samos or not. I hardly cared about anything as long as I was in this powerful woman's presence. I stood for a moment, scanning an immense spire of rock, poking into the clouds. At the base of the spire was a cave, with a wide, squat entrance. I began to realize why they call this place Fertility Rock—the peak was as phallic as a maypole, and the slit at the base of the mountain was equally suggestive.

A soft mist crept over us, as if a cloud had chosen to act as our curtain, shutting us off from the outside world. No one passing by this remote place would ever see us, and our voices carried no farther than a whisper. Netha took my hand and led me over a flowered crest, into the low mouth of the cave. As our breathing and pounding hearts echoed off those dark walls, we lay down on a bed of thick moss. Outside, the mist danced and swirled.

I unloosened her gown, as Netha smiled up at me, sweet and trusting. No words were spoken between us, and I had never known a woman intimately before, but I knew instantly which caress would soothe her, and which would inflame her. Her mind was my mind, her body my body. Under my fingers, her loins were like the strings of a harp, and I remembered what the muse, Erato, had said on the day when I was granted my voice: "I give Aesop the power to see into the souls of women and know what pleasures them."

I was suddenly so thankful for my blessings that I began to cry, and Netha touched my face, her hand trembling. "I too am thankful," she wept.

A moment later, I entered her, and all thoughts were banished in animal lust. We spent one another totally, then lay in the swirling mists until the sun was no longer high in the sky, and shadows darkened the mouth of the cave.

Netha stirred gently in the crook of my arm. "Tell me a story, Aesop," she cooed.

I smiled, as a fitting tale formed in my mind. "A man and a woman were once lovers, but unmarried. So the man went secretly to the woman's house several nights a week. In case a friend or relative was visiting her, he would always stop outside her door and bark like a little dog. If she was alone, she would lower the lights so no one could see, then open the door and let him in. This went on for some time, and another man of the village began to notice these strange comings and goings. He hid in the shadows one night and saw how the man gained access to the lady's bed. The next night, this interloper went to the lady's door and barked like a little dog. At once, the lights lowered, and the door opened. He slipped inside and made love to the woman, who quickly decided that two secret lovers were better than one. But the next night, when the new lover was lying with the woman, the old lover came to the door and barked like a little dog. The new lover jumped out of bed and ran to the door, where he growled and barked and carried on like the most ferocious hound imaginable. Thinking the woman had tired of him and bought a large dog to keep him away, the first lover left and never returned."

Netha sat up, her luminous eyes staring at me with mock accusation. "And what is the moral of that story, Aesop? That the one who barks the loudest deserves the prize, or that women are fickle?"

"I only tell them," I shrugged, "not explain them."

Netha chuckled huskily and began to pull her garments around her. "Come, Aesop, or it will be too late to find our way back."

I didn't understand why we couldn't blink our way back on a magical wind, as we had done to reach the jagged peak. But Netha insisted we walk, and I was soon glad we did. Despite my earlier doubts, we were still on the isle of Samos; the rugged site of our lovemaking was a long walk, but not totally inaccessible. As the highest point on the island, Fertility Rock lay hidden most of the time between banks of clouds. Netha showed me an easy trail to reach the place, saying it was good for me to come here alone to think and meditate, and that I would often find her here. Already we were ordaining this as our secret rendezvous, and I began to think of the fable I had told and its true moral: The trappings and secrets of a love affair are often more intriguing than the affair itself.

I was suddenly intrigued by Samos as well. Seeing a new part of the island and experiencing its primitive attractions firsthand, I felt a new love for Samos. As we made our way into familiar countryside, I saw the rugged hills, lazy villages, and emerald shores with fresh eyes. There really was something magical and special about this place, and I'd been a fool not to see it. It truly was the oasis of the Aegean, with ships of every flag calling in port. Some came for trade, but most were seeking a peaceful haven. Even Xanthus's school boasted an international flavor unknown anywhere else. He had students who were the best of friends who would have been warring enemies on the mainland. All grievances and territorial feuds were suspended on this sunny speck in the blue of the Aegean.

Netha handed me her basket of leaves and flowers. "Here, Aesop, so that you are not beaten for staying away so long, take the herbs you have collected."

She left so quickly I couldn't move until I watched her totally vanish from sight over the high ridges leading to the craggy interior of the island. Even then, I wasn't sure if she was a dream or not.

CHAPTER 10

The Omen of the Great Seal

Once I became enchanted with the island of Samos, my life fell into a pleasant routine. I filled in for Xanthus in his classes whenever the professor was detained elsewhere, or hung over, which was much more frequent. I performed mild household tasks, such as chopping vegetables and polishing silver, and avoided strenuous labor at all costs. On occasion, I had to take an ax to the woodpile, but I rather enjoyed the exercise.

I often extricated Xanthus from gambling debts, but I no longer demanded my freedom each time. I knew how much Xanthus depended upon me and how highly he valued me. Many times, a visiting dignitary would offer Xanthus ten or twenty thousand gold pieces for the property known as Aesop—one even offered to trade Xanthus a yacht! But each time, Xanthus would decline, saying that no monetary value could be placed upon my services. I still longed to be known as a freeman, not a slave, but I could think of no place I would rather be than my beloved Samos.

Netha's presence also curbed my wanderlust. I couldn't often free myself for the entire day, but when I did, I rushed to those barren hills. Sometimes the path took me to Fertility Rock, sometimes it took me to the door of her humble hut, but it never failed to transport me into a realm of peace and, occasionally, mystery.

A very special visit occurred on Election Day in my fifth year on Samos. The island had only one elected official, the Guardian of the Laws, and it was mainly a ceremonial post. Occasionally, the guardian was called upon to interpret an obscure law, but everyone on the island knew the law as well as he: When on Samos, don't disrupt the peace and serenity. Offenders were usually put on the next boat out, and serious offenders were banned from Samos forever. Everyone, from pirates to heads-of-state, upheld this law and defended the peace of Samos.

Nevertheless, the election of a new guardian was cause for much feasting and celebration, and I knew it would be a good time for me to slip away. I was almost skipping along the familiar path toward Netha's house, when my nostrils were assaulted by the sweet aroma of her pungent incense. I rounded the rock wall and saw her house engulfed in a weird red mist, as if it were on fire but not burning. I knew that high magic was taking place inside, and I almost ran in the opposite direction, as I had before when not wishing to disturb the sorceress at work. But a voice in my subconscious urged me to overcome my fear and go on. So I strode through the brambles of her overgrown garden, held my breath against the intoxicating odors, and entered Netha's domain.

I could see her in her dark hood, lizard-head necklace, and regalia, a purple fog swirling all around her. She stood upon my entrance and stretched out her hand to me. "Come, Aesop, I have been waiting for your arrival. You must see this, for our very lives depend upon it!"

She grabbed my hand, and for the first time in her touch, I felt fear. She hauled me through the mists, out the rear door, and she almost flung me over the edge of a small but deep well. I had seen the well before but had never paid it much attention. Now Netha was excitedly pushing my head over the dry clay walls, hissing, "Look, Aesop! As I feared—it is Croesus, king of Lydia!"

I saw nothing in the strange black waters for several moments. Then a glint of reflected light, or so I thought, took on the shape of a man's face. It was a thin gnarled face, with a bald dome over which ran several terrible scars. It was not an altogether cruel face, but I wouldn't want to meet this determined warrior under any circumstances. Nevertheless, I knew I would meet him and that he controlled my immediate fate. Netha gripped my hand as he began to speak.

"I welcome my Advisory Council. Our new navy must have a foreign port, one from which we can strike at Africa and Asia. After careful study, our captains suggest the island of Samos, in the Aegean. The natives are well-known to be soft and peaceful. They would probably not take much persuasion, and they would make good slaves. We have many spies already in place on the island, ready to soften the resistance, should any develop. What do you, my advisers, say to this venture—the conquering of Samos?"

The other voices were like the buzzing of mosquitoes, and not a single one rose to contest the cruel plan. Samos, the most peaceful place on earth, was to be conquered and enslaved for no better reason than to berth a crazed dictator's navy! We didn't have an army or even a militia to defend us! Netha gripped my hand as Croesus spoke again.

"Very well. We will plan a War Council this very afternoon . . ." I leaned so far forward that I knocked a loose bit of clay into the dark waters of the well, and the sudden ripples scattered the image into the depths of the pool. I looked at Netha, and her face was as white and ghastly as a bone.

"This is the end of all we know." She lowered her head, pulling her hood around her face.

"No!" I said. "We can fight this! There must be some way!"

But I could no longer see her face as she replied, "I must go to protect myself, Aesop. Warfare is the most vulnerable time for me. Return to your people, Aesop—they need you."

She touched my hand briefly before whirling around and disappearing into the swirl of incense emanating from her house. I stood watching for a moment, tempted to follow her, but I knew instinctively that she was gone to a place I couldn't find.

I ran almost all the way home, expecting to beat Xanthus, Lady Xanthus, and his celebrating students by many hours. The townspeople would be celebrating the new guardian well into the night. For all I knew, Xanthus might be given the honor, as he had served as guardian several times in the past. I hardly expected to see Xanthus pacing in his garden, his shoulders as stooped as an old pelican's.

"Aesop!" he gratefully cried upon seeing me. He quickly regained his composure, his face drooping into a dour expression. As I approached, I saw that his expression was truly dour and not something made up to trick me, as was usually the case.

He gripped my hands and peered into my face with terrified eyes. "Something monstrous has happened today! I don't know where to begin . . . I don't know what to do!"

"Calm yourself, Master, and simply start at the beginning. You went to elect a new Guardian of the Laws."

"Yes, yes," he said, struggling to think. "We were all gathered—all the people—in the town square. Milrod, the butcher and the old guardian, brought out the Public Seal with its beautiful golden ribbon and was about to present the Seal to the new guardian, Osriah, the town librarian. Osriah was so proud! But before he could take the Seal, a huge demon of an eagle swooped down and snatched the Seal by its ribbon! Then this monster sped off so fast we lost sight of it in seconds. A dark cloud passed overhead, and we knew this was a sign from the gods. Aesop, I swear we had all but given up seeing the Seal again, when the eagle suddenly swooped back overhead, still carrying the Seal, and dropped it!"

His face really became ashen now, and his grip tightened on my robes. "The Great Seal of our island," he shuddered, "landed in the lap of a *galley slave!* This pathetic, emaciated slave, who was given a moment's respite on shore before dying, suddenly held the Great Seal in his bleeding hands! We were all stunned, and the people beseeched me to interpret the omen!"

"I can tell you exactly what it means."

Xanthus shook my shoulders. "Please, Aesop, I am no interpreter of omens. What does it mean? What is to befall our island?"

I shrugged. "You know my fee for consultation work."

Xanthus slumped even more pathetically. "Your freedom," he replied. "So many times I have cheated you out of it. But, Aesop, my slave, my friend, you must know by now that I cannot exist without you. I have only half the wisdom you have—a *tenth!* I am a fraud. You've been my redemption from the moment I saw you in the slave market. You, with your advice, your clever stories, and your good nature, have made my work possible and have made my home a happy place. I am reluctant to free you, not because I wish to deny you freedom, but because I wish not to deny myself your company."

I could see the honest anguish in his face, but this was the time to be resolute. "If I am to do what I have to do, you must grant me my freedom. Take me before the people now, and I will interpret the omen."

Xanthus suddenly drew himself up to his considerable height. "I'm sorry, Aesop. I'm too selfish to let you go. But I know it isn't fair to ask you to solve this riddle for me. It's high time I face up to my own responsibilities! Go now," he commanded, "and leave me in peace to interpret the omen!"

"Xanthus," I pleaded, "just as no man can stop the tide, no man can stop the tide of events. Grant me my freedom and let me interpret the omen."

"No!" he snapped. "Go now!"

For three days, Xanthus prowled sleeplessly through his garden. By nightfall, he knew the paths so well that he needed no lamps to light his way. I heard him cursing to himself in little muffled sighs, and I felt sorry for the man. But I could not soften now if I were to have any impact on the situation.

Shortly after midnight of the third night, I heard a crash and some much louder cursing. I rushed from my window and leaped over a row of hedges, reaching Xanthus just as his kicking feet were about to smash another flowerpot. He was hanging from an olive tree, his belt slowly strangling him to death.

"You fool!" I shrieked, leaping over twice my height into the air and snapping off the branch with one pull. He thudded to the ground in a pathetic pile, the tree limb hanging from his neck. I kicked him angrily. "You fool! You could have actually killed yourself!"

He sat sobbing on the ground. "I am a fraud, Aesop! An utter fraud! I am not a philosopher, not a wise man! I am, like you say, a *fool!*"

I had to laugh at his melodramatics. "True fools are usually the last ones to hang themselves!"

"Why did you stop me?" he wailed. "With me dead, you would have your precious freedom!"

"I don't wish your lifeless body to mar my freedom. You may not be much of a philosopher, Xanthus, but you are a very good teacher. As such, you impart wisdom, which is just as important as possessing it. For example, I know you are writing down my fables, which is something I would never think of doing myself. You will reach more people with these writings than I could ever hope to reach with my voice. Now whose is the greater gift? Among your countless students have been philosophers, physicians, and historians—you opened their minds to the great thinking of the ages! Yet you keep your own mind closed tightly to selfishness."

He shook his head miserably. "Very well, Aesop. Interpret the omen tomorrow, and you shall be freed."

"No tricks?" I asked.

"No tricks," he sighed.

The crowd in the town square was in a very ugly mood, especially for Samians. Not that they were prone to violence or demonstration—they were just concerned and frightened, and they showed it by bickering among themselves. Never before had the Seal and laws of their island been so threatened. Not one single person doubted that the incident with the eagle had been a sign—they just wanted to be assured that their worst fears would not be realized. Unfortunately, I was here to tell them just the opposite.

The clouds remained dark and stormy overhead as Xanthus took the podium. The crowd stopped their murmuring and turned to the tall professor, who patiently motioned them to silence. "My fellow Samians!" he began regally. "After much consideration, I have concluded that the interpretation of omens is an art contrary to my scientific training. Therefore, I have assigned this important task to my slave, Aesop, whom many of you know to be possessed of uncommonly good sense. Thusly, I give you Aesop!"

Xanthus stepped aside, as I pushed my way through the crowd to a podium that was twice my size. Someone in the crowd shouted, "Give him to us? We don't want him!"

The murmurs intensified, and I decided to convert the podium to a platform by climbing upon it. Another loudmouth shouted, "We want a *learned* man to interpret the symbols!"

"Are there no learned men among you?" I countered in my most forceful voice. The crowd silenced somewhat, and I went on. "I see many here who claim to be scholars. Why have none of them interpreted this event? Because they cannot. I, on the other hand, am not burdened by philosophical and scientific training. Just as the value of a wine is determined by its taste rather than its bottle, judge me not by my appearance. Judge me by the value of my words."

"Ugly as he is, he always speaks the truth!" screamed one of my admirers.

"I will interpret the omen on one small condition," I announced. "It is not proper for a free people to be advised by a slave. Therefore, you must prevail upon my master to set me free."

"Free him, Xanthus!" shrieked the crowd. "You've more than got your money's worth!" The chant was instant and overpowering: "Free him! Free him!"

"Very well," shrugged the professor. "But I'll not take the blame if he's wrong. By the witness of all present, Aesop is freed!"

The crowd cheered perfunctorily, and I experienced a rush of excitement. I was finally a freeman! But I couldn't avoid the irony of having been freed in the face of enslavement under a merciless conqueror. And I couldn't spend any time savoring my freedom.

"I truly wish my freedom had come under better circumstances," I admitted, "for the omen of the Great Seal is not good. The eagle, King of Birds, represents the ruling king of a powerful nation. The fact that the Seal was stolen and then returned to a slave can only mean that a king will attempt to conquer Samos and, if successful, will enslave the entire population."

"No! No!" the crowd cried. "We don't believe it!"

"You must believe it!" I insisted. "Even though it hasn't happened yet, the time will come, and we must be prepared! When a fox once spied a boar intently sharpening his tusks on an old mill wheel, he said, 'Why do you work so hard this beautiful morning? No huntsman or tiger is about.' And the boar replied, 'The time to sharpen my tusks is now. When the danger comes, I won't have time.' Likewise, Samos must prepare! We have been at peace for many years now and are ripe for conquering!"

The crowd exploded in frenzied debate, and I was still trying to restore order when a roustabout from the shipyard rushed into the square, pointing frantically toward the dock. "A royal barge has landed!" he screamed. "It contains an emissary from King Croesus of Lydia!"

Now the discussion reached a fever pitch and would not subside until the emissary himself, replete in purple robes and a silver headdress and surrounded by armed sailors, strode purposefully into the square. "Where is the Guardian of the Laws?" he asked in a strange accent, brandishing a large scroll.

Milrod, the plump and likable butcher who had wielded the Seal of Samos for the past year, held out his trembling hand. "I am the guardian," he squeaked.

The emissary slapped the scroll into the butcher's hand and crossed his arms, waiting. The sailors pulled into a tight circle around him, as if expecting to be attacked by this unruly and surly mob. In a shaking voice, the guardian read the scroll.

"From Croesus and the Kingdom of Lydia, to the people of Samos and their leaders: From this day forward, I command you to pay taxes and tribute to the Kingdom of Lydia, which claims dominion over the seas in which you reside. If you do not pay immediately, I will move against you with the full power of my armies and navies. Signed with the Seal of Croesus, King of Lydia."

The guardian lowered the scroll, and the people gaped at one another. "Aesop was right!" said one, and several murmured their agreement.

A woman bellowed, "We must pay the taxes and avoid the war!"

An even fiercer debate ensued, and I could see the emissary stamping his foot impatiently. He finally pointed an accusing finger at Milrod. "You are the leader—what do you decide?"

"I . . . I don't know." He looked beseechingly at Xanthus, who turned helplessly toward me.

"No!" I shouted. "I say to you, *no!*" The strength of my voice quieted the fearful crowd. "This request is merely a test. If we pay the tribute, Croesus will know we are weak and will move at once to attack and enslave us. If we refuse to pay, he will give it some thought first, and we will gain some time."

Xanthus strode to my side. "Aesop was right before! Let's listen to him now. King Croesus began this course— let him finish it!"

Surprisingly, the crowd cheered their support, proving that even peace-loving people will rally in defense of their freedom. Milrod took the scroll in his powerful hands and twisted it as if strangling a chicken. "No tribute! No taxes! Nobody owns Samos but the Samians!"

The crowd roared their approval, and the grand emissary of Lydia was forced to escape with pitchforks and clubs at his back. Several of his sailors did not make the journey back to Lydia with him.

When the commotion died down, people started wandering away, fear and solemnity weighing heavily upon them. Xanthus turned to me and warmly touched my shoulder. "Aesop," he smiled, "we must get you to the smithy's shop and have that bracelet removed."

CHAPTER 11

Farewell

I returned to Xanthus's house that night, and he was gracious enough to let me stay there. Technically, as a freeman, I could have slept anywhere I wanted. Unfortunately, I didn't have any money or a bed anywhere else. Thusly, I learned the first truth of life as a freeman: You don't necessarily have a place to sleep.

I kept rubbing my naked wrist, having never seen nor felt the flesh beneath the crude copper bracelet I always wore. Now the bracelet lay upon the junk pile in the smithy's shop, and I felt as if my whole past life lay there with it.

No one in Xanthus's household commented upon, nor seemed particularly interested in, my new station in life—they were too busy watching the clouds of war that had drifted over our peaceful island.

"What on earth would Croesus want in Samos?" wailed one of the maidservants. "He has palaces and slaves enough!"

"A port is what he wants," said Lady Xanthus. She turned worriedly to her husband, who stood staring out the door at the gentle rain. "We won't have to close the school, will we?"

"If war breaks out, we certainly will," replied Xanthus.

"We can't expect parents to keep their children on an island which is besieged."

Lady Xanthus touched her eyes with her handkerchief, and I could tell that, for once, her tears were genuine and not calculated for her own purposes. "This is the end of everything we know," she sighed.

Her words were uncomfortably reminiscent of those spoken by Netha. "I beg to differ," I said. "Even in warfare, even under enslavement, basic human nature doesn't change. We Samians will find some way to triumph!"

Lady Xanthus was touched by my patriotism. "I am glad you consider yourself one of us now, Aesop. I never truly considered myself to be Samian either, but the thought of destroying the harmony of all we have built here . . ." She sighed heavily. "That would be devastating to me."

Xanthus went to his wife and laid his hands comfortingly on her shoulders. "The lure of Samos herself is largely responsible for the success of the school—we've known that for many years. Who wouldn't want to send his children to such a peaceful, progressive island? I only hope we can preserve it."

This solemnity was becoming oppressive, and I quickly decided to lighten the mood. "Did I ever tell you of an actual occurrence I witnessed in Phrygia? It is a famous tale, and perhaps you've heard it—the king who taught a group of apes to dance!"

At once, grateful smiles appeared on the faces of all present, which included town dignitaries and slaves alike. I only hoped my tale would be good enough to make them forget their dread.

"This king was known to be loath to part with a single shekel. Nevertheless, he wanted to stage a tremendous feast to celebrate his tenth anniversary in office. He knew he had to have suitable entertainment, but he refused to pay the prices asked by even the most mediocre of dancing troupes. Apes were plentiful in his kingdom, so the king had a group of them rounded up. Through diligent practice and rehearsal, he actually taught those apes to dance! You should have seen them pirouette and prance!"

I paused to let a bit of laughter die down. "He put powdered wigs upon their heads, masks upon their faces, and long purple pants to hide their hairy places! No one could tell these graceful dancers were not human. Then the big day of the festival came, and the concert got under way. The apes were performing marvelously, like the greatest court dancers, when a small child spilled a bag of peanuts upon the stage. At once, the apes ripped off their disguises and fought each other for the prizes. That king is a laughingstock to this very day!"

One of the maidservants laughed, and then cried. "Leave it to you, Aesop, to find a way to make us laugh!"

Xanthus nodded somberly. "It is true, Aesop, that you can't hide a person's true nature." He brightened suddenly. "That is why I am so happy that you are finally a *free* man! Each morning, it was an inspiration to me to know that you were in my service. I feared deeply to lose you, but now I know the true value of freedom. On this day, when we have learned the cost of our own liberty, it is fitting that you have finally attained yours! I propose we pour some wine and drink a toast in Aesop's honor!"

The shouts of pleasure were deafening, and Lady Xanthus strode forcefully to me, leaned down, and hugged me. "I thank you, Aesop, for speaking up in defense of our lovely island. Let us put aside any differences we may have had and move on to our common goal. We must *all* remain free. As of this day, I also free my maidservants, who may stay in our employ if they so wish. But they may also feel free to pursue the callings and journeyings to which their souls hearken."

Now I was the one who began to cry, and I was joined immediately by the four maidservants. We all hugged one another, weeping with joy, and it was one of the most stirring moments I have ever felt as a human being. It certainly rivaled the moment Isis and the Muses visited me. It was not as good as lovemaking with Netha, however. But I reveled in the shared experience of winning our freedom, although the irony was not lost upon me: What freedom we were winning was very nebulous indeed. Word would spread quickly that Lydia and Samos were at war—as, in fact, we were. Shipping would halt on the island, and we would be shunned like the plague. In case you don't know it, Lydia was the supreme power in the Aegean in 600 B.C., and Croesus was as ruthless a conqueror as they come.

I slept fitfully that night, and I kept dreaming the same dream of the eagle, swooping down and stealing the Great Seal. And I could see the eagle again, swooping back and depositing the Seal in the bloody hands of a dying slave. Was there ever an omen more easily read? Though I hadn't been present, I knew each detail of the incident as if I had been the eagle. King Croesus was also a major fixture of my dreams that night, but I never saw more than his bald scarred head and cold eyes, reflected in the shimmering well behind Netha's house.

All I knew was that slavery was an abomination. And the enslavement of Samos would be doubly worse, like enslaving the earth! My whole being bristled at the idea, and I remembered Xanthus saying that freemen are not all that much more free than slaves.

The next morning, I searched for the mysterious path to Netha's house. I cannot remember a time when the path was harder to find; even my first accidental visit was easier. I had the feeling I had walked a very long way by the time I reached her house. Netha's grapevines and herb bushes seemed withered and neglected, and I couldn't understand how things had got this way in such a short time. Her house looked as humble as always, though perhaps a bit too quiet. Etiquette seemed silly under the circumstances, so I banged her door open and rushed in.

Netha was in a deep trance in the center of her living room. She also looked ill, as if she hadn't eaten for days on end. I rushed to her and instinctively shook her out of her trance, and she blinked at me as if she'd never seen me before. "Isis," she muttered. "Isis."

"What about Isis?" I asked, suddenly scared.

Warm recognition came into Netha's eyes, and she grabbed my shoulders. "Aesop, you are no longer protected by Apollo. You must beware!"

"Screw Apollo!" I shouted. "I'm tired of taking orders from that *excuse* for a god! I'm a freeman now, and that's the way I intend to stay!"

"You will never return to Samos!"she wailed.

"Never return?" I asked. "But I'm not going anywhere! This is my home!"

She shook her head sadly. "No, you are leaving. Go to the back and look in the well. Remember, you no longer have any god's protection, save that of Isis."

"Isis is enough for me!" I retorted. "Isis and the Muses gave me my voice, and I require no more from any god!" Angry, I strode out the back door.

The well loomed before me, like a secret altar. I slowed my stride and approached it, fearing to see again the warrior king, Croesus. In my heart, I knew he could take my life as easily as yawn. I stepped cautiously up to the magical well.

At once, a dizziness overcame me, pulling my head over the edge of the clay wall and riveting my attention upon the dark sparkling waters. I again saw the visage of King Croesus, scars running across his brow like a poorly drawn map.

"That is your full report?" he grumbled. "That one man, a freed slave, stands between me and my prize!"

I saw the emissary, the one who had barely escaped with his life, and I hardly envied him his job. "Oh, Mighty King," he bowed, "the man they call Aesop is a formidable leader. He is practically ruling the island."

"What said this Aesop?" snapped the king.

"He said your letter was a test, that if they paid the taxes and tribute, you would know they were weak and would attack."

Croesus nodded. "Of course, he is right. But I hadn't expected clever leadership on such an insignificant island. What do my generals and captains say? What would be the cost of an assault on Samos?"

"A dozen ships," said one.

"Five hundred men," said another.

Intoned a third, "Twenty chariots and eighty horses!"

"It would be a costly venture with no guarantee of success," said the first general.

"Particularly if the Samians have able leadership," agreed another.

Croesus scowled, "Like this man Aesop."

"Precisely!" chirped the emissary.

King Croesus shrugged amiably. "Then our course is clear. We must get rid of Aesop. To defeat a people, you must first defeat their leaders. Emissary, return to the island of Samos with the rank of Ambassador!"

"Yes, Your Highness?" said the emissary doubtfully.

"Tell the people to send Aesop to us, for the purpose of negotiating a treaty. Or some such thing." Croesus smiled evilly. "Make it very plain that if they send us Aesop, we will trouble them no more. Then we will execute the man and mount our attack. Now, go tell them to forget the taxes and send us Aesop!"

The emissary, now ambassador, bowed and scraped himself out of the royal chambers, and the image disappeared into the fathomless depths of Netha's well.

I rushed back into the house and confronted the sorceress. "What does this mean?"

Netha avoided my eyes. "It means that you will never return to Samos."

"No!" I cried. "That can't be true! I am a freeman now, and I can come and go as I wish!"

"Would that life could be so simple," she sighed, finally meeting my eyes with her own. "You were warned. You were told that the gods protected you as long as you were a slave. Now you have made your own path, and no one knows where it will lead."

My anger melted in her obvious concern for my well-being. "Netha, I only wish to live my own life—nothing more. If I must deliver myself unto Croesus in order to defend Samos, then I will do so."

"You will never return," she said gravely.

This was no time whatsoever for talk, and I bent low over her mat and took her in my arms. She kissed me desperately and held me as if I might blow away any minute. "I don't want you to go!" she cried.

"I'm here now," I breathed, gripping her even tighter. Our kisses dissolved into lovemaking, and we spent ourselves as if we knew it would be the last time together. I fell asleep, and when I awoke, Netha was gone. I called her name a few times, but I knew Netha and I had already made our farewells.

In a daze, I wandered back down the path to Xanthus's household. I felt my life changing, evolving, by the moment. From a field slave in the desert to the defender of the loveliest island on the earth, thus had my life advanced in five short years. The weight of my responsibility overwhelmed me almost as much as my freedom. Netha represented the island of Samos to me, and I felt as if both she and the island were my wives, my absolute responsibility. Again, I felt no loss from Apollo's abandonment—every time I thought of Apollo, I saw that stinking sphinx, ready to bite my head off if I didn't answer a stupid riddle.

Each day was a morass of anxiety until the arrival of Lydia's new ambassador. Several of Xanthus's students left when their fathers' barges called for them, summoning them back to relative safety. All the students vowed to return, when the "trouble was over." Xanthus and Lady

Xanthus watched them go, starched smiles on their faces, bravery their first emotion. Two of the maidservants left, intoxicated by their new freedom; but the two eldest maidens remained, now paid monthly for their services, as was I. The money I never spent but gave back to Xanthus, in order to maintain the household as always.

The ambassador set up sham offices on the waterfront and kept a number of fast boats waiting for his escape. I still would not have wished for his job. He went to see Milrod, who remained Guardian of the Laws, and asked him to send an ambassador to King Croesus for the purposes of negotiating a treaty. Preferably, this ambassador was to be Aesop, whom all knew to be possessed of uncommonly good sense. Milrod first talked the proposal over with Xanthus, and the two of them approached me together.

"Croesus wants to speak privately to you in Lydia," said Milrod bluntly.

"I bet he does," I smiled.

"Don't go," warned Xanthus. "It is far too dangerous."

I smiled at the distinguished scholar, who was now my best friend. "Do you remember the fable I told you of the North Wind and the Sun?"

"Of course," he nodded. "Do you think you can shine gently on Croesus and cause him to lose his clothes?"

"We have no alternative but to try," I answered. "But while I am gone, you must both promise to fortify the island and form a militia. If I am unsuccessful, you must promise to defend Samos."

"I will," promised Xanthus sternly.

"As will I," said Milrod. "But you don't have to go, Aesop. We can send others."

"And their heads would come back on a spit," I replied. "I am the only one who can reason with him." I had no idea how I knew that, but I said it anyway.

Xanthus bent low and embraced me. "The speed of Hermes to you, my friend. We shall keep the altar fires burning until your return."

"Thank you, Xanthus," I replied. "If I never return to you again, my heart is with you forever."

CHAPTER 12

The Court of Croesus

As soon as Milrod informed the Lydian ambassador that I was willing to parlay with Croesus, the armada withdrew. I had no time to visit Netha again, and I prayed to every god I'd ever heard of that I could reverse her prophecy and return to Samos. I had no chance to relay a message to her either, as I was surrounded by armed guards from the moment I reached the quay until we set sail. But I maintained my dignity and did my best to ignore completely whatever indignities were heaped upon me. I knew I had a long journey ahead, and I had no wish to disrupt it early on. I began to long for the protection of my second master, Pelaphus, who was as handy with a sword as I was with words. I knew he could cut down ten or twelve of these sailors at the knees before they could tell the wind had changed.

So frightened was I, traveling for the first time as a freeman and delivering myself to a king who I knew wanted to kill me, that I was unable to speak a word the entire journey. The steward of the immense Lydian barge kept me well supplied with food—I suppose someone forgot to tell him that I was to be killed the moment we reached shore.

Some days later, we did dock in a sprawling port city, larger than anything I had ever seen. Gigantic temples graced the hillsides, statues towered into the sky, and I re-alized for the first time that I was glimpsing the Greek mainland. Houses climbed the hillsides like a myriad of steps, glinting in the sun, and I could sense the power of this land and her people, as represented by a conqueror king. I feared him yet had hope that he would listen to rea-son.

I didn't have long to wait, as I was brought before Croe-sus instantly. The throne room was gigantic, the size of a grain elevator in Phrygia, and as ornate as a temple to Aphrodite, with jewel bedecked statuary in every corner. Hundreds of people, in glorious gowns of purple, red, and blue, parted and formed an aisle for me to enter. With their stoic faces, these courtiers really did look quite like the apes who tried to dance like humans. Only they weren't dancing—they were very still, studying me as if I were some marked-down vegetable. I didn't fear these people anymore—I pitied them.

At the rear end of the vast hall, towering over the col-orful assemblage, stood an immense throne of the most ravishing scarlet silk. With torches blazing at its sides, the throne looked like a sunset perched on a carpet. I almost shielded my eyes, except that the presence seated on the throne was the most arresting and exciting sight I had ever beheld. I almost gasped, as did his Highness upon seeing me. There, in all his imperial splendor and fierce visage, was the king of Lydia, Croesus! His feet barely touched the floor, and the back of the throne dwarfed him, as well it should.

Because King Croesus was a *dwarf*, barely taller than I!

I bowed low, trying to hide my amusement and relief. "May I present myself," I announced. "I am Aesop, emis-sary of Samos, a peaceful haven in the Aegean."

The ferocious bald head, with its welts and scars, nod-ded in my direction. The eyes studied me with a certain amount of amusement too, or so I imagined. I glanced at his generals and advisers, and they glanced nervously at one another, as if my misshapen appearance was mocking their king. Of course, I had a hunched back, an indignity spared King Croesus—his body was as fit and taut as a fighting hawk's. I could well imagine him in battle, chopping foes at the knees and the belly, his bobbing head the only target. That thick dome had certainly received the brunt of his opponents' blows, or so the scars testified.

"This is Aesop?" he grumbled. "The mighty warrior?"

I bowed again. "I am no warrior, Your Highness, but a simply storyteller."

He scoffed, "How does a simple storyteller command the allegiance of an entire island?"

"Because Samos is a simple, loving place, and my stories reflect truth and common sense." I saw no reason to spare his feelings, even if he was a dwarf. "You, Sire, with all your power and might, are never told the truth, because your advisers tell you only what you want to hear. On the other hand, I, your enemy, can be entirely truthful, because I have nothing to gain by currying your favor."

Croesus waved down several of his advisers, who were about to protest. He smiled wryly, "You have your life to preserve, Aesop."

I shrugged. "By coming here, I have already surrendered my life. My only request is that you allow me to tell you a story before you order my execution."

"How can I refuse such a simple request?" he asked, settling back and almost disappearing in the cushions of his gigantic throne. I could barely see his feet.

"Many years ago," I began, "when animals spoke the same language as men, a man had the idea of catching small insects, called hummers, and pickling them in brine. The hummers made a pleasing sound, which was easy enough to follow, and the man soon collected enough hummers to fill several jars. As he caught the last one between his fingers and was about to kill it, the tiny creature spoke up and said, 'Please, sir, don't idly kill me. I harm neither the grain nor the fruit, and I pollinate the flowers.

And when I put my wings together, I make a harmonious sound which is pleasing to all men. I give solace to the wayfarer.' The man, who had many more insects than he needed, was moved by her plea and let her go free."

Croesus leaned forward, and I could see the weariness in his face. A stay on Samos would certainly do him some good, I thought. "I suppose *I* am the man who already has more than he needs?"

"Some things," I observed, "no man may own. The sun and the stars belong to no one—they are free for everyone to enjoy. The island of Samos is such a place. In its solitude and serenity, it harms neither man nor god but offers a haven to weary travelers of all nations. It belongs to the world and all who travel by sea. Your kingdom is already great and would hardly be the greater for the addition of a tiny island. But the world would be a lesser place with the loss of Samos and the sanctuary it offers to all who risk their lives upon the sea."

Croesus scratched a broad scar which ran the length of his hairless skull. "I myself visited Samos once, when returning from battle with the Minoans. I was feverish and bedridden from a blow to the head, but my men carried me ashore. They sought out a sorceress, who cured me." With sudden urgency, he asked, "Does that sorceress still live?"

"As long as Samos remains free to all," I answered.

Croesus hung his head, looking chastised. "Perhaps you are right, Aesop. I am so busy making war that I forget the joys of peace. There is so little peace in this world, how can I deprive anyone of a safe port?" He turned to his stunned advisers. "Send the royal engineer and his builders to Samos and instruct them to build a temple to Poseidon. This temple will also serve as a symbol of the friendship between Samos and Lydia." He waved, and the advisers scampered off.

I slumped gratefully to my knees. "Thank you, King Croesus. Peace is the greatest present I could take back to my people."

"Who says you are returning?" he scowled. "I have need for a skilled emissary like you. In ten years of rule, you are the first to ever dissuade me from my chosen path with mere words." The king clapped his hands and was surrounded by well-armed men, some of whom glanced at me suspiciously. Samos may have been safe, but I certainly didn't feel like *I* was.

"Are the maidens from Macedonia cleaned and dressed?" he asked the sergeant-at-arms.

"Yes, Your Highness," said the man with a bow.

"Present them before the court!" Croesus ordered. The man rushed off, followed by several other guards.

I rose slowly to my feet and inched toward the throne, waving to get the king's attention. "Excuse me, Sire, but I was very happy in Samos, where I often lectured at the school of Xanthus, the noted philosopher. Perhaps you've heard of Xanthus, who is . . ."

"Philosophers don't interest me very much," he muttered. "Whatever he was paying you to baby-sit his spoiled students, I will better by ten times." His attention was suddenly distracted. "Ah! Here are the women!"

The guards escorted eight stunning women into the throne room and lined them up before the king. They were all young, maybe even virgins, and they had obviously been handpicked for their beauty and voluptuous figures, which the filmy gauze of their gowns did little to conceal. I had thought Hippolyte and the women of the circus were beautiful, but these maidens were just as fair and possessed a freshness of face and limb that was more appealing. I, frankly, could not take my eyes off them.

Croesus jumped down from his throne and inspected each maiden in turn, his nose barely reaching the crests of their youthful and exciting bosoms. (Only an extremely short man can appreciate such a vantage point.) Surprisingly, the women did not flinch from this frank appraisal but seemed to welcome it, as if they were in competition

for the king's favors. After a moment, Croesus motioned
to me to join him, and I can't say I hesitated.

In a very chummy manner, Croesus put his arm around
my shoulders, and it occurred to me that this was not a
maneuver he could perform with many other men. "Aesop,
these women were given to me by the king of Macedonia.
All were raised to be king's concubines, which means they
are well schooled in the arts of lovemaking."

"That's quite wonderful!" I said with honest apprecia-
tion.

"It is, isn't it?" he remarked. "But I have many wives
and concubines, and don't need all these."

"That's a pity," I agreed.

He winked. "You may choose any two to take to bed
with you."

"Choose *two?*" I gulped.

"You are right!" he growled, slapping me on the back.
"Mustn't be stingy! Take *four* of them to bed with you,
and keep them as long as you stay in my service!"

Had I not looked at anything that moment but the swell-
ing breasts of a Macedonian maiden twice my size, I
might have resisted King Croesus and returned to Samos.
But I didn't resist. I succumbed.

Having my pick of women was hardly the only change
in my life—but it was the most exhausting. I lay sated for
days in a luxurious apartment granted to me by King
Croesus. Besides my four maidservants, I had kitchen and
court servants waiting on me as well. I must admit it was
somewhat disconcerting to switch from the role of slave to
that of pampered master. At first, I wouldn't allow the four
beautiful young maidens to wait upon me—I was grateful
enough to have them in bed each night. But they insisted
and became downright angry when I fended for myself, by
filling my own goblet or trimming my own nails.

Still thinking like a slave, I soon realized that the maidens considered me easy duty and feared worse at the hands

of Croesus or his guards. From what I saw around that palace, I hardly doubt they were right. The Lydians were crazed warriors and required a constant stream of women, men, goats, camels, anything upon which to vent their sexual energy. Boredom made them attack their neighbors. From long experience, the neighboring states kept them well supplied with women. What were a few maidens, they reasoned, when peace was at stake?

Another subtle form of diplomacy had developed among the rulers of that era. Kings tried to collect tribute from one another by any means they could invent, including conundrums. When one king wanted to increase his coffers at the expense of another, instead of waging war, he would send the other a riddle. If that king's advisers couldn't answer the riddle, he'd be forced to turn over some gold, maidens, or maybe a contested piece of land. On the other hand, if the petitioned ruler successfully answered the conundrum, the sender was forced to pay the tribute. It was a silly game, but preferable to war.

This, of course, was my new job. After a week in the palace, Croesus sent for me in the dead of night and had me escorted at once to the throne room. To my surprise, we were left alone. I stared up at my fellow dwarf on his giantic seat of power.

"It's time you start earning your keep, Aesop," he scowled. "My other advisers are totally stumped by a conundrum from Nectanabo, the pharaoh of Egypt. If we fail to answer, we lose two thousand talents of gold. Do you know how much money that is, Aesop?"

"It would probably buy two thousand maidservants."

"Exactly!" he screeched. "You've got to help us, Aesop!"

"You should have called me sooner," I yawned, still exhausted from my week in bed. "What is the question?"

Croesus steeled himself. "The question is worded thusly: What river runs to no sea but stays constant in length until it disappears only to appear in another place?"

I laughed out loud, nearly doubling over. "You, King Croesus, should know the answer to that better than any other man! For you have been inflicted with so many."

He cocked his head curiously, growing a bit impatient. "If you know the answer, say it."

"A wound," I replied. "A wound flows blood, never increases in length, eventually goes away, but may reappear elsewhere on the body. I don't know if that is the answer you seek, but it certainly fits the question."

"Yes," Croesus smiled slowly. I could see him ordering two thousand more slave girls from Egypt. "Yes, Aesop, I believe that will suffice. Are you as good at inventing these philosophical queries as you are at answering them?"

"I don't know," I shrugged. "I've never tried."

"Try now," said the king. "I will send scribes to your apartment in the morning, and you are to form as many conundrums as you can. I will instruct them to copy down your amusing fables as well."

"Fine," I said. As jobs went, this one certainly beat peeling vegetables. I returned quickly to my bed, knowing four luscious bodies were keeping it warm.

Days pass quickly enough in poverty; in luxury, they fly like Zeus's thunderbolts. After three months, I had composed one hundred conundrums and committed five hundred fables to paper. My daily work sessions became the high point of the court's schedule, and I was often visited by the king, his nobles, and wives. So many people crowded my anteroom that I had to ask the king's permission to work in the throne room. Surprisingly, permission was granted, as long as I didn't try to sit on the throne.

One afternoon, I arrived in the throne room just as Croesus was dispensing justice to wrongdoers. A rich nobleman was accused of stealing his neighbor's daughter, imprisoning her, and repeatedly ravishing her. He was sentenced to give the poor maiden's father twenty head of cattle. Immediately thereafter, a poor wretch was brought before the king and accused of stealing a loaf of bread. He was ordered to have both hands chopped off.

Before the crowd had a chance to disperse, I leaped upon the dais and harangued them: "Gather, everyone, for a special fable from Aesop!" Everyone, the king included, stopped, turned, and looked expectantly at me. Even the wretch who was about to lose his hands blinked at me with a degree of interest. Under my stern glare, they soon quieted.

"This tale is about the trial of the wolf and the ass," I began. "One night, a starving wolf cornered an ass in his stall and was about to eat him. The ass appealed to Apollo, protector of draft animals, and the wolf appealed to Artemis, goddess of the hunt. Both gods appeared to hear the complaint. 'Grant me protection,' said the ass to Apollo, 'for I have done nothing to deserve such a cruel death.' 'Neither have I,' said the wolf to Artemis, 'and if I don't eat tonight, I will surely die.'

"Since it was plain that one or the other animal must die, the gods offered to conduct a trial. They would hear the testimony of each animal's past wrongs, then judge which most deserved to die. The wolf went first, giving a lurid account of the many sheep and goats he had mangled, the thousands of kids and lambs he had carried off, and the dozens of shepherds he had disemboweled. But he was careful to point out that each episode was merely a quest for food, and not a crime. The ass testified next, but search his soul as he could, he was unable to unearth a single instance of wrongdoing. He had merely eaten hay and served his master his entire life. Incredulous, the wolf asked him if his master had never beaten him? The ass finally remembered one distant episode in his youth, when he had reached back and nibbled the leaf of a vegetable from his master's wagon. His master had beaten him severely, and he had never attempted such a trick again.

"The wolf seized upon this admission as if it were a choice young lamb, saying, 'The ass admits to being punished for his crimes, while I have *never* felt the sting and dishonor of the whip! By the laws of man, *he* is more guilty.' The gods were forced to admit the truth of this argument, and they allowed the wolf to kill and eat the poor ass."

The silence, which had once been respectful, was now ominous. All eyes turned from me to Croesus, who wasn't doing a very good job of hiding his anger. "Aesop, do you wish to mock the justice of this court?" he bellowed.

"No, Your Highness," I said. "Such is the nature of justice, that it is seldom just."

"I think," said Croesus, still seething, "it is time for Aesop to deliver one of his notable conundrums to the court of Lycurgus, king of Babylonia. Aesop, I appoint you Grand Emissary to Babylonia. You will leave tomorrow."

Now, at this point in history, Babylonia was about the farthest place in the civilized world from Lydia. The journey would span the breadth of the Aegean and Asia Minor, passing through my birthplace of Phrygia, and encompassing months of travel by land and sea. I instantly regretted my hasty words, especially when I learned that my four maidservants could not accompany me.

In the midst of packing, my spirits were lifted somewhat by the arrival of a letter from Xanthus and my beloved Samos. Excitedly, I tore off the seal and spread the scroll across my bed.

Dearest Aesop,

We cannot thank you enough for saving the precious peace of our little island. In honor of your great accomplishment by unanimous proclamation, we have renamed the town square Aesopeum! I myself have commissioned an artist to erect a statue bearing your likeness. You are truly the greatest hero Samos has ever had.

The Temple of Poseidon, under Lydian construction,

promises to be the most magnificent structure on the island. We praise the generosity of Croesus, though knowing full well that you are primarily responsible. To that end, we would like to reciprocate and construct a shrine upon the Lydian shore, and we would like you to dedicate it. I know your protector gods are Apollo, Isis, and the Muses, and we will build the temple in the name of whichever god you choose.

Daily, my students return, and enrollment swells. Taking a walk a few days ago, I met a woman named Netha, and she asked about your welfare. We miss you terribly, Aesop, and we long for the day when you return, even if briefly. Your return will occasion the greatest celebration in Samos's history! We know your destiny is now entwined with that of gods and kings, but please remember that your greatest friends reside on Samos. No matter what course your life may take, you will always be a hero here.

> Your Great Friend,
> Xanthus

Tears welling in my eyes, I put the letter aside and summoned a scribe. I couldn't let Samos go to the expense of building a shrine on such a faraway shore. I instructed the scribe to ask the king to take my pay and build a shrine to the Muses, in the name of Samos. I debated whether to place a statue of Apollo or Mnemosyne at the center of the shrine, and I finally decided on Mnemosyne. I knew Apollo had many temples and statues, while Mnemosyne, Titan queen and mother of the Muses, had relatively few.

That was my biggest mistake.

CHAPTER 13

The Road to Babylon

I may have been a hunchbacked dwarf, but I was still the Royal Emissary of King Croesus, who, at that time, had the reputation for being the richest man on earth. Needless to say, I was expected to travel to Babylon in style and safety. The caravan consisted of fifty foot soldiers, thirty cavalry soldiers, twice as many horses, twenty slaves and attendants, and four huge wagons with forty oxen to pull them. The wagons carried food, cooking utensils, and three tents as big as those in Hesiod's circus: one was a mess tent, another a dormitory tent for the soldiers, and the third was *my* tent, big enough to house me and the twenty slaves who slept at my feet. With all this, I had to wonder why I couldn't have brought at least one of my maidservants, too.

This cumbersome procession traveled very slowly, mainly because of the gaudy litter in which I was carried by four strapping Nubians. We would go about five miles a day, then stop to make camp, which took several hours. Little children often followed us from the villages we passed; they made so much better time that they could follow us for the entire day, watch us set up camp, and return to their houses before dark.

It wasn't until we left the Lydian borders that I realized what a conspicuous and tempting target the caravan made.

I had no vain notions that the soldiers were along for my protection—they were there to guard the gold which Croesus hoped I would be bringing back from Babylon. For all I knew, they might try to steal the gold themselves! I was valuable only until the tribute was secured from Lycurgus, then I was expendable. I began to think of the emissary Croesus had sent to Samos and how I had pitied him his dangerous job. And all he'd had to do was take a boat ride to a peaceful island with no militia, say a few things, and leave. I, on the other hand, had to cross the entire breadth of the known world—mountains, rivers, seas, and deserts, crammed with brigands and monsters—and deliver myself unto another strange despot. All I had to protect me was the war-ax banner of one of the most despised rulers on the face of the earth.

I knew *I* was being punished, and I couldn't help but feel that the soldiers, slaves, and even the oxen traveling with us had all run afoul of some power in the universe. We were not a cheerful band, as we slogged our way through the Ionian lowlands. When we reached the Aegean, I wished I could have taken a small rowboat over to Samos, instead of the heavy barge which took me back to Ephesus. True, I now returned to the land of my birth wearing the trappings of a king, instead of the bracelet and rags of a slave. But I had no longing to reveal my new station in life to those who might remember me. I stayed in my litter, barely showing my face.

Even when we passed through Phrygia, within a few miles of my original master and my fellow fig-pickers, like Agathopous, I didn't part the curtains of my litter. Local kings and dignitaries tried to pay their respects to me, but I instructed Obares, the captain of the cavalry, to say only that our mission was of extreme haste and secrecy. Anyone watching our progress might question how much haste we were in, but they couldn't doubt the secrecy, since not a single visitor left knowing who was in command of this mysterious procession. I had practical reasons for this as well: I preferred that the local robbers thought a king or great general was in command, instead of a lowly storyteller. Nevertheless, I'm sure I was seen occasionally, moving from the litter to the tent. But I didn't mind if it got out that I was a dwarf, because Croesus himself was known to be one.

My instincts apparently paid off, because we were never attacked by bandits or petty kings. We were only attacked by boredom. I did very little to lift the spirits of those around me; for that, I felt doubly miserable. Occasionally, I told the slaves a fable or two, but it wasn't enough to break the monotony of the journey, which now had lasted through spring and summer. Whenever we passed a fair-sized town, the soldiers would beseech me to let them have liberty. But I always resisted, saying we would have liberty enough in Babylon. I hated myself for these brusque refusals, but the captains of the army always came to me in private and congratulated me on maintaining discipline. They were afraid, as I was, that the soldiers would desert if they discovered what it was like to have a good time again. Of course, these same captains left my tent, returned to their troops, and complained bitterly about the ogre who wouldn't allow anyone a moment's pleasure. I was always made to look the bad guy.

Believe me, the irony of this situation didn't escape me. Here I was, finally a freeman—emissary to the richest king in the world, no less—and I was more miserable than when I had been a slave!

A slave, at least, is secure in the knowledge that he can do harm to his fellow man only with great difficulty. A master can inflict pain in countless ways, from a careless word to torture and death. I was prepared for the comforts of being a master, but not the loneliness, doubt, and fear. Should I be nicer to the soldiers? Is that slave who never looks into my eyes really a spy for Lycurgus? I had no friends, and I felt as though everyone on the caravan hated and envied me. On Samos, I had been the Sun, pressing my points with gentle persuasion; now I was the North Wind, bending others to my will through fear and obedience. Nevertheless, I must have been doing my job: the caravan was making steady if unspectacular progress toward the ancient heart of Mesopotamia, Babylon.

Though we had been following well-worn trade routes, we sometimes lost our way, especially in mountainous country. We were only in serious danger once, however, when passing from Phrygia into Syria through the Kilikian Pass. I say it was the Kilikian Pass, but we really had no idea where we were in the mountains, having been confounded by a sudden snowstorm.

I had been out of my litter for hours, trudging up the rocks with everyone else. The big Nubians were having a hard time carrying the *empty* litter, and if we were following a path, I couldn't see it. The cavalry had dismounted ahead of us; with spirited cursing and whipping, they were trying to move their mounts along. I suddenly realized the horses had considerably more sense than we did.

"Captain!" I screamed into the wind. "Obares!"

The words blew back into my face, but a young slave boy heard them and volunteered his services. "Go tell Captain Obares to stop the caravan and come back to see me!"

The boy nodded briskly and hurried off. I could see him reach the front of the line, where a tall trooper raised his hands and frantically waved at the others. Like a sluggish snake, the column shuddered to a stop. The horses gratefully shook the snow off their backs.

"Yes, My Liege," said Obares, reaching me with several long strides. Snow crusted on his newly grown beard, which he'd let sprout only since reaching the high country.

I tried to moderate my anger and fear. "Captain, I hold no one at fault if we have inadvertently strayed from the trail, but I don't believe we're following a trail at this particular moment."

"But we are going up," he pointed out.

"Yes," I nodded, "but I would rather be going *out* than *up*. I think we should turn around and go back ... only until we find the trail, of course."

The captain shrugged. He was used to hardships and could doubtless bear them for weeks upon end. This duty was no worse than being at war. "Suppose you tell me which way is down?" he asked.

I looked around. The snow was blinding, jagged peaks loomed in the dimness, and we were standing upon rocks which were becoming more slippery by the moment. "Let's continue on," I said finally, "making camp at the first level ground we come to."

Obares nodded and strode off. I had basically given him an order to find some level ground, which was as good an order as any. Obares sent scouts ahead on foot, and they located ground, which we reached within an hour. All of us, man and animal alike, were exhausted by the time we staggered into the clearing. I gave orders to erect the mess tent only, saying we would all sleep there. Parts of the other tents were used to protect the horses and oxen.

Several of the animals were not fit for going on, and the cook suggested we butcher them for supplies. One big ox had twisted his leg in a crevice and looked particularly forlorn, almost as glum as the men. I am not usually the most devout of worshipers, but I felt we needed something to lift everyone's spirits and give us some hope. So I ordered the stewards to build a huge fire, big enough to sacrifice the ox.

Now came the delicate question of to which god to dedicate the sacrifice. The soldiers wanted to sacrifice to Ares, the god of war, but soldiers always want to sacrifice to Ares. Cooler heads suggested Zeus or Hera, and those particularly scared of death wanted to honor Hades, of the Underworld. Of course, I best loved the Muses and Isis, but they hardly applied in this instance, and I didn't think the Greeks would let me sacrifice to an Egyptian goddess

like Isis. So I settled upon my old benefactor, Apollo.
True, Apollo was no longer my avowed protector, not
since I had gained my freedom, but I hoped he would still
have some interest in my well-being. I told the others that
I had chosen Apollo because I wanted the sun to shine and
stop the snow. This was welcomed all around as a fine
idea.

Among the infantry, we had an old soldier who looked
very fierce and holy, so we elected him to slay the ox and
invoke the god. I must say, I didn't care for all the blood,
but it was very exciting when we tossed the ox on the
roaring fire and watched it burn. The smell also made us
hungry, and we cooked and ate some horses right afterward.

With meat in everyone's belly and a huge fire blazing,
we all felt much better, despite the howl of the wind. We
were rather cozy, all sleeping in one tent, and I think some
of the soldiers and slaves became close friends that night.
Obares posted a large guard to watch the horses and had
the men relieved frequently.

Nevertheless, a stranger sneaked into camp shortly before dawn.

I wasn't sleeping soundly, anyway. I had the steward
fetch me a glass of wine, but it didn't do any good. We
had now been months on the road without real incident;
we had even been lost before, and snow was not unexpected in these mountains. But for some reason I felt this
was different, that we were standing on the precipice of a
great cliff, ready to plunge to our deaths.

Before I realized what I was doing, I was on my feet
and throwing on my robe. I had to step over dozens of
sprawled bodies to reach the flap of the tent, but I didn't
awake a single soldier or servant. Seconds later, I was
standing in the snow, staring up at a window of stars in a
swirl of dense clouds. The snow landed like feathers on
my face, melted, and ran down my cheeks like tears.

"My son!" groaned a voice. "Help me!"

I whirled around but couldn't locate the source of the strangled voice. I thought perhaps it was a trick of the wind, or of one of the men. Then plaintively it cried again, "Before they return . . ."

A dread filled me, and before I could stop myself I was scrambling down a rocky slope, slashing my legs on a variety of thistles while avoiding the ice which had hardened over the cold night. "Where are you?" I called, trying to pinpoint the rantings.

"They never give up!" shrieked the voice. "They will be back!"

Ahead of me, beneath a gnarled thorn bush, I spied a bare and bloodied leg. Over my shoulder, I heard one of my own soldiers rushing to my aid, his boots kicking stones into the deep gorge below us. He reached me just as I reached the man in the thorns, and I must say he turned away even quicker than I. There before us lay a man with most of his skin turned inside out by huge scratches. These scratches covered his body from skull to toe but none was apparently deep enough to kill him, because his eyes brightened at our approach.

"Saved!" he croaked. "I am *saved!*" He tried to raise himself on one arm, but his body shook with a great spasm and slumped back to earth. His eyes closed, and I feared he was dead; then, a moment later, his breast moved with the unconscious labor of breathing.

The young soldier with me stole another glance, then jerked his head away. "Fetch a litter!" I rasped, cracking him on the back. Looking grateful, he scampered up the rocks, hollering for the litter bearers. The entire camp would be rousted by his bellowing, but that couldn't be helped if we wanted to save this man's life.

I looked down at the man, who had once been a fine specimen, handsome and muscular, and I saw his hand tighten around a sword tangled in the thicket. The sword was coated with blood, and thick gray fur stuck to it in places. Against what manner of beast had he defended himself? I shuddered and looked around, hoping the litter would be here soon.

How had the man passed the guards, I wondered to myself, trying to keep my mind off the more frightening question. I peered anxiously into the darkness and struggled to keep my footing on the frozen rock. He might have crawled along the rock face for some time, I supposed, before attracting any attention. The guards were not looking for dying men crawling in the bushes. Or he might have even lain here for a day or two, blissfully unconscious as he was now. Growing somewhat accustomed to his ghastly appearance, I studied the man and formed some conclusions. He had clearly been in his prime, a man of substance, judging by the richness of his tattered clothes. What was he doing here in these fearsome mountains? What, for that matter, was *I* doing here? Despite the deep gashes in his face, it seemed the man was unconsciously smiling.

I wasn't smiling until we had carried him up from there and placed him on a cot. The guard around camp was doubled, and we sent for the chief steward, who had some medical knowledge. The steward arrived and carefully probed the man's wounds under our lamplight. Some had dried cleanly, some had festered, and some were still oozing blood. The chief steward looked at me and shook his head. "He may continue to live, but it seems more likely he will die."

Suddenly the man bolted upright in bed and shrieked, "They come at dawn! At dawn!" Sobbing, he lay back down and in a second or two was asleep again, breathing laboriously.

The rest of us were breathing rather uneasily ourselves. Captain Obares paced to the doorway and brushed back the tent flap. He stared at the mauve-colored sky and said matter-of-factly, "Dawn is but minutes away. Shall I prepare for attack?"

"Yes," I gulped, wondering how one prepared for attack against creatures unknown and unseen.

Within minutes, I heard the men falling into ranks outside and taking up posts around our tent. I congratulated myself on having had them erect only one tent, which would be much easier to defend than three. The steward was now applying salve to the man's wounds, and I wondered how long the stranger would live. Personally, I didn't think I would care to live very long with wounds like that.

A chorus of screams sounded on the wind, and I leaped to my feet. Obviously, the lookouts had been taken by surprise. Next came the terrified braying of the horses and oxen, some of which broke from the corral and stampeded against our tent, snapping one corner tent pole in half and collapsing canvas onto several startled attendants. Outside, officers were barking orders, and I heard the rhythmic clanking of armor as the men formed a phalanx to meet the foe. Some of the servants wailed in fear, while others grabbed clubs and kitchen utensils. I had a ceremonial sword which Croesus had given me, and I fumbled inside my clothing chest for it. Upon gripping the shining blade in my hand, I heard war screams from the men outside. I started out to join them when I heard another more chilling sound—like the guttural roar of the sea before it crashes over an embankment. Only this was a living roar, a chorus of deep-throated growls!

With the need to meet one's death face-to-face, I rushed outside into the chaos. In front of me, an ox staggered to his death with two huge gray figures clinging to his broad back. Upon felling the ox, one of them leaped off and snarled victoriously at me. Blood dripped from the jaws of the monstrous gray wolf.

Before the beast decided to do more than gloat, I squirmed under the shields and between the legs of two soldiers, neither one of whom budged to help me. I didn't blame them for not breaking ranks—at the end of the line, the wolves had broken through and were dragging soldiers off. Behind me, a man had a vicious wolf pinned to his lance, and another man was hacking at it with his sword. Another wolf bounded completely over the line of shields, passing so close I could feel the heat of his body. His carcass stank of blood. He landed on the back of a cavalryman, who went down with a scream. At once, his comrades sank six lances into the wolf, but the beast continued to gnaw at his victim until someone chopped its head off with an ax.

It was the most ferocious battle I had ever seen. Only the skill of the archers saved us. At close quarters, the wolves had all the advantage: They could rip into a man's throat with their tremendous jaws and kill him in an instant, while it took several well-placed blows to kill each wolf. Believe me, modern wolves in a zoo bear as much resemblance to these creatures as a house cat bears likeness to a lion. These wolves were as large and lithe as war ponies, with teeth like rows of spear tips and eyes that bespoke evil intelligence. But the monsters made the fatal mistake of regrouping and encircling us, while others broke off to gorge themselves on dying horses, oxen, and men. During this lull, the archers quickly drew their bows and fired a volley of arrows, most of which found their large targets. While few wolves were killed by the arrows, most were slowed down and confused. Upon Obares's command, we broke ranks and charged.

For the first and last time in my life, I drew blood with a sword that day. I was not at the head of the charge, however; the lancers went first, spearing the fittest of the wolves with their heavy lances. They fell back as the swordsmen closed in—I was somewhere back in that pack. I don't know which screamed loudest, dying men or dying wolves. I remember only that a wolf with an arrow in its neck leaped at me and knocked me down, but I was quick enough to plunge my sword between its ribs. Warm sticky blood spilled out of the wound and flowed down my arm, and I was soon smothered by the smell of fur and death. Mercifully, a soldier kicked the carcass off me and stabbed it again. A few feet from my face, the great jaws of the dying animal snapped in a silent imitation of laughter.

By the time I regained my feet and my senses, the surviving wolves were skulking away. In smaller packs, bloodlusting soldiers hunted each one down and slaughtered them unmercifully. I could hear the men's whoops of victory in the distance. The tide of this battle had definitely turned, but that didn't mean there wasn't still unpleasant work to do. As the sun crept over the jagged peaks in front of us, I and my servants began to count the dead and minister to the wounded.

Incredibly, only eleven men were killed outright. About twice as many were wounded, but most had superficial bites and scratches which cleaned easily. Those with deep bites were already among the dead. In a way, the loss of horses and oxen was much more serious, because men would not carry other men or pull wagons. We lost about half the horses, many of which killed themselves on the cliffs rather than face the wolves. The oxen acquitted themselves better than any other creature; only six were dead, and they had trampled to death more wolves than that.

The men returned with bloody wolf pelts slung over their shoulders. After the skinning was done, we counted forty-three pelts, enough to afford almost every man a new jacket. Despite the deaths of their comrades, the soldiers were singing and laughing, and morale in camp was never higher. Obares explained to me that a band of men is never really close until they have faced and survived battle together. Tales of the wolf attack would enliven many a campfire for years to come.

"But I hate to think," he muttered solemnly, "what our losses would have been without the warning. The gods were watching over us when you found that man in the bushes."

* * *

The sun was high in the sky before I found time to return to the tent and check on our unlikely savior. His breathing was worse, like the sound of a broken bellows, and the steward shook his head sadly at me as he left.

Nevertheless, the man awakened at my touch. "The wolves are all dead," I said. "We will make a coat for you from the richest pelt."

He tried a smile, but the gashes in his face opened wider than his lips. "Revenge is enough," he rasped. "Two dawns ago, they killed my caravan ... my entire family ..." His face broke into soundless sobbing.

I patted his shoulder, wishing I could say something calming. "Is there anything I can do for you? Anything which you need?"

After a moment, in which I thought he had finally left us, the man sighed as if recalling a pleasant memory. When he spoke, his voice took on surprising strength. "I am Jhubal of Delphi ... home to the Oracle of Apollo. I know I shall never see fair Delphi again. Would you please make a small offering for me at the cave of the Oracle?"

I wanted to be honest, and I was beginning to wonder if any of us would live long enough to return to Lydia, let alone Delphi. "If my eyes ever behold Greece again," I assured him, "I will make straightaway for Delphi and do as you ask."

"That is all I require," smiled Jhubal serenely, as he died.

CHAPTER 14

Center of the World

We stayed in the mountain pass for two days, until the snow melted and our scouts could locate the trail. During that time, we buried our dead, granting Jhubal of Delphi the same honors we accorded the fallen Lydians. We continued to stuff ourselves on horsemeat, which made us little better than the wolves, but there were so many dead horses we couldn't let them rot. The cavalrymen drew lots to see who would have a mount and who would join the infantry.

Surprisingly, I was now much loved by the men. Before, they had hated me for keeping to myself and denying them liberty; now they knew I had discovered the Delphian and had kept him alive long enough to issue his timely warning. They had also seen me fighting side by side with them against the wolves, although I was totally ineffective and had nearly got myself killed. Nevertheless, I had won the respect of soldiers, never an easy thing for a civilian to do. To cement our bond, I occasionally told them a risqué fable.

"Perhaps you have heard the tale of the sculptor and the old woman?" I asked one afternoon after our usual lunch of horseflesh.

"No!" the soldiers shouted back. "Tell us, Aesop!"

"Well," I replied, lounging back in the chair of my litter,

having had the canopy removed to enjoy a little sun, "a sculptor was walking along a road on a very hot summer's day. He happened to pass an older woman who was going in the same direction, and she was nearly faint from heat and exhaustion. The sculptor took pity on her and offered to carry her, but the only way he could comfortably do so was to have her sit on his shoulders. After a bit, the proximity of the woman's legs about his face caused his penis to go stiff as a chisel, and he instinctively flung her to the ground and began to have intercourse with her. 'What are you doing?' she shrieked. Ashamed, he replied, 'I am a sculptor. You were heavy, so I am trying to chisel some weight off you!' When finished, he picked her up again and placed her back on his shoulders. After they had gone some distance more, the woman tapped him on his head and said, 'If I am still heavy and burdensome for you, put me down again and chisel off some more.' "

The men guffawed and told me some stories for which I dare not take credit. For the rest of our journey, our packs seemed much lighter. Once we reached the Euphrates River, we no longer even had need to follow a trail. We meandered along the lush banks of the ancient tributary until we spied a stack of glimmering dark cubes in the distance. It looked like some careless Titan's child had dropped his building blocks on a great green carpet, so fertile was the plain before us. Like glittering jeweled snakes, the Tigris and Euphrates curled through the valley and among the dark, shiny blocks. Not for nothing was this called the center of the world: Babylon.

In due course, we were greeted by some very regal soldiers, wearing great plumes in their helmets and strong perfume. They didn't look like they would be much in a fight, but they must have put on a grand parade. I was pleased to see that the Babylonians were a dark race of people, though not as dark as I. I kept the Nubians close by me, because I knew they made me look pale by comparison.

Obares glared disgustedly at the popinjay soldiers. At least his men looked, and smelled, like soldiers. "The Royal Emissary of King Croesus of Lydia!" he announced, "to see His Grace, the King of Persia!" Obares was wise not to call the king by name. We had been traveling a long time, and not even a famous king like Lycurgus stays in power forever.

The Persian officer smiled. "You are perhaps carrying gold?"

"Not until we leave here," I said testily. "Now take us to the king, who awaits us!"

The Babylonian wheeled around on his beautifully prancing horse and motioned his men to form a column ahead of us. Our column dutifully followed, and Obares rode at my side.

"We should be out of here as quickly as possible," he said in a low voice. He was less frightened of spies than his own men, who would hardly care to leave civilization again so quickly after eight months in the wilderness. Nothing would be likely to get them out of Babylon but fear, and we had no reason to believe that we would be treated any way but hospitably. On the other hand, where gold was concerned, no one could ever be sure of another's actions.

"Order your men not to eat or drink anything without testing it," I said.

Obares nodded grimly. "Very wise," he said, as he rode off to spread the caution.

I watched him go and marveled to myself at the direction my life had taken since leaving the peaceful service of Xanthus. On Samos, I had rarely been afraid of anything but a mild beating—now I was frightened by the shadow of every decision. Every movement, thought, or deed had become agonizing with the weight of my responsibility to the soldiers and slaves in my company. All of this terror was the result of my unbridled ambition, I told myself. Had I been content to remain free, and not been tempted by a high post and luxuries, I could've returned to my simple Samos, where Xanthus surely would have paid me a comfortable stipend to teach his classes. I would be treated as a hero there, not as the conniving invader I was in Babylon.

Despite my fear, I couldn't help but be awed, and cowed, by the splendor that was Babylon. This was not a real city, I quickly saw. It was the equivalent of the present-day Disneyland, an elaborate garden which can house an enormous number of people, all of whom realize they are guests and not natives. Babylon, with its huge graphite walls and the rivers swirling around it, was also an impressive military fortress, housing an army of colorful charioteers. Evidently, the Persians' way of battle is simply to run their enemies down. Farther east, I heard they used elephants for this task. Either way, the Persian Empire was vast and due to become bigger with the coming of Alexander the Great two hundred years later, and Babylon was its crown, the fortress in the fertile valley from where life was said to have sprung.

We were led to a sumptuous estate, where no one apparently lived but visiting dignitaries. A feast was ordered to be held in our honor, though I am sure a feast was held every night in Babylon. Every soldier was invited, and they were so eagerly looking forward to it that they spent most of their accumulated pay on new clothes. I felt a bit sorry for the slaves and servants, who wouldn't be invited anywhere. But I know firsthand how inventive slaves are and how they would manage to see more of the city unobtrusively than we could see as honored guests.

So we put on our best finery and strolled en masse across the vast garden, many cubits in the air on a high black wall. We were utterly lost in the various levels of the city and would have been captured in moments had we tried to elude our guard. But we had no cause to do so. We had been groomed well and now were about to be fed well, like expensive horses. The lights of the guard towers glimmered in the sweet smelling darkness, rife with the scents of food, perfume, and flowers. This was truly an enchanted city, and none of us were in any hurry to rush through our examination. After our long march, we were content to sample the delicacies of Babylon one at a time. Also, this was hardly a rude village where men could go running around like a pack of jackals—this was a cultured city where men behaved with gentility and grace. Besides, we had hardly seen any women and had yet to see a single prostitute.

The word had already been passed on to us that Lycurgus was on his way to Babylon from the East, where he had been keeping the rajahs in line, I suppose. We knew he kept various abodes in his vast kingdom, and we hadn't been certain of catching him in Babylon. I almost wished he would be delayed, for I had no desire to start a process which might end with me dragging large quantities of gold from one side of the world to the other.

We reached a great dining hall, and the soldiers were seated at tables running lengthways down the sides of the room. My officers and I were seated at a table which joined the others at the top of the room and formed a long horseshoe. I assumed that the center area was left free for the servers, who were already pouring the wine. Some soldiers drank unhesitatingly until their fellows elbowed them, reminding them of the decree not to drink untested fluids. They stopped, embarrassed, and looked at Obares and me. I honestly didn't know what to say or do until a tall older man, who reminded me slightly of Xanthus, strode into the center of the tables. As if on cue, he picked up a random cup of wine and began to drink. The men laughed with the sudden smashing of the tension, and I hoisted my cup to the man and smiled. The servers were busy pouring wine after that.

"I am Hermippus," said the man, approaching our table,

"Adviser to the king and regent of Babylon. And you are the wise Aesop?"

I bowed. "Not half as wise, I'm sure, as the noble advisers of King Lycurgus." I didn't know who my competition was, and I didn't want to step on any toes.

"We Persians appreciate modesty," smiled Hermippus. "And honesty."

"As does every just man," I agreed. "Are you to dine with us?"

"Alas, not," sighed Hermippus. "Perhaps you have heard, the king is expected back tomorrow, or the next day at the latest. We must make ready the Palace," he said gravely.

My Persian not being too good, I couldn't tell whether he had said *palace* or *city*. Either way, I knew he meant Babylon, because that's exactly what it was—an elaborate palace, staffed by a city of people. "We await at the king's convenience," I said, bowing solemnly.

"You await," Hermippus relied, a twinkling in his eye, "in comfort and amusement, I trust." He bowed politely and backed away from us. Every soldier watched his graceful exit, which blended perfectly into the rush of white-robed servers, who surrounded us with heaping platefuls of exotic food. I am told I ate peacock that night, but I have no idea which of the delicious fowl dishes it was. We ate goat and mutton too, unusual scented rice, and many large tubular vegetables which tasted like a combination of nectar and fresh bread. The wine was the finest I ever tasted, and I was soon sated enough to sleep for a hundred years. But the delicious dinner was only the preliminary attraction—soon the real entertainment began.

After an efficient filling of our cups, the servers melted into the curtains, and the room quieted expectantly. The far corner of the vast hall filled with musicians, most of whom were drummers and harpists. As the drummers slowly began to play, several hand-held torches were lighted, casting a kaleidoscope of moving shadows on the

parquet floor before us. Into this swirl of shadows and
drums rushed a dance troupe of lithe youngsters wearing
short yellow tunics which did nothing to hide their supple
legs.

The twenty or so dancers sprawled on the floor and began wailing and clicking their tongues to the music in a
way that was quite uncanny. It was the odd timbre of their
voices that was so strange, too high to be male yet too guttural and husky to be female. By their bodies, they appeared to be young women on the verge of full blossom,
and the men leaned forward eagerly. The dancers rose
slowly and gracefully to their feet, lissome hands caressing
dark faces, black curls accentuating painted eyes. They
may not have deigned to stare at us for very long, but we
certainly stared at them, especially as they began to sway
in elegant unison to the soaring music. I had seen professional dancers in the circus, on Samos, and at the court of
Croesus, but not since gazing upon the Muses had I seen
such delicate and assured movement. Children though they
may have been, these were great masters of the dance.

Then the amazed whispers began to sound on both sides
of me. Irritated, I turned to bark my displeasure when a
single word assaulted my ears. This single word, from one
of my most revered and experienced officers, did much to
explain what we were seeing. *"Eunuchs!"* he gasped.

I now studied the closest dancer with a policeman's
gaze. He still appeared more female than anything else, as
sweet and pure as a twelve-year-old princess, but his
movements were far too assured and athletic for such a
child. The lithe hairless legs, slim unformed breast, and
angelic face all bespoke youth and unfulfilled femininity.
Of course, unfulfilled masculinity might look the same, as
far as I knew. Vaguely, I remembered stories about socie-
ties which routinely castrated a certain number of male
children for the purpose of keeping them youthful, but I
had never really believed such primitive behavior could
exist. Now the results were dancing before me, and I was

astounded that such barbarism could spawn such beauty. The world was a strange place with strange practices, I reminded myself.

These remarkable dancers performed for over an hour and then mingled with our soldiers, whom I had never seen so bashful. Some of them apparently understood that eunuchs were specially trained in lovemaking, but they didn't know how to proceed with such exotic creatures. More than one would have sooner taken a goat in his arms. Nevertheless, toward midnight, a few of the men could be seen slipping off with the small dark lovelies, or gazing fondly, and drunkenly, into their eyes. (Denied receiving pleasure themselves, eunuchs can lavish more attention on their partners; or so the theory goes.)

In Lydia, honored guests would have been offered women for the night, or men if they had insisted. So only the neutered sex of the participants was an oddity here. I was beginning to think the Babylonians did without women altogether—the only ones we had seen were a few old crones in the marketplace. But a well-traveled veteran explained to me that wealthy Persians collected women and kept them hidden away in harems. The king, for instance, might have sixty wives and a couple of hundred concubines. With this in mind, the practice of creating so many eunuchs began to make perverse sense.

I personally didn't find the eunuchs either appealing or appalling, so I paid them no more mind. I busied myself worrying about my mission. I didn't fear failure in this conundrum business—I feared success. The Persians were hospitable now, but what would they be like after parting with five thousand talents of gold? What would the soldiers be like after being forced from luxury back to the trail, with the intoxicating smell of gold under their noses? What would all those petty chieftains and kings, who had let us pass so peacefully, do upon our return?

I called Obares over and asked him to sit beside me.

"The men are enjoying themselves," he said grimly.

"They deserve a bit of pleasure," I said. "The trip back is going to make the trip here look like a jaunt in the plaza. We can't spend as much time getting the gold back as we spent getting ourselves here. It's just too tempting."

I agree," said Obares. "But what can we do?"

"Tomorrow, send your most trusted man to the nearest seaport on the Mediterranean. I would imagine it is Tyre on the Phoenician coast. Tell him to learn the workings of the dock until he learns how and where to charter a fast ship. Once we have the gold in our possession, the entire force will march quickly to Tyre—from there, you, I, and a few trusted men will return to Lydia by ship, with the gold."

Obares leaned forward excitedly. "And the rest of the force?"

"Will return to Lydia over the land route," I replied, "carrying the litter and acting as a decoy."

Obares scratched the unaccustomed stubble on his chin. "The men might desert if left to themselves."

"The men won't desert if they want to collect their shares."

"We run the risk of pirates," he grumped.

I sighed impatiently. "Pirates will have no way of knowing who we are or what we are carrying. Besides, nobody has a bigger navy than Croesus—with any luck we'll run across one of his ships to escort us."

"These are not our orders," said Obares finally.

"You can conduct a gold parade across those mountains if you like," I shrugged. "But I'm not going."

After several moments of contemplation, Obares awarded me a very rare smile. "I once thought that this was an accursed assignment, but now I believe that your leadership will see us through. This will make all of our careers!"

"I'm only interested in saving my neck and my sanity," I muttered. "After this is over, I'm going back to being a schoolteacher. Just don't tell anyone about this."

"Yes, My Liege," Obares nodded soberly. He rushed off, and I looked out over the empty dance floor. Most of my men had vanished into the night with their new friends. They were on liberty, and I didn't blame them. Unfortunately, there was no liberty for me.

CHAPTER 15

Old Friends and New

The Babylonians treated us lovingly over the next few days, but they kept us shut up in the visitors' estate under constant guard. Our soldiers were much disappointed and longed to have free run of the city and all its hidden charms, but we cautioned them that they were all emissaries from a strange foreign power and, as such, easily mistaken for spies. If our hosts suddenly turned on us, they could cut us down in the labyrinthian streets as easily as a farmer mows his hay. Of course, our slaves, who went out daily to replenish our supplies, had free run of the city; they mingled with the Babylonian slaves and learned much. They returned with wondrous stories of a great and sumptuous harem deep in the Palace, a network of gruesome dungeons even deeper in the bowels of the city, and a conservative populace who seemed to value decorum above all else.

To keep up the spirits of the soldiers and the household servants, I assembled them all each afternoon, and we amused ourselves with fables and ditties. Those who could play instruments played them, and those who could sing sang; but we in no way approached the splendor of the dancing eunuchs. Nevertheless, our parties attracted a few visitors on their own merits. Hermippus came by nearly every afternoon and sometimes brought other Babylonian dignitaries with him. One time, he astounded us by bringing a woman with him. Not only was her sex a rarity in our company, she was easily the most beautiful and exotic mortal I had ever seen.

Her skin was like brown teak, but her eyes were the crystallized purple of amethyst. Her hair was sleek and black and flowed down to a trim waist wrapped in yellow satin. Her face was arresting—youthful yet wise, calculating yet serene. I thought she must surely be the queen or a princess.

"The king's concubine," the water boy whispered as he plumped the pillows behind my back. "Her name is Astrah."

"If that's one of the concubines," I replied, "what must the wives look like?"

"Not nearly so good." He smiled and hurried off.

Hermippus bowed and seated his guests himself, as he always did. We had taken to leaving him some choice seats in the front, should he suddenly show up. "Excuse the intrusion," he said solemnly. "There has been no sign yet of the king's party. Please, go on with your address, Aesop."

I nodded and tried to take my eyes off Astrah the concubine long enough to acknowledge his presence. "We were just discussing how King Lycurgus must be a great king to rule such a cultivated kingdom. He must be very proud of Babylonia, and Babylonia of him."

"Thank you," bowed Hermippus. "Babylonia has always been blessed by the gods with good fortune and good rulers. But, please . . . go on with your lecture . . . we never meant to interrupt you."

When I saw he wasn't going to introduce the lovely lady, I had no choice but to go on. "Since we are talking about gods and rulers, I have a curious tale to relate. Many years ago, the frogs became annoyed that they had no one to govern them. So they sent a petition to Zeus, asking him to furnish them a ruler. Not having much respect for frogs, Zeus sent them a block of wood, which he assumed would float on the pond and keep them amused. At first, the frogs were frightened of the block of wood, then the bravest ones began to swim close to it and touch it. Finally, they became contemptuous of the block, sitting on it and kicking it. They complained to Zeus that their ruler was too pliant, too complacent, and they wanted a tougher one. Losing patience, Zeus sent them a water snake, which gobbled up thousands of frogs before dying of old age."

For the benefit of my guests, who were also my hosts, I translated my tale into Persian. Upon finishing, I caught a trace of a smile on the lovely Astrah's face, and that was reward enough for me.

Hermippus looked mildly amused. "If you told that story in the presence of a ruler who was not as benevolent as ours, you might have a serious problem."

"How could a story about frogs frighten a king?" I asked.

"It is the truth which frightens," Hermippus replied.

"The truth is different to each person," I observed. "For instance, a man and a lion were once traveling together, and they soon began to brag about which was better able to rule. They came upon a statue of a man strangling a lion, and the man turned to the lion and said, 'Do you see how much more powerful we are than you?' The lion sniffed, 'If lions cared about carving statues, you would see many more statues of lions eating men.' "

Hermippus and his elegant guest smiled appreciatively, then she bent over and whispered something into his ear. Hermippus lowered his voice to speak. "The lady, whose name must not be mentioned, asks if these stories have a name?"

"Fables," I replied.

Astrah spoke again to the lucky Hermippus; he smiled and turned to relate her question. "She asks if all Greeks are as wise as you?"

"Alas, no," I replied.

Before we could continue with this pleasant if somewhat limited repartee, a messenger barged into the room and spoke urgently to Hermippus. At once, he rose to his feet and waved at his entourage to precede him from the room. "I beg your pardon," he bowed politely, "but the king has been sighted and may well arrive this evening. I will try to arrange an audience for you tomorrow."

"Thank you," I said, more than a little disappointed. I didn't think I would be seeing much more of Astrah if her master was again in residence. The remarkable woman and her dignified escort swept out of the room, and every soldier and servant sighed as one. By Zeus, it was hard to imagine that there were creatures like this around yet not be allowed to see or meet them.

I suddenly felt that maybe we should stay a while in Babylon after all.

If we hadn't known it was the king, we would have thought Babylon was being invaded. All night long, soldiers, horses, chariots, wagons, and camp followers trooped into the city. I wouldn't have thought the city could hold so many new arrivals, but it obviously had resources and depths unknown to us. The din was terrific, and even by midmorning it hadn't stopped. I looked out my bedroom window at a narrow side street far below and watched what must have been the thousandth column of soldiers to pass. Their headgear, plumes, and costumes varied, and I presumed that each distinct group represented a different section of the realm. Obares stood to my side and clicked his tongue ominously. I could tell he was counting, estimating the enemy's strength.

"If we get the tribute, do you think they will allow us to leave?" he asked.

"We can only hope they are honorable," I shrugged. "If they aren't, we are dead no matter what we do."

"I'm ready to leave anytime," muttered Obares. "I don't mind telling you, Aesop, I'm afraid."

I looked up at the taciturn face of the captain, a man whom I had grown to trust and admire yet hardly begun to know. I put my hand on his shoulder. "When a fisherman pulls his net in, he catches only the big fish. The small fish easily slip away to safety. So it is with men—only the great ones need to be afraid."

Obares managed a grateful smile. "If we must depend upon words alone to guarantee our safety, we can thank the gods we are under your care."

I would have liked to assure him that everything was going to be fine. More than that, I would have liked for someone to come in and reassure *me!* But we were on a mission, an adventure; and the nature of adventures is that they never turn out the way you think they will. In fact, surprise is probably the overriding law of the universe.

A knock sounded at the door, making us both jump. "Enter!" I snapped.

My servant boy scuttled into the room and bowed before us, looking scared to death. "The captain of the Guard requests an immediate audience with you."

"A Babylonian captain?" asked Obares.

"A *huge* Babylonian captain!" the boy replied.

"Then we better not keep him waiting," I shrugged. "Show him in immediately." The boy hustled out, and I turned and smiled wanly at Obares. "I hope your man has got to Tyre all right and picked us out a good boat."

Had Apollo's sphinx strode into the room at that moment, I could not have been more surprised. The door slammed open and there before me stood the grinning visage of my second owner, Pelaphus. Though thinner and much better dressed, he still looked more like a slovenly monk than a fierce warrior. But I well remembered his dispatching six Ammorites at a bazaar in Faba; they were all legless beggars now, teetering around on little boards. A rush of memories and emotions swept over me, and I suddenly felt safe and secure basking in Pelaphus's warm grin.

"Pelaphus!" I cried, rushing toward him and grasping his arm.

He pounded me roundly on the back and gripped my shoulders. "When I heard your description, I wondered! Is that the same Aesop I know? But how many hunchbacked dwarves named Aesop are there?"

"Few!" I agreed.

"Especially those who have become great orators," Pelaphus nodded with admiration.

"How do you happen to be captain of the Guard to Lycurgus?" I gaped. "When last I saw you, you were a trader!"

"Always a mercenary, Aesop, you know that!" laughed the giant, slumping into one of my couches. He took a handful of figs from the bowl on the table and threw them down with one gulp. "I only took the dye as payment for a little job I did, and I only bought you slaves to help me carry it."

Obares blinked at me, and I suddenly remembered that I hadn't introduced them. "Captain Obares, Captain Pelaphus."

The two captains cordially shook hands, and Pelaphus pointed at me. "He was a very good slave. In fact, he was the foreman of my caravan. Did he ever tell you about the sphinx?"

"How did you come to be here?" I asked bluntly.

"The same way you did," Pelaphus shrugged. "I came here protecting another's interests, and I stayed on when I saw how wealthy they are. Croesus, your new master, is wealthy by Greek standards, but these Persians have wealth and manners beyond belief! This is a very stable kingdom, Aesop, even if the people are a little full of themselves."

"What kind of man is Lycrugus?" I asked.

Pelaphus shrugged. "Wise, just, cruel. But he throws great parties!"

"We have already had a taste of his remarkable entertainment," said Obares.

"The eunuchs, huh?" nodded Pelaphus knowingly. "I'll take you to the dungeon where they chop their manhood off. Then you can tell me what you think."

"You're Greek," said Obares. "Why don't you come back with us?"

"You couldn't pay me what I make here," winked Pelaphus. "I can't stay now—Lycurgus will be waking and will want to make sure his security is tight. In case you don't know, Aesop, captain of the Guard is a euphemism for the king's bodyguard." Pelaphus saluted us and left.

"An interesting man," said Obares. "Can we trust him?"

"As long as we don't try to kill the king."

The king did not look like a man who would die easily. Lycurgus stood as tall as any of his guards, including Pelaphus, and he had a kingly bearing and noble chin which belied his advanced age. Also belying his age was a thatch of unnaturally black hair. I didn't hold that particular vanity against him; even Greek men colored their hair. Obviously, much of Lycurgus's popularity depended upon his appearance, and he worked hard to keep it up. Of course, the purple ostrich plumes, brocaded silk jacket, and flaming red pantaloons did much to convey the majesty of his position. He sat in his great throne chair and studied me with indifference as I approached. Pelaphus cast a professionally wary eye upon my entourage, offering no indication that he ever knew me or cared to know me.

"King Croesus of Lydia sends his friendship and respect to the Light of Babylonia, Lycurgus," I intoned from a bow so low that I was almost prostrate.

Lycurgus nodded condescendingly. His coolness was all part of the game, I knew. "And is Croesus so displeased with the tribute I sent him two summers ago that he must request more?"

This was news to me, but I wasn't surprised to find that these two had played the game before. "The king was honored with your generous gift and wished to offer you a chance to even the score."

Lycurgus smiled, obviously pleased by that idea. "Then it is to be the same wager?" he asked. "Five thousand talents of gold and twenty slave girls?"

"Yes," I nodded, having serious doubts that the twenty slave girls would survive the trip. "Am I to ask the question, or are you?"

"You must be new at this," Lycurgus snorted. "Croesus asked the question last time, and I couldn't answer. But now I have more advisers." He glanced behind him at Hermippus and a dozen other splendidly dressed noblemen. "We have formulated a masterful conundrum."

"Fine," I nodded politely. "I pray to Zeus that I will be worthy to answer it."

Lycurgus leaned forward on his throne and leered triumphantly at me. "What creature grows only one horn in its lifetime, which it then loses in old age?" He sat back in his throne, as erect and smug as any king could be.

"With your kind permission," I said with a bow, "I shall return tomorrow with an answer." Lycurgus confidently flicked his wrist, and I backed away from the throne.

Obares and my officers joined me at the door to the great hall and backed out with me. Obares whispered urgently, "Aesop, do you think you can find the answer?"

"I already know it," I said under my breath. "I don't wish to embarrass him by making it look too easy."

"Is it a unicorn?" another officer wanted to know.

"Unicorns die when they lose their horns," countered another.

I merely smiled and shook my head. A professional wise man doesn't have to worry much about another person's taking his job—the competition is decidedly scarce.

* * *

The next afternoon, I kept my appointment in the crowded hall. Lycurgus leaped eagerly to his feet upon seeing me, perhaps mistaking my grim expression for defeat. In reality, I was miserable about leaving Babylon so soon for what was bound to be a harrowing journey with all that gold. As I made my bow, I caught a fleeting but encouraging smile from Pelaphus. "Have you an answer?" crowed King Lycurgus.

"Yes, Your Highness," I nodded humbly. "I believe I have an answer. Will you please repeat the question?"

"Gladly," grinned the potentate. "What creature grows only one horn in its lifetime, which it then loses in old age?"

"The moon," I said, watching the king's smile crumble. "The new moon grows a single horn which then disappears as it wanes. Is this the answer you were seeking?"

"Yes," said Lycurgus glumly, slumping into the silk cushions of his throne. He glared over his shoulder at a number of noblemen who were shifting about nervously and staring at their feet. "These so-called advisers of mine have much to learn."

"Perhaps Your Highness has heard the story of the ass who was about to be caught by a wolf?"

"No," said Lycurgus with curiosity. "Is this one of your fables, of which I have heard so much?"

"Yes," I nodded.

"Then proceed, Aesop, by all means."

"The ass had been running from the wolf for some time," I continued, "and saw that he would never be able to escape. So the ass slowed down and began to walk with an exaggerated limp. The wolf came bounding up and was about to leap upon him, when the ass held out his hoof and moaned, 'Do not eat me just yet, sir wolf. For I have picked up a thorn in my hoof, and the thorn will surely prick your mouth if you try to eat me.' The wolf believed him and said he would be happy to remove the thorn first. While he was intently examining the ass's hoof, the ass kicked him in the mouth and knocked all his teeth out. 'I got what I deserved,' said the wolf through toothless gums, "for trying to be a doctor when my profession is that of a butcher.' "

The great hall was quiet until Lycurgus began to laugh; then the entire court joined him, with Pelaphus laughing the loudest. Only the chastened advisers refused to join in the merriment. Hermippus, who previously had been one of my greatest admirers, snarled and left the room. The elegant regent must be fairly certain of his position, I thought to myself, to leave the king's audience without even asking his permission. Still, the attitude of the advisers irked me; one should be more gracious in defeat than that.

"May I tell the court another fable?" I asked.

"Please do!" exclaimed the Persian king.

"Many years ago," I began, "the mice of the earth grew tired of being eaten by weasels and declared war on them. The mice elected generals, who became very vain about their positions and insisted upon wearing antlers on their heads to distinguish them from the other mice. No sooner did the battle commence than the cowardly mice broke ranks and ran to their holes. All of them escaped except for the generals, who were devoured because their antlered heads wouldn't fit into the holes anymore."

Lycurgus snorted a laugh, then quickly stifled it. "These fables . . . they have the refreshing ring of truth. I suppose, Aesop, you are in a hurry to take the tribute and return to Lydia?"

"Not necessarily," I admitted. "We've been marching for many months and were hoping for a bit of divertissement before we take our leave."

"Impossible," Lycurgus replied grimly. "Babylon may look large, because so much of it is underground. But we are filled to capacity now and desperately need the quarters your troops are occupying. I promise you, Aesop, I shall grant your troops guaranteed passage to any city in my realm, if only they will leave now. You, however, are another matter."

"Me?" I asked.

"Yes," smiled Lycurgus, "You are going to stay and become my new chamberlain."

"What?" I gasped. I glanced over my shoulder and saw Obares raising his eyes worriedly toward the ceiling. Pelaphus, on the other hand, was beaming at me with his big, round face. I stammered, "I hardly know what to say."

"If you are worried about Croesus, don't be," sniffed the king. "I will throw in an extra thousand talents of gold, which will more than pacify that moneygrubber. I have long waited for a man of your talents to come to my court, and I am not easily dissuaded from what I want. Besides, you come highly recommended." I saw him glance at Pelaphus, who did his best to look noncommittal. Despite the quandary in which I found myself, I couldn't be angry with Pelaphus, who, after all, had been the first man to treat me as an equal.

"Let me get this straight," I said. "The tribute now consists of *six* thousand talents of gold and twenty slave girls?"

"Yes," nodded the king.

"And you will offer your personal guarantee of passage to one of your cities?"

"Absolutely!" agreed Lycurgus. "My captain of the Guard, Pelaphus, will see to it personally."

That was as good a guarantee as I could wish. In reality, I was as much a stranger in Lydia as I was in Babylon, and no one could say I hadn't fulfilled my mission. I didn't know what my duties would be as chamberlain, but I could well imagine the luxuries attendant to the title. "Agreed," I said with finality. "My troops will leave for the port of Tyre tomorrow."

"Excellent!" exclaimed the king, leaping to his feet. He clapped his hands and issued orders in such rapid Persian that I couldn't understand him. As sycophants scurried all about, I turned to Obares, who shrugged and managed a smile.

"Take the extra talents of gold and send everyone home by boat," I told the Lydian. "Give every man a substantial bonus and tell Croesus I will return at the first opportunity."

Obares made a formal bow. "We shall always honor your name, Aesop."

CHAPTER 16

Eight Feet of Bliss

Obares and the rest of the soldiers left the next morning, as promised. Some of them grumbled, but word was passed secretly to them that they would be traveling home by ship, where they would receive substantial bonuses. Obares would probably be made a general. Plus, the presence of the twenty slave girls, who were all quite young and comely, did much to lift their spirits. It was obvious to all of them that a wonderful trade had been arranged: riches and women for one talkative hunchbacked dwarf.

I kept the Lydian slaves with me and had a private meeting with each one, from foolish houseboy to venerable chief steward. I explained to each that he was now free and could stay in my employ for a wage commensurate with that of a soldier, or he could leave as soon as we found a way to sneak him out. With the Lydians gone and an impressive title in front of my name, I had no pretenses to keep up. Maintaining slaves was not going to be part of my operations. Since I didn't require much money for myself, I could easily afford to pay them good wages. Surprisingly, all of the slaves, except a couple of old ones who were ready to retire, elected to stay with me. So grateful were they for their freedom that they offered to share the duty of being my official wine- and food-taster.

I was very touched by this gesture and not stupid

enough to turn it down. Immediately, all my food and drink was sampled by at least two servants in a grisly ceremony that only served to depress me. Unfortunately, the Babylonians were well-known for their prodigious mastery of poisons. As I learned from Pelaphus, two of the last three chamberlains had died under suspicious circumstances.

The main part of my job was, as always, entertainment. I presided at state dinners, which sometimes occurred two or three times a night, and hosted visiting dignitaries. I was, ostensibly, the second most important person in the kingdom, so dignitaries should feel content to be with me if the king was busy elsewhere. Of course, I kept these petty potentates happy and entertained, with more than a little help from the dancing eunuchs.

Occasionally, I also advised the king in private audience. At these times, I could feel the jealous stares as I made my way to the royal study or bedchambers. These rooms had double doors and walls eight feet thick, and nobody could know the nefarious ways in which I was manipulating the king to do my bidding. Of course, I never did any such thing: I only gave Lycurgus the same commonsense advice I would give anyone else.

"A king died in one of my northern provinces," he said to me one night, "and there is no clear descendant to the throne. On one side are the fat old nobles who have ruled the province for eons. On the other side is a family of poor noblemen who claim direct blood ancestry to the throne. I have to award the throne to one of them, or there'll be a war. What do you think I should do, Aesop?"

"A fox was swimming across a river one day," I replied, "and his body became covered with leeches. His friend, the hawk, came swooping by and offered to pull the leeches off. 'No thanks,' said the fox. 'These leeches have already made a good meal on me and don't suck much blood now. If you take them away, a fresh pack will come, all hungry, and take twice as much blood.' "

Lycurgus smiled. "So the old leeches I already know are better than a hungry bunch of new leeches!" He patted me on the shoulder. "I wish I could reason as well and simply as you, Aesop."

"I wish I had your height," I replied.

Lycurgus laughed even louder, then grew suddenly somber. "The weight of always making the right decision . . . it's a curse, Aesop."

"I know," I said. "I was actually happier when I was a slave on Samos. And I was miserable when I had the charge of all those Lydians."

"Leave me now," said Lycurgus wearily. He slumped back onto his cushions and turned into an old man before my eyes.

I took my leave quietly and quickly, gently closing the first of the doors and reaching the second before Hermippus, listening at the keyhole, had a chance to get away. I rocked him soundly on the head with the door and sent him spilling to the floor in a pile of elegant silks. I had to turn away to keep from laughing.

"Sir Regent!" I gasped. "I had no idea you were passing by. This confounded door should be fixed so that it doesn't open outward."

Hermippus scrambled to his feet and slapped on his most dignified mien. He cleared his throat and glowered at me. "You think you are so clever, Aesop, just because the old man is a fool who loves to surround himself with fools! You're nothing but a plaything, Aesop, so don't believe you have any real power around here."

"Did I ever tell you about the ass and the statue?" I asked. "An ass was once pulling a wagon which contained a statue of a famous king. Everyone he passed bowed, and . . ."

"Bah!" snarled Hermippus, swishing away in his elaborate robes.

I shrugged and shook my head, conscious of the gathering of storm clouds. "Maybe I am the ass," I admitted.

* * *

One of my food-tasters died of poisoning a week later. I couldn't prove anything against Hermippus, and, in fact, the servant could have been poisoned purposely by a fellow servant. Servants aren't immune to having enemies and disagreements. My loyal staff rallied around to protect me, taking extra care with my food and drink, testing it with *three* tasters instead of two. They well knew that the only way to prevent subsequent poisonings was to make it clear that such tactics wouldn't succeed. For the first time in my life, I began to lose weight.

Pelaphus returned from Tyre and reported to me that the Lydians had successfully set sail for home with the tribute. As usual, the Lydians had nothing but high praise for me and insisted they would further spread word of my fables and deeds. I would soon be famous the world over, even if I couldn't trust the food I was eating.

I hesitated about telling my old friend about my difficulties with Hermippus. After all, Pelaphus's allegiance was to his employers, not me; I didn't know how closely he might be aligned with Hermippus, who, it must be remembered, was the regent of Babylon and held sway over the city in Lycurgus's absence. Technically, I was second in command of the whole kingdom, but the backbone of the kingdom was Babylon. I finally threw caution to the wind and told Pelaphus that Hermippus was trying to kill me.

His big, round face darkened. "He's a snake all right— jealous of everyone who's close to the king. He's especially jealous of you, because you please the king so much without being obsequious. The king knows you have no designs and only wish to live comfortably, dispensing good advice and goodwill. That's why the king hires foreigners like us for important posts—we aren't as ambitious or cutthroat as his own Persian nobility."

"What am I to do?" I asked. "How can I make Hermippus see I am not a threat?"

Pelaphus smiled and laid his big hand upon my hump. "Even in the face of the horrid sphinx, you were not so afraid. You have only a few weeks more to endure this, as the king will be leaving Babylon when the worst of the winter is past. Do you think *he* likes this constant court intrigue? He can hardly wait to get back to war or to his summer home, both of which are more peaceful than Babylon."

"In the meantime?" I asked.

The captain's smile faded. "In the meantime, Aesop . . . beware."

But my duties demanded I be so many places that I hardly had time to beware. Secretly, I relished the state dinners, because they gave me an opportunity to eat and drink unencumbered by fear; I didn't think Hermippus would poison dozens of visiting dignitaries just to dispatch me. But the constant entertaining, dining, and late nights took their toll; for every extra hour of sleep Lycurgus got, I got an hour less! I seldom went to bed before the last royal guest passed out, and I was expected to be witty, charming, and diplomatic from dawn until dawn! As my stature in the kingdom grew, more and more dignitaries requested private audience with me and asked me to petition the king for this favor or that. I seldom did anything about their requests, but I became an expert on every petty squabble in the kingdom. I can truthfully say I had more of a private life when I was a mute fig-picker in Phrygia.

Why didn't I leave, you may ask? I was, after all, a freeman who could come and go as he wished. The answer to this curious question, dear reader, can be summed up in one word: Astrah. I was in love again. Love is not a relative term, and I can't say if I was more in love with Astrah than I had been with Hippolyte of the circus, or the sorceress Netha. I had felt more kinship and closeness to Netha, and I had only spoken to Hippolyte once in my life, the day she was so tragically swept overboard in the storm. But Astrah I saw often, coming and going from the king's bedchamber. In both cases, our hours with the king were somewhat irregular. There was no doubt at all that Astrah was the favorite from among all his wives and concubines; no doubt she would've been my favorite and every other man's as well.

The only differences between royal wives and royal concubines, I was to learn, were the circumstances of their births. Wives arrived in the palace as the daughters of petty chiefs, and concubines had either been slaves or spoils of war. The king had so many children with all these women that neither I nor anyone else knew who would eventually succeed him to the throne. Half the population of Babylon were direct descendents of the royal line. I never saw most of Lycurgus's women and children, because they were kept in the harem, a well-guarded tower in the northwest corner of the palace. No man with full genitalia ever entered the harem, except for the king. So desperate were these three hundred women for attention that, rumor had it, the eunuchs occasionally serviced them as best they could. Of course, eunuchs were not likely to sire a child who might be mistaken for a royal heir, so such dalliances were discreetly permitted. Sometimes I thought that the dancing eunuchs, the harem eunuchs, and Lycurgus were the only ones in the palace getting any sex at all.

As long as I occasionally saw Astrah, I didn't care if I saw any other women in the palace. She was always perfectly cordial and friendly to me, as we passed through the double doors of Lycurgus's bedchamber or met briefly in the hall. If Lycurgus had fallen asleep, as he often did during both of our visits, we would stop to chat.

"How fare you today, Sir Chamberlain?" she asked in a sultry yet melodious voice.

"Better now that I have seen you," I replied with all sincerity.

"Lycurgus is asleep," she said with a twinkling smile. "I'm afraid he exhausts easily these days."

Easily but happily, I thought to myself. "So now you must return to the secret chambers of the harem."

"Yes," Astrah sighed charmingly. "I am very fond of Lycurgus, but we have so much more freedom when he is away from Babylon." She smiled with happy reminiscence. "I remember the day Hermippus brought me to the villa to hear your fables."

Now it was my turn to sigh. "Ah, yes, so do I."

"Now all I see is the hallway between here and the harem," she grumped.

"That's something I don't understand," I admitted. "In Greece, women are not treated as well as they should be, but they are allowed to mingle with men. Here, it's as if men and women are two entirely different species."

"Well, aren't they?" she asked coyly.

"No," I said. "What do you want that is any different from what I want? A chance to live your life unfettered by tyranny and slavery—that's all anyone wants!"

"Sshh, Aesop!" she said, putting her finger to my lips.

This was the first time Astrah had ever touched me, and it sent waves of molten lava from my lips to my brain and back down to every extremity of my body. I stared into her limpid eyes, and a lifetime of knowledge passed between us. Reflected in her eyes was the truth of what I had said.

After an eternity, she took her finger away from my lips. "You aren't like other men, are you, Aesop? You know much more."

"I know the value of freedom," I said. "I know that both men and women should be free to choose their destinies, without the interference of gods or kings."

"Gods and kings would not agree," Astrah said solemnly, slipping past me and hurrying down the hall and away into the shadows. Her scent, like a sweet harvest of spring fruit, lingered after her, and I was hopelessly in love.

* * *

You must remember, in my first thirty-five years of life, I hardly saw any women at all. And those I saw would hardly have been interested in a hunchbacked mute dwarf slave. Since then, I had tasted the apples of passion, from slave girl to sorceress, and had found them to my liking. To me, free love represents the essence of freedom; of course, I am hardly the first one to harbor that opinion. Moreover, I adored women and found them more interesting than the pompous male company I often endured. I still could think of no one I would rather talk to than Netha, but I was drunk with longing for Astrah.

I thought about killing myself. As wild as my fantasies were, I never dreamed that coupling with Astrah would be possible. It would have to occur either in the king's bedroom or the harem, and I didn't believe that either one would be conducive to lovemaking. Of course, there was always that eight-foot space between the double doors of Lycurgus's bedchamber. Eventually, that was where we took to meeting.

Our first meetings were still accidental and usually nocturnal. Often Lycurgus would summon me, having forgotten that he had also made an appointment with Astrah. As soon as Astrah showed up, he forgot about me. I preferred Astrah's going first, because the king was always asleep after her visit, and she was often flushed from his lovemaking, which, despite his age, must have been fairly expert after all those women.

I surprised her once, just before dawn, when she hadn't fully finished wrapping herself in her gown. A flash of ebony thigh and rosebud nipple greeted my eyes as I opened the inner door.

"Aesop!" she hissed. "Wait outside!"

I slipped out, smiling to myself. She hadn't actually meant outside but only in the eight-foot space between the doors.

She slipped out a moment later, her face flushed and

burning. She was angry and passionate, passionate and angry. "Aesop, you knew I was in there!"

"I knew you were dressing," I replied.

She calmed down a bit. "Well, did you like what you saw?"

"No, the king was not sleeping too soundly. I worry about his sinus condition."

She laughed heartily. I love women who laugh heartily. "You were watching the king?"

"Who else?" I shrugged. "I wanted to make sure you hadn't killed him."

She laughed herself into a somber mood, then stared down at me. "Aesop, do you know we could be put to death for even talking like this?"

"We are as common as the flies around this place," I said. "The guards pay us no attention. We're the king's toys. We deserve much more—we deserve each other."

She shuddered a bit before taking me in her arms. That's one of the advantages of being small: women take you into *their* arms. "Aesop," she gasped, "this is wrong."

"We're free in here," I said, motioning around the barren anteroom, nothing but gray mortar and stone. "We don't need gods or kings to tell us what to do."

"No we don't," moaned Astrah, fondling my hump intimately. I fondled back. Lycurgus may have lighted the flames which engulfed Astrah that night, but I quenched them.

CHAPTER 17

Deeper and Deeper

Although Astrah and I planned many of our meetings, our best times were always accidental. We usually didn't want to take our clothes off, so we ended up ripping them to shreds. In later meetings, we would better learn to judge how much time we could spend together, but it was never enough. Guards, servants, and other interruptions always lurked in the corridor beyond the outside door. Often, we latched the outside door, which gave us a giddy but false sense of security. We refused even to consider the possibility that Lycurgus himself might open his door and discover us.

In retrospect, it seems incredible we didn't get caught sooner than we did. I still have no idea how long Hermippus observed our indiscretions before blowing the whistle, but he had plenty of witnesses with him. Hermippus, who was never subtle, ordered his men to break the door down without even knocking first. As I'm sure he intended, the horrific banging awoke Lycurgus, who had the pleasure of making the initial discovery. I still can see him now, blinking more in amazement than anger.

Half-clothed, we scurried out of the way as the door shattered. Hermippus strode victoriously into our secret lair and grinned at me, "Tell us a fable now, Aesop!"

"Take them away," rasped Lycurgus. He wiped his aged

cracked lips and flashed us both a look of disgust. Though I felt a certain shame about my actions, I resented the fact that this one man could have three hundred women and begrudge me just one of them! I tried to explain this to the guards as they hauled me feetfirst down several flights of stairs. Little did I know, I was about to get my first glimpse of Babylon's famed dungeons.

"Astrah!" roared Pelaphus. "You could have dallied with any other woman in the kingdom without such dire consequences!"

"What exactly is to become of me?" I shuddered. The clammy walls of my tiny cell were already beginning to chill me. Depths above, the sun shined warmly; but in the dungeon, warmth and sun were but a rumor.

Pelaphus shook his head pityingly. "You poor fool ... you are to be killed!"

"What?" I shrieked. "And Astrah, too, are they to kill her?"

"Technically, yes," Pelaphus nodded. "But in reality, she has been sold to a convent in India, where she is to serve her penance. Officially, she will be dead."

"Couldn't I be officially dead and go somewhere else?" I pleaded.

"Fool!" Pelaphus scowled, banging his sword in its sheath. "I myself am charged with running you through with this very blade! How could you ever think you could get away with it?"

I shrugged. "Did you ever hear the story of the ass who fell into the water while trying to cross a stream? He was carrying a load of salt, and it dissolved in the water, leaving him an empty pack to carry. On another day, he came to the stream and decided to try the same thing. Only this time, his pack was filled with sponges, which sucked up enough water to drown him."

Pelaphus smiled understandingly. "So you did get away with it a few times? Perhaps she was worth it. I still say your biggest mistake was seeking your freedom in the first place, when you knew Apollo protected you as long as you were a slave."

"That's easy for you to say!" I snapped. "A man who has been free since birth. If I am to die, at least I am to die a freeman!"

"Brave words!" the warrior gushed. "I like to see a man die bravely."

"Please," I begged, dropping to my knees. "Save me, Pelaphus, if there is a way. I will do anything!"

Pelaphus went to the cell door and glanced quickly down both ends of the passageway. He turned back to me and smiled evilly. "If you are willing to do anything, Aesop, you may have a chance."

"Say it," I beseeched him, "and I will do it!"

"You'll be risking a far more horrible death than my efficient blade."

"Give me a choice," I replied. "That's all I've ever wanted from life, the freedom to choose."

Pelaphus nodded and straddled my meager bed, one beefy leg on each side. Then he drew his face close to mine. "I have heard some legends," he whispered. "This city and these dungeons date from the beginning of time, and they go deeper than any living man knows. Some say they go directly to the Underworld, but I don't believe in such nonsense. According to the legend I prefer to believe, the dungeons lead down to a secret passage out of the city. I have always wanted to explore that far down, but I never had the opportunity."

I gaped at Pelaphus, then at the moldy gray walls. I wanted daylight, not more dungeons. "Can't we escape by going up?"

"You must never be seen again within the walls of the city," intoned the captain of the Guards. "In fact, Aesop, you're already dead."

"Well, if I'm dead," I gulped, "I might as well be on my way to the Underworld."

"Well said!" beamed Pelaphus, slapping me on the back. "I must gather our supplies and leave word that I'll be gone for a week or so.'

"A week!" I stammered. "How deep are these dungeons?"

"I told you, Aesop, no one knows." He strode jauntily to the door and paused to look back. "This is going to be a grand adventure!"

"I hope so," I shuddered.

I paced in my tiny clammy cell, waiting for Pelaphus to return. He had left the door to the cell open, and I realized I could make a dash up the circular staircase at the end of the corridor and take my chances with the guards. I heard their muffled voices from the level above. The guards undoubtedly knew that Pelaphus had thus far spared my life, but I couldn't expect them to do the same. As Pelaphus had said, I was dead. As long as no one ever saw my face again in Babylon, I was safe. Some safety, I thought ruefully, abandoned in the bowels of the world's foulest dungeon, there to die of hunger, rats, pestilence, or unknown terrors, never again to feel the warmth of the sun!

Of course, I was being dramatic, but I did feel dramatically trapped. Even as the most miserable of slaves, I had always had the wonders of the earth to cheer me—the afternoon breeze, a furry moss bed under a tree, and an endless canopy of sky over my head. Now all I had was a dank ceiling, dripping putrid slime onto my hair. The oppressive dungeon frightened me more than the howling of the snow in the mountains; the weird muffled sounds were worse than the growls of the wolf pack. Here in the depths, I had nothing to comfort me except a sputtering torch in the black passageway outside my door. Had Pelaphus not seen fit to leave that torch, I would have stood in total darkness, racing toward madness.

Unconsciously, I found myself cursing Apollo. Why did I feel that my old benefactor was to blame for my current predicament? No god had perched at my shoulder encouraging me to pursue Astrah. No god had sent me to Babylon—Croesus and my own greed had accomplished that. The blessings of the Muses and Isis were all the comforts I needed in the outside world, but they seemed irrelevant down here. Somehow, I felt as if I were still being tested, as the sphinx had tested me in the desert of Phrygia. The irony of my timely reunion with Pelaphus almost served to confirm these suspicions. Apollo, or some fabric of the universe, had prepared a massive test for me and might not be disappointed to see me fail.

But perhaps this is the true nature of freedom—to be tested constantly and to test oneself. Slavery makes life simple, but slavery denies the freedom of choice upon which real testing depends. Life is not true-or-false; it's multiple-choice. Even now, I reminded myself glumly, I had the choice of which death to embrace: Hermippus would be glad to furnish me with a dram of poison; I could attempt my escape through the city and fall to a phalanx of anonymous blades; I could prevail upon Pelaphus to fulfill his orders and dispatch me with all his skill and alacrity; or I could confront unknown death in the catacombs. Life was full of choices!

I suddenly heard a commotion, and I saw Pelaphus half running, half stumbling down the staircase, dragging a bundle of wooden torches, backpacks, and weapons with him. "Hurry, Aesop!" he barked. "Hermippus has demanded to see your body! He's right behind me!"

As I bolted from my cell into the hall, I heard angry voices and footsteps upon the circular staircase. Pelaphus thrust an unlit torch, a sword, and a pack into my hands and pointed me toward a dark crevice at the end of the passageway. "Move quickly—they mustn't see you!"

I padded down the damp stones. My height made it easy for me to dash into the crevice, which appeared to be natural. Had I not moved so quickly, I might have avoided the slick slope which waited beyond. At once, I was on my rear, sliding straight into darkness, gripping the torch and pack desperately to my chest. The sword clattered along beside me, and I groped for it to keep from accidentally running myself through. I needn't have worried about that, however, as an overhanging ledge caught me squarely on the forehead and sent me into a dreamless sleep where no god or man could touch me.

I felt a light feathery touch on my cheek as I reached that enchanted state between unconsciousness and wakefulness. "Astrah," I panted, imagining it to be my beloved's silky hair brushing across my cheek.

"Don't move!" insisted a brusque male voice.

This was not at all part of my dream, and I moved despite the warning. At once, the feather on my cheek became a claw, pinching my left eye socket. I pried open my right eye only to see a huge black spider perched across the bridge of my nose. As I froze in terror, its pincered mouth snapped leisurely at me, and it shifted its grip slightly. As if to echo the warning not to move, the spider tipped a long furry leg at me. Actually, screaming was more on my mind, and I gripped my chest to stop from shaking.

"Hold still," said the familiar male voice. Pelaphus knelt beside me and took a small stiletto from his boot. "If he bites you in the eye, you'll surely lose it," said the warrior cheerfully.

Fainting was a real possibility now, and I found myself slipping back into blackness. But the feel of cold steel on my forehead forced me to remain conscious. I watched from entirely too close a vantage point as Pelaphus, with all the skill and confidence of a surgeon, slid the stiletto between the spider's legs and under its body. At first, the spider resisted the blade's intrusion, then it snapped at the blade and curled several legs lovingly around it. At once, Pelaphus flicked his wrist and sent the spider hurtling into the air. I never moved quicker, rolling completely out of the way before the beast hit the ground. Pelaphus's boot was on top of it a second later, grinding it into a mushy pulp.

I was still panting uncontrollably when he turned to me and laughed. "I'm glad you started dreaming about Astrah, or I never would've found you."

I was suddenly mad at him for his cavalier attitude. "How could you thrust me into that dangerous pit? I was nearly killed by the fall, then by hitting my head on the rock!"

"I doubt that," scoffed Pelaphus, "but I'm glad you're safe. I've never been down here, except to peer down with a torch, but I knew it wasn't a total drop-off. They aren't likely to follow us into this cozy spot."

I did manage to remember that Pelaphus had probably saved my life at least twice today. "What's our plan, Pelaphus? Where are we going?"

"I said I had tossed your body into this hole and had gone to look for it," the big man shrugged. Hermippus may hang around for a few hours, but the dungeons aren't his style. We'll just keep going down this cavern until we find the hidden passage out."

"What if it doesn't exist?" I shrieked. "You've never seen it, and you don't know where it is!"

"Legends," he reiterated. "The legends are very clear about it."

"What about the Underworld?" I asked. "Isn't that part of the legend?"

Pelaphus rolled his eyes. In the flickering torchlight, I couldn't tell if he was thinking or ignoring me. Finally he answered, "You don't have much choice, do you, Aesop? And didn't Orpheus escape from the Underworld? Either way, we get out of Babylon—I've found that place pretty stifling lately."

"What if we get *killed?*" I roared in astonishment.

Pelaphus winked. "Then we won't have so far to walk."

He slapped me soundly on my hump. "Let's get going, what d'ya say?"

I peered into the gloom, barely illuminated by Pelaphus's torch; the darkness undulated down the slimy rock walls and blossomed into total blackness. "Lead on," I gulped.

Pelaphus did so, cautiously poking his torch into each new crevice and around each corner. With nothing much else to occupy my mind, I studied the walls and foundations of these strange catacombs. Before, I had thought they were natural, but now I saw that the twisting passageways were man-made, or at least carved. But they had been carved so crudely and in such antiquity that rubble and seepage had transformed the walls back into natural rock. I couldn't for the life of me imagine who they had got to go this deep in the earth to carve passageways out of sheer rock—even an army of slaves would be hard put to perform such a task. There could be no doubt, however, as to the purpose of the strange catacombs: They led straight down with no turnoffs.

Despite the gloomy surroundings, I was already beginning to feel better about our little trek. We had been traveling several hours, encountering nothing but the same winding corridor, and we had to be many miles from Babylon and Hermippus by now. Much as I would miss the splendors of the court, especially Astrah, I was somewhat relieved to be a free agent again. I was already formulating a plan of action for the rest of my life, should this escape be successful. I would make my way to Delphi, there to visit the famed Oracle and make a sacrifice for the Delphian who had saved us from the mountain wolves. If Delphi was to my liking, and I fully expected such a revered and ancient city to be most enlightening, I would pass some time there. But my final destination was my beloved Samos, where I planned to teach, think, and study for the rest of my life. If Netha could be coaxed down from her mysterious retreat, I might even marry. No more grandiose titles, dangerous missions, and court intrigue for me. I was going to be a poor but happy scholar.

Pelaphus stopped suddenly, and I nearly bumped into him. Slowly, he moved his torch across a large indentation in the rock wall, while I took a moment to reposition my pack. (Carrying a backpack is rather difficult with a hump.) Occupied with my pack, I didn't see what Pelaphus was staring at. "Aesop!" he hissed. "Come and look."

"At what?" I asked suspiciously. The dark hole had a vaguely unpleasant smell about it, and I couldn't imagine what was in there that I would want to see.

He motioned with the torch to several splinters of wood around the low entrance, and the light glinted off two rusty triangles. My eyes widened in amazement. "Hinges and a door!"

My curiosity piqued, I peered under my companion's arm, past the remains of the door, and into the low chamber. The torchlight shone on a pile of chains draped over a larger pile of indiscriminate bones. I couldn't tell whether the bones were human or animal, and the odor of rotting flesh didn't make me want to stay around long enough to examine them. I backed out of the circle of light from my friend's torch.

"What kind of cell could this be?" Pelaphus asked rhetorically. "It's too small to be for humans."

"I don't know," I shuddered. "Couldn't we be going?"

"Yes," laughed Pelaphus. He took a few long strides down the corridor, shoving the torch into several other low burrows. "This hall is full of tiny cells. We're definitely in some kind of dungeon."

"I never thought we were in a garden," I snapped, the sight of all those bones and chains making me testy. "Let's keep going."

"We should check out each of these cells," the warrior insisted. "After all, any one of them may lead to a secret passageway."

"Fine," I said, sitting on a low rocky ledge. "You check them out, and I'll wait here." Suddenly, the rock shifted out from under me with a loud grinding noise, and I fell unceremoniously onto my rear. Behind me, a whole wall of rock kept moving and so did I, scuttling out of the way as the rock transformed into a doorway, with another black passageway beyond it. I scurried to my feet and gaped at Pelaphus.

He was grinning triumphantly. "See! There *are* secret passageways down here!"

"Well," I remarked cheerfully, "now at least we have a choice of directions in which to travel."

As I peered bravely around the corner into the newly discovered passage, a low unearthly howl sounded from far away, but not far enough away. I stumbled backward. "What's that?"

The howl was joined by a nerve-racking chorus of howls, forming a weird minor chord. The hollow catacombs echoed and reverberated with the strange sounds, which seemed to come from everywhere at once. Pelaphus drew his sword and backed up close to me. I drew my sword too, but my hand was shaking so hard I could barely grip it. The howls were perceptibly louder now; either that, or we were just listening more intently.

"Dogs!" Pelaphus breathed. "That's what these cells are, kennels!"

"What kind of dog lives underground?" I asked, knowing I didn't want to know the answer. My mind flashed back to the horrid wolves we had faced in the Kilikian Pass; their howls had been unearthly too, and they had appeared just as mysteriously, like an avenging force from the gods. I glanced around the grim catacombs and wondered whose terrain we had trespassed upon now?

"We must get out of here," I said.

"But which way?" asked Pelaphus. "The way we were headed, or this new way?"

Now growls were interspersed with the howls, and we

heard what sounded uncomfortably like rapid footsteps converging upon us. "In here!" I exclaimed, pushing Pelaphus into the newly opened doorway. "Try to get that rock pushed back in front!"

Pelaphus handed me the torch, stuck his sword in the dirt, and put his broad back to the stone. Strong as he was, he couldn't budge it, and the ferocious growls echoed ever louder in the caverns. Of course, if I had guessed wrong and the unseen creatures were coming from behind us, closing the door would only hasten our deaths. But I had no time for such thoughts as I waved the torch over the floor of the cave, trying to find the switch which would trip the door. Finally, with the footsteps so loud we could hear claws scraping stone and growls so fierce we could sense the hot breath behind them, I spied an iron ring on the floor. "Pelaphus!" I cried. "The ring!"

Immediately, he stopped his futile pushing on the rock and dived for the ring. A monstrous black figure skidded past the doorway only a few feet away from us; had the floor not been so slippery and the beast so eager to eat us, we might have died then and there. But Pelaphus was pulling with all his substantial might, and the stone door slowly groaned back into place. Before it closed, a second more nimble beast joined the first, and its three heads snapped and snarled at us through the disappearing doorway. Mercifully, the door closed before I had to see much more. I turned and stared at Pelaphus, who was still heaving from the force of his exertion.

"Did that dog have three heads?" he panted.

I gulped, "I'm afraid so. This is some place you've brought me, Pelaphus."

"I'm sorry, Aesop," he shrugged good-naturedly. The big warrior shouldered his pack and retrieved his sword. "Unfortunately, we can't go back the way we came, so we might as well go forward. Say, Aesop, how did you know the dogs would be coming from the other direction and not this?"

I wondered about that myself, though I considered it a brilliant maneuver. "It seemed likely, I suppose, that the dogs were watchdogs who happened to be temporarily away from their kennels. Intruders might be expected to get this far, but they surely couldn't be expected to find the secret passageway. And dogs, no matter how monstrous, can't be expected to open a door. They are probably chained in their kennels most of the time."

"Chained by whom?" Pelaphus asked, his eyes glimmering even in the dim light. "And who let them out?"

Who indeed, I wondered, as I absentmindedly walked forward. But I didn't get a chance to think about it very long, as a slab of stone disappeared from under my feet and I again found myself hurtling into an abyss of cold darkness, the wind whistling by me. I screwed my eyes shut and prepared to meet my death.

CHAPTER 18

Beyond the Veil

When I didn't die after a few seconds, I realized I was not really falling into a black pit. I wasn't falling at all, in fact, but was floating, as much in the clouds as underground. The space around me remained dark, but that might be accounted for by the fact that I was afraid to open my eyes—I still expected to hit the ground at any moment. I stuck out my hands but could feel nothing but a slight breeze flowing from above, as if both the air and I were being sucked into a mild vortex. After a few eerie moments of this, my heart stopped pounding, and I began to relax, though not enough to enjoy the experience.

More than actually see, I could feel Pelaphus's presence nearby, and I knew he could no more avoid the trap than I had. "Pelaphus?" I squeaked. "Are you here?"

"Wherever *here* is!' he grumbled.

Our voices broke the spell, and I suddenly felt firm ground under my feet again—it materialized just as suddenly and mysteriously as it had disappeared only seconds earlier. I unscrewed my eyes and found myself staring at Pelaphus, who looked every bit as confused as I felt. His torch remained in his hand, miraculously still lighted. Our weapons, however, had disappeared, as had our packs. "We seem to be traveling lighter," I observed.

Pelaphus waved the torch around, desperately trying to

find his sword. "Blast the gods!" he cursed. "They've done this! They're always doing things like this!"

While Pelaphus stomped and cursed, I took a moment to study our new surroundings. Despite the fact that we hadn't fallen anywhere, we had arrived somewhere—this was a different hallway, wider, better kept, and clearly man-made. One thing was the same about it, though: with a wall at our backs and not a single doorway in sight, there was no direction to travel but downward.

"Come," I said to Pelaphus, suddenly full of unexpected confidence. "Let's keep going."

"But our swords!" he muttered. "My shield!"

"They won't do us any good," I said, starting down the corridor. I motioned for the big warrior to follow me and, disgruntled, he brushed by me and took the lead. As we walked, I again spent my time studying the walls and floors, looking for any clue as to who had built these mysterious catacombs. The walls were flat and plastered; instead of rubble and damp mold, they bore smudge marks and the twisted remains of torch holders. I felt like I was in some long-forgotten wing of a king's castle rather than leagues underground. I expected to turn the corner and walk out on a parapet, staring up at a sky full of stars. But, no, all we had to look at was a vast stretch of nondescript corridor, sloping ever and depressingly downward into the unknown.

Neither one of us talked very much, because we hardly cared to give voice to our fears. Thanks to the loss of our packs, we were now without food or water, which frightened us more than the tomblike silence. Once the torch burned away, we would be in darkness, too, where we would more than likely go mad before we died of thirst. If possible, Pelaphus was even glummer than I. Of course, a warrior feels naked without his weapons, and Pelaphus distrusted the gods considerably more than I did. I didn't expect them to help us, but I had the feeling that gods were as powerless down here as we were.

My gigantic companion was striding several yards ahead of me, obviously thinking that the faster he walked, the faster he would get out. Suddenly, as he passed under an archway between two beams, Pelaphus stopped, gasped, and scrambled backward. *"Two prongs!"* he stammered. "The staff with two prongs!"

"What are you babbling about?" I asked, jumping out of his way.

"There, there!" he croaked, jabbing his torch at the archway. Once he held the torch still enough, I could see a deeply engraved line with what appeared to be a "U" above it. The sign meant nothing to me, but Pelaphus was still beside himself. The sight of the big man shaking with fear was almost comical.

"If that's a staff," I observed, "it's an unusual one."

Pelaphus glowered at the simple but ancient engraving. "Hephaestus made two staffs, one for each of Zeus's brothers: a three-pronged staff for Poseidon and a two-pronged staff for Hades. It's the symbol for the god of the Underworld!"

"I thought you didn't believe in the Underworld," I reminded him.

"I didn't," he murmured, "until now that I'm here!"

"Better to be in the Underworld," I shrugged, "than lost, wondering whether we'll die of hunger, thirst, or fall into a hole. Let's see if anybody lives here." I cupped my hands and shouted, "Hades, Persephone, your servants and slaves—Aesop has arrived!"

Pelaphus cringed. "Are you crazy," he hissed. "Don't tempt the gods of the dead!"

I wanted to explain that a mortal who was merely alive and minding his own business was already a serious temptation to the gods, who hardly needed an invitation to meddle in business which wasn't theirs. But before I could speak, a low sultry feminine laugh sounded directly behind us. Both Pelaphus and I whirled around, and Pelaphus slapped at his empty scabbard, cursing when he found it empty. For my part, I could only stare at an extraordinary apparition which emerged from the dense shadows of the torchlight. A winged woman leisurely glided toward us.

In the flickering light, I could barely see the winged woman's face, but what I saw was aged and ravaged. Her movements, however, were remarkably fluid, like a young girl's, and the wings greatly enhanced the image of grace and beauty. But a second later, when I saw the true nature of her undulating limbs, I recoiled so quickly that I smashed into Pelaphus's chest and knocked him back a step. I blinked and stared again, but my eyes weren't failing me: The winged lady had huge serpents instead of arms and legs!

As she slithered toward us, her arms snaking about her torso and snapping annoyedly at us, Pelaphus wrapped a beefy arm around my shoulders and shoved me behind him. I could see him girding for a fight, even if all he had to use were his bare hands, and I realized that a warrior prefers to fight in any tense situation. Fierce as Pelaphus was, without blade, he was hardly a match for four huge serpents with a woman attached to them. But the fight did not materialize, as the strange female stopped politely a few feet from us and bowed.

"Aesop," she purred, "and Sir Captain of the Guard. King Hades welcomes you to his palace and his kingdom. It has been a long time since we have had such distinguished visitors who, shall I say, have not yet passed officially beyond the veil."

"And who might you be?" Pelaphus scowled.

"Alecto," bowed the winged creature, her snake limbs undulating gracefully. "I am known as 'She who rests not.' With my sisters, Megaera and Tisiphone, we are known to mortals as the Furies."

"We're glad to see you!" I interjected. "We are lost and are trying to find our way to the surface. If you could just indicate ..."

"Nonsense," the aged one sneered. "No one seeks the

surface by going ever deeper. You are here because you are fools, pure and simple. But this is a place which suffers fools gladly. Now, storyteller Aesop and warrior Pelaphus, follow me deeper."

The Fury lifted her majestic wings and fanned them between her face and ours. As she had suggested, a veil formed over my eyes, and I was once again disoriented. Blindly, I floated to yet another location within the mysterious kingdom of the Underworld. But I didn't really feel as if I were under anything—I didn't trust my own mind or senses at all anymore. My limbs ached resoundingly from all the walking, my stomach growled insistently, yet I could have sworn I was in a dream. Try as I might, though, I couldn't wake myself. I could only hold my breath and try to quell my pounding heart until the veil passed, leaving me in semirecognizable surroundings: a king's throne room.

It was not even as regal as Croesus's throne room and certainly paltry when compared to Lycurgus's. Only the drab wooden throne, flanked by sooty torches, gave us any indication that we stood in the receiving chamber of the king. The sickly torches revealed very little of our surroundings, and once again I couldn't tell whether we were in a palace hall or an immense natural cavity. All in all, my impression was that we had fallen into the cave of a disreputable exile, so dreary and impoverished was this place compared to the royal chambers of the surface.

Pelaphus and Alecto stood beside me. The Fury was so still she seemed like a statue; even her serpentine arms and legs barely twitched. In the immense silence, we heard footsteps approaching, and I could see Pelaphus's eyes darting from side to side, trying to find the direction of what he assumed would be an attack. Again, no attack materialized in this peaceful kingdom—instead, a smallish man with a bald head and wizened face strode out of the shadows, nodded formally to us, and took his seat on the throne.

Alecto spoke at once. "Visitors from the Outerworld, My Lord. The orator, Aesop, and the warrior, Pelaphus. They came directly from Babylon, and I had to conduct them beyond the veil."

"Thank you," nodded the little man, his voice warm and appreciative.

At once, Alecto bowed and snaked out of the room, leaving us alone with the little man in the simple black robe. "Congratulations," he said, waving his sleeve in our direction. "Few even attempt the trip down here nowadays, and even fewer succeed. Men no longer want to explain death, as they once did. Now they are content to ignore it."

"Then you truly are Hades," I replied. "And this is the Kingdom of the Dead."

"A quaint concept," smiled our host. "But I am the keeper of this place, also known as Hades. We are not as important as we once were, of course, but many souls still want to come here before moving on to a new existence." Hades motioned around the vast hall, and his voice took on a note of irony. "This is what you mortals expect when you die, so this is what you get . . . some of you."

Pelaphus, who looked as white as the flame in the center of his torch, could contain himself no more. "Your Deity!" he stammered, dropping to his knees. "It is by accident that we intrude upon your domain—please let us go back to where we belong!"

"But it's too late," shrugged the god. "Alecto brought you beyond the veil, beyond the place where a soul has need of a body. If the two of you weren't so stubborn, you'd realize you're already dead."

"What did we die of?" I asked, annoyed that I had apparently missed my own demise.

"Well, perhaps you aren't entirely dead," Hades admitted. "That can be remedied fairly quickly. The point is, you have already made the journey, and the Outerworld already thinks you're dead. Aesop, believe me, you are better off dead, accursed as you are by Apollo."

"What did I do to Apollo!" I wailed.

Hades clucked his tongue. "You disobeyed his edict that you remain a slave, you built a temple to the Muses and not to him, in which you erected a statue to Mnemosyne and not to him. Both you and Pelaphus insulted his emissary, the sphinx, and you worship the Muses and Isis instead of him. Apollo was complaining to Zeus about you just the other day . . ."

"Stop!" I screeched. "This is ridiculous! Apollo has never done *anything* for me except to proclaim himself my benefactor. Then he promptly sent a monster to try to kill me! All I ever wanted was to be free, and the Muses and Isis afforded me that chance with their generous gifts. Why shouldn't I pay homage to those who have done the most for me? Thanks to them, I have been the confidant of kings and the instructor of brilliant minds. I have known love and hate and every other emotion worth having. If you tell me I'm dead and I can find no way to disprove you, I'll accept that. But don't tell me I have to atone for the way I've treated Apollo! I've never done him half the wrong he's done me! In fact, I proclaimed a great feast in his honor the night we conquered the wolves, and I was on my way to Delphi to sacrifice to his Oracle. I'd like to honor Apollo, but he's given me more reason to hate him than thank him!" Exhausted by my tirade, I hunched my shoulders and stared repentantly at my feet.

"I'm inclined to agree with you," Hades admitted after a moment's thought. "But Apollo felt you should be content with your remarkable talents, instead of lusting after power and women. You're not here by accident, Aesop—you were escaping his vengeance. Believe me, I can make your death quick and painless down here and then send you to a place where gods are nothing but puffs of wind." Somberly, he rolled his eyes upward toward the earth. "Above us, Apollo has you at his mercy. Knowing that, does life still hold such attraction?"

"I once knew an old slave," I replied, "who had been worked like an ox all his life, with nothing but beatings as his reward. As usual, he was carrying a heavy bundle of wood up a hill, when he collapsed. Thinking he could go no farther, he called Death to come immediately. A second later, he looked up, and there was a skeleton in a long dark cloak, grinning down at the old man. 'You called me?' asked Death. The old man scrambled to his feet and struggled to pick up his bundle. 'Yes, I was wondering if you could help me put this wood on my back!' "

Hades chuckled, and his deeply creased face looked almost human. "I know how much you mortals value that fragile illusion you call a body, and it is true that a short candle burns brightly. But death is not the end of experience—it's the beginning of creation. If you would stay here with me, Aesop, I could teach you so much!" He shook his head sadly and gazed off into the flickering shadows. "Of course, this place holds few attractions, and I realize it. At one time, we had many visitors."

"We'll send lots of people down to you!" Pelaphus offered. "Live ones, dead ones—whatever you want. Just let us go back to the surface!"

The god looked pained. "Chances are I would just see you down here again, under much more unpleasant circumstances. Your friends, Hermippus and Lycurgus, are very anxious to find you."

"Let them find us," I said suddenly. "We'll deal with them.'

Pelaphus gaped at me. But Hades smiled knowingly. "That is your one other option. You can go back to Babylon to meet your persecutors, but I don't believe you'll find their reception as cordial as mine."

"Send us back," I insisted. "Neither Pelaphus nor I are going to die without a fight, each in his own way."

"Brave words," said the god of the Underworld. "I like

you, Aesop, and I shall try to put in a good word for you
with Zeus ... next time I see him. He doesn't come down
here very often either." Hades sighed with the weight of
his thankless job, then raised a long sleeve, which he
pointed in our direction. I could see no trace of a hand or
finger in the black swirls of cloth. "The veil of death is the
greatest of all mortal mysteries. Passing back requires
great energy, not just on my part but on yours. Think now,
the two of you, of how dearly you love life and how
dearly you wish to cling to your mortal shells. Think of
the seas and mountains, women and wine, and all the other
attractions of the living and try to place yourself in that di-
mension."

I closed my eyes and tried to envision the glory of
Samos on a sun-kissed day, with warm ocean breezes
blowing the purifying smell of the sea even to the island's
highest peaks. I saw the mysterious Fertility Rock, jutting
proudly into the sky, and I envisioned Netha, her serene
face in my hands. So vivid was my vision that I barely noticed that I was again floating in the dark ether, somewhere between living and dead, earth and sky. I knew
instinctively that I had to maintain my vision if I wished
to complete this difficult journey, and I lost myself completely in the memory of Netha's lovemaking, still sweet-
est of all. These thoughts brought immense longing to my
soul, and I began to weep over the foolishness which had
kept me away from Samos for so many years. Perhaps
Apollo was not the real villain—maybe it *was* my own
greed and ambition. Whatever it was, I cried for the loss
of the paradise I had so taken for granted.

"Wa-a-ah!" screamed Pelaphus, as we were dumped unceremoniously onto the gray cavern floor. I found myself
sitting on his chest, and I quickly scrambled off. At first,
I wanted to curse that subterranean charlatan, Hades, because we were still in the dreary catacombs, not the lovely
sun-drenched island I had imagined. But I quickly realized
that we were in the *outer* catacombs, the ones we had

walked to on our own power. In fact, we were surrounded by the strange kennels we had discovered.

"Wonderful!" cried Pelaphus, hefting his beloved sword and slashing the air a few times. "We have our weapons back, and our packs, and we can make our escape!"

Before I could rejoice, a low howl sounded directly behind us, and it was quickly joined by a number of other howls, forming the same discordant chorus we had heard on our initial foray to this spot. I knew the clawed footsteps couldn't be too far behind, and I had no desire to think about what came after that.

"You can wait for the dogs," I said. "I'll take my chances with Lycurgus." I immediately grabbed a torch and bolted back up the corridor.

"Wait! Aesop! Wait!" shouted the warrior. He waved his sword after me, but I could already hear the sound of growls and rapidly approaching footsteps. With several long strides, Pelaphus caught up to and passed me. "I can't let you go back alone!" he panted.

CHAPTER 19

Resurrection

Relieved to be heading up at last, I was cheerful as we trudged our way out of the catacombs. Pelaphus was glum, however, and I began to realize how bored he must be in the rarified atmosphere of Lycurgus's court. He was a man of action, a warrior, and he would rather be fighting and living off the land than lounging about on silk pillows, guarding the life of an aging potentate. Plus, in executing my escape, he had taken me under his protection and guidance; now he was forced to retrace his steps, the escape a failure. Though we hadn't found the secret passageway out of Babylon, I felt as if the trip had been entirely successful: I had met a god, a monster, and a three-headed dog—and lived to tell about it! More importantly, I had bought myself some time, and time can be very beneficial in matters of anger and the heart. I could only hope that Lycurgus would be as content with my immediate exile as with my lifeless body. At any rate, I no longer feared death so much. Hades had said he could send me to a place where gods were no more important than puffs of wind, and I was all for that.

Had I known what was transpiring in Lycurgus's throne room that very instant, my relief would have been total. Lycurgus was receiving an envoy from Nectanabo, pharoah of Egypt. Of course, Egypt had slipped somewhat from her glory days, but she was still a force in the world, especially in cultural affairs. Rightly or wrongly, every ruler on earth still felt inferior to a genuine Egyptian pharaoh.

I heard every detail of this conversation later, so I believe I can recount the scene with some accuracy.

"What!" Lycurgus roared at the serenely smiling Egyptian emissary. "Nectanabo refuses to pay the tribute he owes me?" Lycurgus glared at the man, then recovered his kingly demeanor and sat down. Those in attendance say they had never seen the king madder, even in the days when he personally led his troops into battle.

"Oh, the pharaoh will pay, Sire," gushed the emissary. "Five years' tribute as was agreed. He was very impressed by your engineering feat, and the irrigation canals worked as specified. You Babylonians are very skilled in the art of shaping water to your needs."

"We have many rivers," shrugged Lycurgus. "We simply observe how they work and channel the water into our deserts. But what has this to do with anything? Where is the first year's tribute?"

The Egyptian bowed humbly. "Nectanabo wishes to increase the bet to *ten* years worth of tribute if you will perform another task."

Lycurgus smiled slyly and leaned forward. "Double or nothing, eh? What is this task?"

"Something simple for your skilled magicians," purred the Egyptian. "Construct a tower which touches neither heaven nor earth."

Lycurgus shrugged and glanced around at his ashen advisers. "I don't believe that would be too difficult. All we would need are a few winged men. But I believe this should be a separate wager, not connected with the previous one. In other words, you pay me that first tribute, as agreed, and I will assent to the second one, the tower which does not touch the ground."

"I see," said the serene emissary, scouring his mind for

an alternative proposal. "If you will send a man to answer whichever question we pose, and winged men to build the tower, we will give you *twelve* years' tribute. If you cannot perform these simple tasks, you need only give us five."

"We will consider it," mused Lycurgus, rising to his feet, which indicated that the audience was over. Everyone in the room bowed, the Egyptian lowest of all, as Lycurgus swept out of the hall. Like a row of chicks following the hen, Hermippus and the other advisers traipsed after him. The procession wound its way silently through the palace to the king's bedchamber, where no one could hear them talking thanks to those infamous eight-foot walls.

"Winged men?" wailed Hermippus, flapping his arms.

Lycurgus looked crestfallen. "You mean, we don't have winged men? Our mythology is full of them!"

"Have you ever seen any?" countered the regent. "Even if we could find a way to build a tower which didn't touch the ground, why should we build it in Egypt? These accursed Egyptians are taking advantage of us, getting free engineering help for all their projects!"

"Twelve years of tribute could hardly be called *free!*" The king waved his arms helplessly and began to pace. "If only we had Aesop here to advise us!"

"Aesop is dead," Hermippus scowled. "And so is that traitor Pelaphus. We are better off without foreigners in court. I say we demand what is owed to us by the Egyptians and put an end to these pointless conundrums!" The other advisers quickly harrumphed their agreement.

"If only we had Aesop," muttered the king.

A knock sounded at the door. Annoyed, one of the junior advisers crossed to the door and admitted a palace guard. "What can you want?" he snapped irritably. "Can't you see, the king is in urgent conference."

"Extraordinary news," shouted the guard. "Aesop and Pelaphus are alive! They have been found just now, in the deepest part of the dungeons!"

After we bathed and changed our clothes—which, believe me, was a process long overdue—we were given an audience with Lycurgus at his private supper. Hermippus was nowhere in sight. The thought of poison crossed my mind as I surveyed the sumptuous spread of meats, fruits, wines, and pastries, but I decided I would prefer to die on a full stomach. Pelaphus decided likewise, so we scarfed down all the food in sight, as the king picked at a bowl of grapes.

"I wish I could eat like that," he sighed wistfully. "You know, I should order you both killed, but I'm too fond of you to do that again. At first, I was rather relieved to hear you had escaped. Then everyone kept telling me you were dead, that no one ever returned from the ancient catacombs below the dungeons. I didn't know what to think. But now you've come back, and you come at a most opportune time. These crafty Egyptians are trying to gyp me out of payment for a canal I built for them."

"Five years' tribute, right?" asked Pelaphus, his mouth full of pheasant.

"Yes," smiled Lycurgus, his aged eyes brightening at the thought of fine Egyptian jewelry. "To avoid paying, they want to up the ante to twelve years' tribute. All we have to do is build a tower which touches neither heaven nor earth and answer any question they choose to pose." He shrugged and looked down at his hands. "I thought, since you two owe me your lives . . ."

"We shall serve you anyway we can!" I chirped, my cheeks bulging with lamb.

"Then go to Egypt and bring me back at least one year's tribute and the pledge of more, if you can get it. That is really your responsibility, Aesop. You, Pelaphus, are to kill this jackal of a pharaoh if he refuses to pay. We'll let the world know what happens to those who welch on Babylonia!"

"Leave the collection to us," Pelaphus announced grimly.

"Twelve years' tribute isn't unreasonable," I added.

"Fine," nodded Lycurgus. He slumped back into his ornately brocaded dining chair, and the vibrancy drained from his face. A cascade of years descended upon him, and he coughed wearily. "Now tell me about the Underworld and to what I can look forward."

We told him about Hades and the veil and the Furies and the promise of a new existence upon death, which was really nothing but another form of creation. Lycurgus slept peacefully that night, and I was glad to have given him some comfort.

I spent three miserable months trying to train eagles to fly with boys on their backs. The thinking was: If we could produce the winged men Lycurgus had promised, then maybe we could convince the Egyptians we could build the tower, without actually having to build it. Exhibiting winged men ought to be worth *something*, we figured, and we would insist upon partial payment up front. Even Hermippus left us alone, realizing that someone ought to attempt to collect from the Egyptians, and it certainly wasn't going to be him. You may choose to believe this or not, but we actually trained four eagles to carry small boys aloft for short distances. We did it by clipping the eagles' wings and letting them grow accustomed to carrying the boys on the ground. Then, the theory went, as the eagles gradually returned to the air, they would take the boys with them. We went through several sets of boys and eagles trying to perfect this, but both species proved remarkably resilient.

Finally, with little in the way of good-bye or official ado, Pelaphus and I shoved off for Memphis. A crack squadron of the king's personal guard, handpicked by Pelaphus, came along to escort both us and the expected tribute. I can't say it was a particularly rough or interesting journey, because most of it was by boat. Many days, I stood on the bow of our sailing ship, looking out at the shimmering Mediterranean and thinking about Samos. At long last, the course of my path was as clear as the translucent sea: I would collect the debt from Nectanabo, paying off my own to Lycurgus in the bargain; then it was on to Delphi to sacrifice at Apollo's temple and study with the masters of that learned city; then home to Samos, there to remain for the rest of my life. No matter what riches Nectanabo offered to heap upon me, I was getting out of the royal emissary business.

When we entered the famed delta of the Nile, we were met by a regal barge. The Egyptians wined us and dined us and were exceedingly kind. And why not? We had just built them a wondrous canal system for nothing. But that was about to change. We took their food and drink, and I regaled them with fables, but we in no way considered them anything but the enemy. Pelaphus, in particular, took great care not to socialize; he was mentally preparing himself for the possibility of slaying the pharaoh, and he wasn't going to be dissuaded by anything like pity. He sharpened his sword constantly and kept an equally sharp blade in his boot. I remained hopeful that we could collect at least part of the sum owed us and avoid bloodshed, but I was prepared to beat a hasty retreat should diplomacy fail. Pelaphus had already insisted that I should have time to escape before he finished off the pharaoh, and I wasn't about to disagree with him. The pharaoh was supposed to be an immortal god, but I had no doubt that he would be a pile of linen in a sarcophagus should my cheerful friend decide to terminate him.

Illusion, of course, was also part of the plan. We kept the specially trained eagles in sumptuous velvet-lined cages, and soldiers guarded them from prying eyes day and night. Their riders we passed off as serving boys. I had my doubts whether anyone would be fooled by these "winged men"; but I had recently met a winged woman in the bowels of Hades, and she was very convincing. The Egyptians, in fact, were noted for preferring gods who had both human and animal features. They even thought Isis had a bird's head, although I knew differently.

As we floated leisurely up the Nile toward Memphis, Nectanabo must have been in conference with his royal advisers. I can well imagine what they told their trusting pharaoh.

"Don't worry about Aesop," they assured him. "We have a question so brilliant, so deceptive, that even *he* cannot answer it."

"What is it?" Nectanabo asked hopefully.

"Simplicity itself," answered the chief adviser. "We will ask him, 'What is there which we have neither seen nor heard?' "

The pharaoh's eyes glinted greedily. "Yes, and what is there which you have neither seen nor heard?"

"We have seen and heard everything!" grinned the chamberlain. "Because whatever he offers, we will say we've seen it and heard of it!"

Nectanabo clapped his hands and chuckled gleefully. "Excellent! He cannot possibly win! My advisers, you have outdone yourselves. When the Babylonians send us the booty, you shall all share equally!"

The advisers bowed to their pharaoh and smiled sneakily at one another. "Aesop will wish he had remained dead," whispered the chamberlain.

CHAPTER 20

Mysteries of the Pyramids

Our entire company stood on the deck of the ornate barge as it washed into the port of Memphis. From the shore, slaves showered us with orchids and lilacs, disguising the worst odors of the packed harbor. We looked beyond the morass of ships, dockworkers, and slaves, and gaped at the immensity of the monuments which decorated the lush valley. Greeks are accustomed to tasteful statues of recognizable humans, used to decorate gardens and the foyers of temples, but most Greek gardens and temples would fit *inside* Egyptian statuary, none of which looked remotely human. In the center of the port itself stood an imposing statue of Ra, with his bare legs, broad shoulders, and hawk's head glaring down at us. On a bluff overlooking the city sat two gigantic sphinxes; the temple they were guarding seemed almost an afterthought. Along the mountains which edged the valley, more winged gargoyles dwarfed their respective temples. Farther away, the great pyramids rose from the desert, looking like a mountain range carved by a god obsessed with perfection.

I wanted to jump off the boat and lose myself in exploring these remarkable monuments, but I had business to attend to. Pelaphus nudged me as the barge lumbered into its berth. "How long do you think we'll be here?" he asked.

I shrugged. "How long does it take to build a tower which touches neither heaven nor earth?"

"I may die here," said Pelaphus grimly, staring off at the awesome sights of the Egyptian capital.

"No, you won't," I answered. "The question is, once we win the tribute for Lycurgus, what do you want to do? Return to Babylonia?"

"No," snapped the round-faced warrior, shaking his head emphatically. "I'll never be fully trusted there again."

"Then come with me," I said. "I'm going to Delphi from here and then to Samos. I can't promise you much adventure or money, but I think you might find some peace of mind."

"Delphi?" Pelaphus mused. "Y'know, Aesop, I've never been there. Maybe the Oracle will tell me how to make a living without hurting people."

I clasped my friend's brawny arm. "Come with me. We've both made mistakes in our lives, but we're not doomed to keep making them. All it takes is the desire to change and grow. Delphi represents the last debt I have to repay before I can start living my own life—after that, I'll be truly free. Why can't you do the same?"

Pelaphus smiled ironically. "Seems like there's always one last debt either to collect or repay. I promise you, Aesop, if our business is concluded satisfactorily here, I'll go with you to Delphi and then to your precious Samos."

"Good!" I exclaimed, pounding the big man on the back. "Now, let's make sure they don't discover our 'winged men' before we have a chance to prepare them."

I couldn't believe it. For once in my life, my luck actually held. We were given sumptuous quarters with more than enough room to disguise the nature of the beasts in the covered cages. The Egyptians watched these cages with extreme interest as we unloaded them, and I again marveled at the way secrecy can often accomplish more than an army of soldiers and diplomats.

Pelaphus and I went in alone to see the pharaoh, having left the soldiers to guard the eagles. We tried not to let the splendor of the court dazzle us; as extraordinary a civilization as the Egyptians had, to us they were just freeloaders welching on a bet. We had no illusions that we were anything more than pawns in a game between kings, but we had the power and determination to end the game for good. Nectanabo reminded me of Lycurgus—a none too bright but personable politician who ruled by dint of looking good in the royal robes. Nevertheless, Nectanabo was a considerably younger and more energetic man than Lycurgus; he was still in the process of building up his empire and reputation, as proved by the unscrupulous gang of advisers with which he surrounded himself. Two of them in particular, a fat chamberlain and a callow youth who called himself chief adviser, studied me with unbridled hostility as I walked in, and I knew something of my reputation had preceded me.

I marveled at the way Pelaphus remained cool and nonchalant, letting me do all the speaking for us, while underneath plotting how many steps he would need to charge the pharaoh and lop off his head. The guards were numerous, but I suspected they could be taken by surprise; and I tried not to think of how many Egyptians Pelaphus would take with him before they cut him down. I appreciated the fact that Lycurgus had spared our lives, but sometimes I think Pelaphus took his loyalty too far.

"King Lycurgus sends his warm welcome and regards!" I announced to the pharaoh and his court, scraping the ground with a graceful bow. Pelaphus graciously joined me in this obsequious behavior, probably estimating how many Egyptian kneecaps he could split from the prone position.

An interpreter intoned, "The Great Almighty Pharaoh Son of Ra, Nectanabo, greets the emissary of Babylonia, Aesop!"

The pharaoh stood before me, blinding in a gold lamé

outfit which could have been worn by Elvis Presley in his prime. He moved stiffly, trying to support a solid gold headpiece which crested into a swooping crown. "Rise, Aesop," the pharaoh spoke, stretching his arms like the rays of the sun god he represented.

We rose, and I indicated Pelaphus. "This is my comrade, Pelaphus, Captain of the Guard." I knew they would assume he was my personal bodyguard and nothing more.

"Where are the winged men?" the pharaoh asked snidely.

"Back in their quarters, resting for their labors," I replied matter-of-factly.

"I am Lord Kriptin," said the fat chamberlain, "and we have reports that the birds arrived in cages."

"Not birds," I said. "Birds would be ill-equipped to perform the skilled labor needed to build the tower. What you saw were closed litters, not cages. Our winged men are very well treated."

The hall erupted in quizzical whispering, and I knew these superstitious Egyptians wanted to see what was in those cages more than just about anything. That's one thing I quickly loved about the Egyptians: their wild imaginations. Their golden jewelry was also quite fetching.

The handsome chief adviser smiled like a viper. "We have heard much of your prowess and wisdom, Aesop, but we doubt the existence of these winged men."

"The winged men are very real," I replied, taking a deep breath. "Much more genuine than the promises of Nectanabo."

The hushed whispering was no more, and the throne room erupted in shocked cries. The interpreter quickly restored order, his big voice booming, "The pharaoh is speaking! The pharaoh is speaking!"

But he wasn't really speaking, he was studying me intently, probably measuring my resolve. To him, this was a game; and he had only lost once and was playing with the house money. "We realize we have incurred a debt. We only wish a chance to erase it with another conundrum."

"A man once formed a friendship with a fox," I replied, "and they took up housekeeping together. As soon as winter came and it got cold, the fox noticed that the man often blew on his hands. When he asked him why he did that, the man said he was just trying to keep his hands warm. Later, at the dinner table, the man took some hot porridge in his spoon and blew on it, and the fox asked him why he did that? To make it cool, the man explained. At once, the fox got up from the table and started out the door, saying, 'I'm sorry, but our friendship is over. I can't trust a man who blows both hot and cold from his mouth.' "

The hushed crowd didn't dare to laugh or even breathe, until their stone-faced pharaoh spoke, "Then you don't trust me, it's as simple as that. Very well, let's simplify this entire matter: Forget about building the tower between heaven and earth—I'll have my own winged men do it. But we would like to meet your winged men, to compare them with ours. The wager becomes simply this: If you answer the question we shall pose, we agree to pay Lycurgus and Babylon ten years' tribute, two years' tribute to be paid immediately. If you *cannot* answer the conundrum, you will nullify our debt to you and agree to pay *us* five years' tribute."

"I agree to that," I said instantly.

Nectanabo glanced back at his advisers, who smiled rapaciously. When he turned back to me, he sneered, "Are you ready to hear the question?"

I agreed, "This is as good a time as any."

In order to make sure I heard the conundrum correctly, the pharaoh motioned to the interpreter to perform the honor. He intoned importantly, "What is there which we have neither seen nor heard?"

"What is there which we have neither seen nor heard?" I repeated. The pharaoh nodded slowly and sagely, mimicked by his advisers. I thought of the fable of the dancing monkeys but decided I'd better save it for another occasion. "A worthy conundrum," I replied instead. "I shall return in three days to answer it."

The obnoxious chamberlain leaned forward. "Why do you need three days?"

I shrugged, "To see the pyramids."

Toward sunset, Pelaphus and I walked in the Valley of the Kings, surrounded by towering monuments, the pyramids making a surreal backdrop. Three Egyptian guides followed discreetly behind us, and several less obvious spies, disguised as shepherds and camel drivers, moved ahead of us and parallel to us. I whispered to Pelaphus, "Approximately how much is ten years' tribute?"

Pelaphus scratched his dimpled chin. "It could consist of goods, gold, slaves, or even women. Measured purely in gold, I would say ten years' worth is about ten thousand talents of gold."

I whistled. "That's a lot of money."

"The cost of a pharaoh's neck," Pelaphus observed sanguinely.

Ahead of us, the pyramids shimmered so brightly in the salmon-colored sunset that I could swear they were made of glass. They looked like sleek icebergs jutting from the desert floor. I found my step quickening as I was drawn in the direction of these giant obelisks. Pelaphus silently followed, and we began a determined march toward the pyramids. Our Egyptian guides hurried up to us and began jabbering that it would be dark before we reached them, but we just shrugged and kept on walking.

It *was* dark by the time we reached the nearest pyramid. I couldn't imagine how inflated an opinion a man must have of himself to build such a thing, but I could certainly admire the results. The workmanship was extremely impressive, and I could barely see the seams between one level of stone and another. Of course, in those days, the pyramids were covered with metal sheets which kept the weather and vandals at bay. Today, an Egyptian pyramid is still impressive, but compared to its former glory, it's like the skeleton of some extinct animal. Pelaphus and I walked around the base of this immense monument, not speaking a word to one another. Our guides and watchers stood in the shadows at a discreet distance; they must have recognized our need for this private communion with the pyramids. A silver moon cast ample light upon the hallowed site, and I could feel the presence of great mystery. Egyptians didn't build these things just to amaze men, I thought; they built them for the gods. The pharaohs, I reminded myself, were supposed to be divine, but that didn't entirely explain the unspoken power of the obelisks they built. Perhaps the pharaohs themselves had no idea what wonders they had wrought—I could certainly attest to the way the gods manipulated humans to their own designs.

While I wandered, lost in my own thoughts, I failed to notice that Pelaphus had apparently wandered off in another direction. And so had our escort. In other words, I was totally alone in the ghostly shadow of the great pyramid. (Even in the darkest night, something that big makes a shadow.) Pelaphus and the guards were only around the corner, I told myself, and all I had to do was walk over there. But as soon as I started to reverse my steps, a weird force gripped my legs and held them, and I staggered against the pyramid. The ground shook directly under my feet, and a comet seemed to streak out of the sky and barrel directly toward me. I covered my eyes as the light exploded into a shower of sparks. When I opened them, I saw a handsome and ageless woman, bathed in a radiant glow which seemed to pulsate from the stars.

"Hello, Aesop," the goddess purred. "Considering how you've flirted with death lately, you look very fit."

"Isis!" I fell to my knees and clasped my hands. "Finally, all is to be well!"

Isis frowned and looked oddly melancholy. "I don't know about that, Aesop. Contrary to popular belief, I cannot see into the future. You have powerful forces allied against you."

"Then watch over me, Isis!" I begged. "I've already quit seeking personal gains—I only want to go back to Samos."

The goddess shook her head knowingly. "As always, Aesop, you want too much. Nobody, not even a god, can go backward in time. Your special place is now the future."

Well, at least I have a future, I thought with relief. A second later, I finally remembered my manners. "But excuse me, Your Graciousness, I don't want to appear ungrateful. If you never did another thing for me, I would worship you eternally for freeing my voice, which enabled me to free myself."

"We'll see how much you'll want to thank me," she replied. "At any rate, I'm glad you were able to come to my home, the bed of the Nile. Wondrous things have been done here, secret things the likes of which will never be seen again. But the Egyptians are too worldly now—forgetting the spiritual path and becoming more like other men and women." She glanced worriedly behind her. "If *he* finds me here, it could go badly for you."

I snapped, "Why doesn't Apollo show himself? If I could only reason with him . . ." I shook my fists in frustration.

"He doesn't have to show himself, so he doesn't," she sighed. The shimmering light around Isis began to waver, and her face grew sadder and older. "I have taken great pleasure in your doings, Aesop, and I am proud to have been of assistance to such a noble orator."

I'm afraid I began to weep, and in the blink of a teardrop, the blinding light of Isis disappeared. I never saw her again, except in my dreams.

After three days of uneventful sight-seeing, Pelaphus and I returned to the grand palace to answer the pharaoh's question. During those three days, I had been observing Egyptian art and had become a real enthusiast, so I studied the typically bizarre murals as we strode through the anterooms and hallways of the palace. I couldn't help noticing that the dog-headed god of the Underworld, Osiris, looked vaguely familiar.

Pelaphus jostled my arm. "What should I expect?" he whispered.

"Expect them to be mad," I admitted, as a sea of spectators parted before us. We strode up to the pharaoh's dais and bowed, causing the pharaoh to grant us a nod. "Mighty Nectanabo, we have returned with an answer to the conundrum."

Nectanabo smiled confidently, and I could see his advisers struggling to look disinterested. Finally, the fat chamberlain stepped forward and sneered, "What is there which we have neither seen nor heard?"

I turned to the king. "I presume, Your Highness, the 'we' in this case are your advisers?"

"Yes," said the pharaoh impatiently. "Now what is it?"

"This piece of parchment," I said, producing the cheapest scrap of parchment I could find. There was a tiny bit of writing on it.

"We've seen it!" crowed the fat chamberlain.

"We've heard of it!" snapped the smug chief adviser.

"It's not news!" they cheered. "You lose!"

The pharaoh looked at me and shrugged. "They've seen that."

"I'm so glad they have," I replied, showing the piece of parchment to the interpreter. "Because this is a pledge from Nectanabo to Lycurgus promising to pay ten thousand talents of gold. Upon demand."

"No, no!" sputtered the pharaoh. "I wrote no such pledge!"

"But your advisers have just verified it, saying they've seen and heard of it."

Nectanabo turned to his advisers and shook with rage,

berating them with the foulest epithets I am ever likely to hear in Egyptian or any other language. I could sense Pelaphus tensing for battle beside me, or maybe he was just convulsed with laughter. Whichever, I could not bear to look at him for fear that I might burst out laughing. Mercifully, the interpreter took it upon himself to read the note aloud, and his booming voice soon drowned out the pharaoh. I gathered that no one in the court was all that unhappy to see these popinjays bested, and they had still got their money's worth with the canal system. I also still intended to give them a show with the winged men.

Nectanabo collapsed onto his throne. "All right, Aesop, you have won. I shall arrange for immediate payment. But please, Aesop, I cannot afford to deal with the Babylonians while you are in their employ. I am willing to offer you substantial inducements to switch your allegiance over to me."

"Thank you, Sire," I bowed, "but I have an even better plan which will cost you nothing. Guarantee Pelaphus and me safe-conduct to Delphi, and I will promise never to work for another monarch or potentate for as long as I live."

"Done!" announced Nectanabo. "But your men and the winged men . . ."

"My soldiers will accompany the gold back to Babylon. And the winged men will give an exhibit in front of the great pyramids at sundown today!"

A cry went up in the throne hall, and we were surrounded by appreciative courtiers, soldiers, and even advisers. Over the din, I heard Nectanabo shout, "We must have a feast in honor of Aesop! Start the feast!"

I must say, our Winged Men Show was better by far than anything I saw in Hesiod's circus while I was employed there. Those four boys were the bravest acrobats I have ever seen and, having triumphed over a multitude of dangers and obstacles, richly deserved their moment of recognition. More for them than anyone else, I arranged the show in front of the pyramids for the pharaoh and his guests. The boys' mounts were noble beasts, too, the largest and strongest tamed eagles in the known world. Carrying boys since chickhood, the eagles didn't seem to mind the extra weight and inconvenience, but they were still prone to unpredictable dips and swoops which could dump an unwary boy several feet to the ground. Needless to say, the boys were very careful not to let the eagles soar too high, and they kept a close watch on their endurance.

I purposely chose sunset as the hour of our demonstration, knowing the dim light would give away less of our tricks. Also, the setting of the great pyramids at sunset was bound to enhance what I hoped would be an awesome spectacle. I had my soldiers set up a viewing area for the Egyptians, who were glad to cooperate, considering they were getting the show for free. Then I had the covered cages containing the eagles brought to the rear of the farthest pyramid, where I had more soldiers guarding against prying eyes. The pyramid itself served to mask the preparations, which included outfitting the eagles with reins and lifting the boys upon their backs. Pelaphus oversaw these operations, while I waited with Nectanabo and the rest of the audience, hoping that the show would get under way while there was still light enough to see it.

While we waited, I entertained Nectanabo and his party with a fable. "This is a story," I began, "of a flute player who had been traveling for many days and was very hungry. He came to a stream and could see fish swimming in the waters. Being a very talented flutist, he thought he could play his flute and make the fish come out to dance, whereupon he would grab one for his dinner. Though he played with skill and charm, the fish ignored his music. So the man wove himself a net, cast it into the stream, and pulled out dozens of fish, which he dumped upon the bank. As he watched them flop and wriggle about, he sighed, 'You are truly dumb creatures. You don't dance when you hear music but only when you are dying.' "

"That's a sad fable," Nectanabo observed. "It's about death."

"It's about many things," I replied. "I choose to think the fable tells us to have fun and enjoy ourselves when we have the opportunity. It is too late for dancing when we are headed toward death."

"We Egyptians don't believe in death in the usual sense," said the pharaoh. "We believe it is a passage to another lifetime."

It's a passage, I thought, but to where I wasn't sure. Before I had a chance to debate this topic further, a glimmer of movement appeared in the richly hued sky over the pyramids. I pointed excitedly, "The winged men—there they are!"

The regal audience gasped in unison, then seemed to hold their collective breath as four astounding creatures darted skyward between the sleek tips of the pyramids. I gasped, too, for I had never seen the boys fly their mounts so high and with such reckless verve. This was their sole performance, and they were going all out! My heart swelled with pride for their achievement. Even the most cynical observer could see nothing more than a flash of powerful wings and lithe male torsos. My mind flashed back in time to the first appearance of the sphinx, winging leisurely toward our caravan over the Phrygian desert. These boys and eagles had the same grace and confidence, and they put on an exhibition of unified flying that would shame a flock of geese!

I glanced at Nectanabo and his closest advisers; they smiled with wonderment, and many of them had tears in their eyes. Despite all the half-human/half-beast creatures in Egyptian mythology, I doubted if many of them had ever seen one before. Today's exhibition would give their artists and storytellers inspiration for years to come. I toyed briefly with the idea of taking the Winged Men

Show on the road, appearing before all the crowned heads and so on, but I knew in my heart it was a one-time phenomenon. To attempt such a dangerous undertaking on a regular basis for financial gain was sure to tempt retaliation from the gods. As it was, I couldn't help but feel that even the gods applauded the incredible achievement of these brave boys and their noble eagles.

The show ended all too quickly, but it ended with a flourish. The flyers soared to the tip of the very highest pyramid, hovered there for a moment, then began to make lazy circles around the pyramid. They picked up speed until one was right on the tail of another, and the flyers soon blended into a sweeping blur, like a flying serpent chasing its own tail. Down the glimmering face of the pyramid they raced, the furious beating of wings now audible across the still desert. No one dared to breathe. Almost in unison, the last rays of the sun and the last winged man disappeared, leaving the Egyptians gasping and applauding.

"Bravo! Bravo!" screamed Nectanabo. He clapped so hard his mammoth crown nearly fell off. "I must meet them, Aesop! I must see them again!"

I bowed apologetically. "I am sorry, Your Highness, but that isn't possible. As you have no doubt surmised, the winged men are magical beings—even I do not converse with them. They cannot be coaxed into performing more than once every hundred years or so."

The pharaoh looked crestfallen, but he managed a smile. "Aesop, you have more than fulfilled your obligation to both Lycurgus and me. Lycurgus must indeed be the greatest monarch on earth to command both your allegiance and that of the winged men. Not only will I pay ten thousand talents of gold immediately, I shall continue to pay tribute to Lycurgus for as long as I live, and my armies are available for the defense of Babylon whenever he so ordains."

I bowed much lower. "The Almighty Nectanabo is generous indeed."

The pharaoh cocked an eyebrow. "If you would change your mind about coming to my employ, you would see how generous I am."

"I'm sorry," I said with a touch of real regret, "but I have urgent business in Delphi, and I have not seen my homeland in many years and many miles of wandering."

"I can understand that," Nectanabo smiled. "My royal barge will take you and your companion there personally." He then astounded me and everyone watching by touching my hump with warm regard. I had never heard of a divine pharaoh touching an unclean cripple. "Aesop, we shall forever revere your name, as I have heard they do in Greece, Babylonia, Lydia, and the rest of the civilized world. In Egypt, the name Aesop will be synonymous with wisdom and truth."

I took flight as well, only this time I was fleeing *to* something rather than away. On the same day that Pelaphus and I bade good-bye to the soldiers who would be taking Nectanabo's tribute to Babylon, we set sail in an Egyptian barge destined for Delphi. This parting from my royal guard was much less painful than parting had been from Obares and the soldiers of Croesus, for we had been through so much together. My best friend, Pelaphus, was coming with me, and the only other Babylonians I would miss were the brave boys who had ridden the eagles to such acclaim. Had it been up to me, I would have awarded them the entire ten thousand talents of gold, but all I could do was write a letter to Lycurgus praising their efforts on his behalf and hoping he would reward them handsomely. As for myself, I needed no money—I was thrilled to have finished my duties as emissary and have my life my own again.

As on the previous cruise, I stood on the bow of the boat for hours on end, watching the sea swirl and the clouds billow. When it rained or the wind blew heavily, I merely crouched in a bulkhead or threw a bit of tarpaulin over my head. I never tired of watching the sea's endless turmoil and listening to the shriek of the wind. At times, I thought the sea and the wind conspired to whisper words to me, words like, "Delphi. I am here. Come to me." But I dismissed those thoughts as the product of an overly active imagination. Still, I felt the tremendous draw of our destination, the hallowed home of the Oracle. Delphi.

Pelaphus, who didn't overly care for sea travel, usually stayed below nursing a queasy stomach, but one afternoon he joined me on deck. "How can you stay up here so long?" he muttered. "And what in Hades' name are you looking for?"

"In answer to your first question," I replied, "on my first journey by sea, when I was still a slave, I noticed that the sailors who worked on deck were never sick, while the passengers who stayed below always were. I am a great believer in confronting a nemesis rather than hiding from it."

"All right," the warrior nodded grudgingly, "I can see some wisdom in that. But what are you searching for?"

I sighed, "The one place where peace and reason prevail. Do you think Delphi is such a place?"

"I don't know," shrugged the hefty giant. "But the Greeks say Delphi is the center of the world."

"I know the story," I agreed. "Zeus released two eagles, one flying east and one flying west, and they met at Delphi. Thus, he knew that Delphi was the center of the world. I feel both attracted to the place and obliged to go there. I have told you about the Delphian who warned us of the wolves and saved our lives."

"Yes," Pelaphus answered. "But that's not the only reason you're going. What do you expect to find there?"

"I don't know," I admitted. "A question, an answer, an event. There must be scholars and centers of great learning in such a place. I have never been a great believer in fate, but in this instance I am positive I am meant to go to Delphi."

"The Oracle is supposedly worth the trip," Pelaphus said cheerfully. "You can learn your fate from her."

"My fate is to return to Samos," I said hopefully. I turned back to look at the sea, wondering if there would be some answer for me there.

"Delphi," it whispered. "Delphi."

CHAPTER 21

Delphi

We could see the city of Delphi from some distance out to sea; it commanded an imposing fog-enshrouded cliff which plummeted to a phalanx of huge jagged rocks. The crashing of the sea against these rocks did little more than sharpen them into deadly spears, and I noticed that the captain of the Egyptian barge gave the rugged shoreline a wide berth as he looked for a place to dock. We watched the ancient city as we glided slowly past, but all we could see in the fog were the vague outlines of thick columns jutting into the gray clouds and vanishing. Finally, the captain, who had no knowledge of this dangerous coast, gave up his search and commanded that we be put ashore in a dinghy.

The air was cold and misty as we stumbled from the little boat into freezing surf, our luggage on our heads, and staggered ashore to a tiny spit of sand. I turned to wave good-bye to the departing Egyptian sailors, but they had already been swallowed up by the encroaching fog. For the first time, I realized that I had grown accustomed to marching into strange cities at the head of an entourage of hundreds of soldiers and attendants, and I had mixed emotions about our humble arrival. The chill in the air and my sopping clothes did little to lessen my doubt. Perhaps I should've returned to Babylon and convinced Lycurgus to send me here as part of a diplomatic mission. But I hadn't—I had just dropped in.

I turned to Pelaphus and shrugged. "This is a rather inauspicious start."

Pelaphus scowled. "I had forgotten why I left Greece in the first place—the lousy weather!"

"The islands are beautiful," I countered, "especially Samos."

"Don't start with me about Samos," he growled. "If you had wanted to go there, we could have gone there first. But you wanted to come here."

Yes, I thought to myself. Why had I done that, when I had longed to see Samos with every waking breath? Was coming to Delphi really part of my destiny? Not necessarily, I argued—I was merely honoring an obligation to the Delphian who had saved my life. I hadn't gone to Samos first, because I didn't ever want to leave home again. There was actually very little mystery about my purpose here; I would simply sacrifice at the temple in the Delphian's name, then go on about my business. Curiously, I thought of how few times in my life I had made sacrifices to the gods, though I had been "privileged" to meet several of them. Ah, well, I decided, perhaps devotion is best left to the unprivileged.

Pelaphus jabbed my arm. "Come on, let's go meet the Oracle."

"Yes!" I exclaimed with false cheer. "Let's also find a fire and get something to eat!"

By the time we reached a road, the sun had peered from the clouds and was giving the indication of providing some warmth before the day was over. We were cheered considerably at this sight and were even more encouraged to see a substantial two-story building on the road just ahead of us. Even more blessedly, the building appeared to be an inn, and the outlines of the city were visible just beyond it.

Our step quickened as we sauntered up to the welcoming structure. The door was wide open, and we heard raucous laughter booming from within. "They have wine, I bet!" grinned Pelaphus.

They did have wine, and also five or six scruffy patrons who studied us with obvious interest as we walked in. The bartender waved jovially. "Pilgrims? Here to see the Oracle?"

I shrugged, supposing we could claim no other distinction. "Yes, but we are hungry and thirsty."

"Then you have come to the right spot!" beamed the jovial innkeeper. "We also have rooms for the night—much more reasonable than those in town."

"Well, I don't know about that," grinned Pelaphus, engulfing a barstool. "But I do want a goblet of wine!"

Every bartender I have ever seen pours first, then holds out his hand for payment. But this one did it in reverse order. "That'll be ten denarii, in advance, please."

"Ten denarii!" snarled Pelaphus. "I don't want a *case* of wine, just a goblet!"

Meanwhile, one of the scurvy patrons had sidled up to me. "You'll be needing a goat to sacrifice at the temple. I got some lovely ones, very reasonable."

"No thank you," I replied.

"I got some chickens, too. Work just as well."

"No," I said forcefully. "I don't want any."

"Cheapskate!" the Delphian snapped.

"Let's get outta here," growled Pelaphus, grabbing my arm. We were out on the road a second later. "That's another reason I left Greece!" he wailed. "High prices!"

"I'm sure we'll do better in town," I said, pointing to the noble city ahead of us, glimmering in the emerging sun.

Delphi did have some very pleasant buildings and sumptuous residences, but one could hardly see them for all the stalls and vendors lining the street. Every stall was piled high with filthy cages crowded with half-starved animals, all loudly protesting their condition in life. There were squawking chickens, bawling calves, bleating goats, mewing cats, braying asses, and vendors and merchants who made nearly as much noise. Those shops not selling sacrificial animals were selling food or religious trinkets, and the smoke from the barbecues nearly gagged me. What a commerce, I thought to myself—if the animals died before being sold for sacrifice, they were merely slapped on the barbecue.

Luckily, we were not the only pilgrims wandering around in a daze, so not every vendor had time to assault us. Pelaphus got distracted by some scantily clad ladies hanging from a balcony, and before I knew it, he had vanished and left me with the luggage. I wouldn't have talked to anyone at all, except for the fact that I wanted to find the temple. I knew from experience Pelaphus would be occupied for hours, and I thought I could finish with my business and be back in time to get out of Delphi before nightfall. I had no desire to stay a minute more than necessary, and I no longer expected to find any scholars in Delphi, unless they were for sale in cages.

"You a pilgrim?" hissed a man of about my height. "Need a room for the night?"

"Yes, I suppose so," I lied, thinking I might get some information from a man of such noble stature.

"My brother's got the best rooms in the city," he whispered. "Only eighty denarii a night."

"Eighty denarii!" I shrieked in astonishment. That was considerably more than I had ever been worth as a slave. "That's terrible!"

"Whadya mean?" the dwarf snarled. "That's also the *cheapest* in the city." He scowled and walked away. "Stupid pilgrim!"

A dazed young man wandered past me, and I reached out my hand to stop him. "Excuse me, sir, do you know the way to the Oracle?"

He stopped, blinked at me, and, when he realized I

wasn't trying to sell him anything, came out of his coma. "Sure, go to the top of this street and take a right up the hill. Look for some tall columns."

"Thank you," I said, starting off.

"But you can't go there now!" the man called after me. I stopped. "Why not?"

"Because it's closed on Tuesdays."

I shook my head incredulously. "Closed on Tuesdays?"

"Thursdays and Saturdays too," he shrugged. "But this is the slow season. In the summer, it's open every day."

"Is this Delphi?" I finally asked.

"Sure, what did you think it was?" he laughed. "But look, you don't have to go to that Oracle. I know a guy who runs an oracle on the other side of town that's just as good. A lot cheaper too."

I blinked in amazement. "You have to pay to go to the Oracle?"

"Not unless you want to wait around for a few days. But if you slip the priests a couple of denarii, you'll get in a lot faster."

"I can't believe this!" I gasped. "Why does anyone come to this foul place?"

"Reputation, man," the stranger muttered. "Nothin' but reputation. I don't like it here myself, and I'm trying to get enough money together to go to Athens. You ever been to Athens?"

"No," I said dazedly, backing away. I wandered off down the street. In my stupor, I collided with a young woman.

"Watch it!" the girl snapped. She looked like she would be pretty if she ate more regularly.

"I'm sorry," I said. "I'm a bit dazed."

"Could you spare a couple of denarii?" she asked. "I'm waiting for this job to open up."

"What kind of job?" I wondered.

"As a priestess at the temple of Apollo!" she beamed

proudly. Then she frowned. "You're supposed to be a virgin, but I hear they don't check it too closely."

I gave her a couple of denarii and started to wander off again, more glum and dispirited than I could ever remember being. Then I felt a familiar tug on my hump; to my great relief it was Pelaphus.

"What are you doing here?" I asked.

"You wouldn't believe how much those strumpets wanted!" he wailed.

"Yes, I would," I said through gritted teeth. From the corner of my eye, I saw a pedestal that supported a statue which had been broken off at the knees. Those two forlorn calves sticking up in the air seemed to represent all that was rotten about Delphi, and before I knew what I was doing, I found myself climbing the pedestal and waving my arms.

"Delphians! Delphians!" I screamed. "Listen to me! Listen to me, you scum!"

Even with all the noise and activity on the street, a hunchbacked dwarf screaming insults at the top of his lungs was bound to attract some attention. Several vendors and pilgrims turned around to face me.

"Get off of there!" one of them shouted. "Who do you think you are?"

"Aesop!" I shouted back.

"Sure, and I'm Homer!"

Several of the rabble laughed in hearty approval, and I decided to address not this one scoundrel but every Delphian within reach of my lungs. "Yes, I am Aesop the fabulist. Even your little children, if you have any, know my name and recite my fables. I had intended to come here and perhaps deliver a series of lectures, but now I'll deliver just one. Delphi is like a piece of driftwood floating on the sea—it looks like something worthwhile from a distance, but when we approach it we see it has no value whatsoever. I now know the true meaning of the Delphic Oracle. Greed! Ask it a question, and it screams, 'Pay me!

Pay me!' You prey upon the helpless pilgrims who have been duped into coming to this worthless scavenger's den. Well, no more! From this day hence, wherever I go throughout the world, I shall tell every person I see about the abomination that is Delphi! In a year's time, not so much as a cockroach will venture into this city."

I jumped down off the pedestal into a sea of stunned faces, sliced through them, and marched up the street. I could hear the murmurings behind me, but I walked so hard in my anger that even Pelaphus had a difficult time catching up with me.

"Aesop!" he whispered. "Was that wise? They far out-number us."

"We are leaving here immediately," I seethed. "I shall do the minimum offering of some incense at Apollo's temple, then we are gone!"

Dutifully, Pelaphus followed me up the hill, keeping a wary eye on our rear and a beefy hand on the hilt of his sword. He had good reason for such precautions, I saw, as a mob of Delphians followed us all the way. They looked far too cowardly to attempt anything physical, especially with Pelaphus glowering at them, but I knew we wouldn't be safe until we got far out of town.

I realize Apollo's temple at Delphi was renowned in ancient times for its beauty and grandeur, but I was too angry to give it much more than a cursory inspection. Twelve huge columns formed a ring around a circular courtyard, the floor of which was inlaid with intricate marble designs and dominated by a statue of the deity himself. Urns and sacrificial braziers surrounded the statue of Apollo, which was black from the smoke of centuries. As befitted the sun god, the temple was open-aired, a feature which allowed the almost constant burning of animals, incense, and torches. At the rear of the temple, dour priests guarded the entrance to a natural cavern which housed the Oracle, I assumed. Despite the fact that the Oracle was taking the day off, a line of chanting pilgrims waited patiently with their luggage on a crude stairway which led down from the cave to the sea. Their chants and the bleating of the animals were all but drowned out by the constant thunder of the breaking waves.

Pelaphus and I took incense from our luggage and started walking toward the massive statue of Apollo. At once, we were confronted by brawny attendants who pointed to our luggage. Not having anything of value in the bags, we let the attendants take them. One of the priests pointed toward Pelaphus's sword, but he just smiled and shook his head. I gave the priest a few coins from my pocket, and that seemed to satisfy him. I turned to Pelaphus and shrugged, "That's my cash offering in honor of Jhubal of Delphi. Let's make our offering to Apollo and be gone."

We shouldered our way past the animals and pilgrims to the rear of the statue, where we found a small brazier which wasn't in use. The sickening smell of smoldering animal flesh guaranteed that our worship would be brief. I knelt and lighted my incense, and Pelaphus did the same. I looked up at the huge blackened thighs and hindquarters of Apollo and shook my head sadly. "We could have been friends instead of adversaries. All I ever wanted was my freedom."

At once, a monstrous wave crashed against the cliff and spewed water hundreds of feet into the air, drenching the waiting pilgrims and the floor of the temple. I looked down at my incense—it had been doused.

Pelaphus got to his feet and shook the water off his robe. "Let's get going," he said worriedly.

"Right." I stumbled to my feet, slipping on the wet marble. Unwarranted fear chasing us, we rushed from the temple and would have left our luggage there had not the attendant chased after us and thrust the bags into our hands.

Pelaphus gave him a small tip. "May Apollo be kind to

you," the priest smiled obsequiously. "Especially you, Aesop."

The priest slithered away, and I gaped at Pelaphus. "What did he mean by that?"

"Who knows?" the warrior shrugged. "These are all strange ducks here. I'll be glad to be rid of them."

"We can go south to Phocis," I said, "and get a boat from there."

"I don't care where we go," snarled Pelaphus, "as long as we get away from *here.*"

Despite our hunger and thirst, we made no effort to stop until we were far from the stench of Delphi. If that was the center of the world, I thought ruefully, I was happy to stay on the outskirts. We purchased some wine and cheese from a farmer who offered to let us sleep in an empty silo, as night was approaching. Needless to say, we were both exhausted from our adventures of the day and glad for the peaceful respite of the farm. I fell asleep with the sweet aroma of fresh-cut hay in my nostrils, and it reminded me of the sun-drenched pastures of Samos. I slept peacefully that night, dreaming of the island I so longed to see.

So deep was my sleep that I didn't hear the soldiers at all as they surrounded the silo, not even as they opened the squeaky door and thrust swords under our chins. Pelaphus, too, was taken totally by surprise, a mortifying experience for the seasoned warrior. In fact, we had slept so peacefully I wondered if our wine had been doctored. I saw Pelaphus eyeing his blade propped up against the wall, and I knew he was estimating what his chances would be in a fight. As we had not been run through and nothing was stolen, I presumed this was simply a case of mistaken identity. Or maybe they just wanted to question us. "Let's see what they want," I cautioned Pelaphus.

"Right," the big man grumbled. "Do you boys have a good reason for waking us up?"

The captain of the soldiers shrugged disinterestedly, but

his men didn't move their sword tips one centimeter. "A charge has been made against you—we only wish to see if it has any merit. You are Aesop, are you not?" he asked.

"Yes," I replied. "But what charge can possibly have been made against us? We've only been in this country for one day!"

"But you went to Delphi," said the captain, picking up our luggage. He shook the heavy linen bags. "Are these your bags?"

"Yes," I answered. "But what can you want with our bags?"

He opened the drawstrings of Pelaphus's bag, turned it upside down, and began to shake it. "The Delphians say that a sacred golden cup is missing from their temple. They are very particular about such things; you might even say obsessive." While he talked, he had emptied Pelaphus's bag upon the ground. He poked through the huge garments with his sword.

"Not in your luggage," he said to Pelaphus. He hefted my slightly smaller but newer bag. "Your bag is heavy," he smiled.

"Not with golden cups," I replied.

The captain loosened the drawstring and inverted the bag. A few rags of clothes tumbled out, along with a gleaming golden cup.

"Oh, shit," I muttered.

I saw Pelaphus clench his jaw, and I knew the lives of every man in that cramped silo were in immediate danger. "Let my companion go!" I barked, defusing the tension. "His bag was empty!"

"No!" growled Pelaphus. "We are innocent, both of us!"

"A court will determine that," said the captain. "But I see no reason to hold both of you." He motioned to Pelaphus. "You are free to go."

I could see Pelaphus didn't want to go without taking the smug captain and several of his soldiers with him, and where he intended to take them there would be no return.

I gripped my friend's brawny arm. "Go, Pelaphus. Go and get word to Xanthus on Samos to come to my aid. He can defend me."

Pelaphus gritted his teeth and shook his head. "I don't want to leave you."

"I don't want you to go," I admitted. "But we can't get help if both of us are in a cell. Go. Find Xanthus."

Pelaphus snorted angrily and turned back to the captain. "Where are you taking him?"

The captain cocked an eyebrow. "Back to Delphi."

CHAPTER 22

The Trial

I was marched straight back to Delphi in the darkness, allowed to speak to no one, and shoved underground in what appeared to be a wine cellar, minus the wine. The dark if spacious cavern reeked of olives, and the only exit was up some creaky stairs to a heavy wooden door which was bolted from the other side. I paced most of the first day and ate a few pears someone had been considerate enough to toss in. Nobody came to talk to me, and I fought the temptation to scream for attention. There is nothing quite like a silent jail cell to cause a person to think, and I came to the conclusion that I had been arrogant in my approach to the Delphians. After all, scoundrels have to have a place to live as well as decent folk. And certainly this wasn't the only place on earth where the religiously devout were fair prey for hucksters. I would make my peace with the Delphians when given the chance, I decided.

That opportunity came on the second day of my captivity, when four aged priests were escorted into my cell. They turned up their noses at the musty smell and looked at me as if I were somehow responsible.

"Hello!" I said cheerfully. "I'm glad to have a chance to speak to someone!"

"You had no trouble speaking your mind in the public

square," the most cadaverous of the priests remarked, as his fellows smiled approvingly.

"I spoke rashly," I admitted. "I was weary from a long journey and hunger. Surely, you didn't take me seriously!"

"We take attempts to impugn the name of Delphi very seriously," intoned the tallest priest.

"What could I do to Delphi?" I laughed nervously. "I, a simple storyteller!"

"Not so simple," responded a third priest. "You are world renowned as a distinguished orator, an orator with a biting tongue, I might add. People listen to you."

"No one listens to me!" I scoffed.

"No one will have the opportunity," smirked the final priest.

"Wait a second," I said desperately, "I am willing to make my peace with you and rescind what I said. Let me speak to the Delphians in the square again, and you'll see I mean what I say."

"We could be certain that you will speak highly of us while you are here," the elder priest observed. "But elsewhere, we would have no control over your wicked tongue."

The gravity of my situation was beginning to sink in. "Wait a minute, what are you planning to do with me?"

"Try you for stealing the sacred cup from Apollo's temple," answered the tall priest.

"But I'm innocent!" I protested. "I never saw that cup before."

The priests shrugged in unison, and I could tell they were oblivious to such mundane details as justice where matters of civic pride were concerned. "What is the punishment for this crime?" I muttered.

"Death," said one.

I gasped, "For stealing a *cup?*"

"A *sacred* cup," they reminded me.

I dropped my pretense of cooperation and glared at them. "Before you decide to kill me for speaking my mind, let me tell you a story: A fox was trying to make his escape from a hunter, and he scurried up a wall. Suddenly, he slipped and grabbed hold of a brier bush to stop his fall, but the thorns cut his legs and flanks and were worse than the hunter's arrows. 'Dear me!' he shrieked, 'I am worse off now than I was before!' The brier bush answered him, 'Yes, my friend, you made a bad choice when you laid hold of me, for I lay hold of everyone myself.' "

The eldest priest snarled, "Are you threatening us?"

"I have many friends among the rulers of the earth—Croesus, Nectanabo, Lycurgus—and they could squash this little burg like a walnut."

"So they could," the priest admitted. "That is why your trial will be public and straightforward. No one can accuse us of unfairness, not with the evidence we have against you."

"False evidence!" I shrieked. "That cup was *planted* in my luggage!"

"We shall see," smirked the fourth priest.

I forced myself to remain calm. "All right, if I must have a trial, who are to be my judges?"

"Why," smiled the eldest priest, "ourselves."

I was kept underground in that cellar, secluded from all, until the day of my trial. I hoped against hope that Pelaphus would be able to find Xanthus and bring the elegant scholar to defend me, but I knew there was no way he could bring Xanthus there from Samos in less than a fortnight, even by the swiftest sailing ship. Perhaps, I told myself, I should have sent him to fetch Croesus, who could have come to my rescue with an army, but that, too, would have taken the better part of a month. I had some faint hope that word of my unjust imprisonment had spread on its own accord and that some higher authority would prevail upon the Delphians to set me free. Unfortunately, there was no higher authority in Greece at this time than the Oracle, through whom it was said Apollo himself spoke. Would that *I* had a chance to speak with the god—I would have given him an earful!

These thoughts only served to depress me and remind me of my sublime stupidity. Had not my friends, Pelaphus, Xanthus, Netha, and even Isis, warned me constantly of Apollo's growing resentment? Instead of avoiding the god's wrath, I had come to his very den and insulted those who owed him their livelihoods! No dog or monkey in any of my fables had ever behaved so stupidly. Though I could now curse the Delphian, Jhubal, for planting the seeds of my undoing, I could hardly blame him for the brutish way I had behaved. I could have simply sacrificed at the temple with the hundreds of other pilgrims and gone on my way, cursing the Delphians under my breath instead of to their faces.

The other irony of the situation was that my own fame had doomed me. I certainly wasn't the only pilgrim to become indignant at the Delphians' greed, but I was the only one who could make good a threat to disrupt their slimy commerce. Aesop, the Great Orator, I thought with disdain. He can advise kings, teach boys to fly, and hoodwink a pharaoh out of ten thousand talents of gold, but he can't manage to keep himself out of trouble on a simple visit to a temple. Still, I wondered how many others had fallen prey to the "sacred cup in the luggage" routine? No matter—it didn't ease either my mind or my plight to think that others had been similarly mistreated. Freedom, the one commodity I valued most of all, was again lost to me.

Is true freedom too much to ask? Why should this, the simplest of concepts, be so hard to attain and even harder to hold? Forget money—people are much more jealous of another person's freedom. They'll do anything to take it away. Usually the freedom-takers are so intent upon denying others that they have no freedom themselves and, thus, cannot control their jealousy. It's a vicious circle, one from which I had yet to find an escape.

In the middle of rambling thoughts such as these, the

door was unbolted and soldiers came to take me to trial. I have always admired the professionalism of soldiers, even if it is often misdirected, and these soldiers on hire from Athens were no exception. Their orders were not to speak to me as we walked, and they didn't. They did laugh, however, when I told them this story:

"Do you know how stupid I've been?" I asked rhetorically, shaking my head. "There was once a very simple farm girl whose mother was always accusing her of having no sense. One day, she walked outside and saw the village idiot coupling with a mule, and she said, 'What are you doing?' 'I'm putting some sense into her,' the boy replied. The girl immediately got a bright idea and lifted her gown. 'Would you put some sense into me too?'

"Not questioning his good luck, the idiot threw off the mule and deflowered the girl. Later, the girl was overjoyed when she returned home and told her mother that she had finally acquired some sense. Her excited mother asked how and was told a man had injected her a with long sinewy pink thing. 'My child,' wailed the mother, 'you've lost what little sense you had!' "

Once I had the soldiers laughing, I finished off the story and them. "Of course, their child has since become the regent of Athens."

With difficulty, the soldiers rearranged their grins by the time we reached the tribunal, held—where else?—in the temple of Apollo. The tribunal did indeed consist of the four dour priests, with numerous other priests from other temples and cities in attendance. Ostensibly, I was told, these additional priests were here to verify to their home provinces that Aesop had been given a fair trial. I seriously doubt whether any of them knew how trumped-up the charges were.

Several witnesses testified that they had seen me slip into the cave—past several priests, I might add—and emerge later carrying a bag. When the sacred cup was found missing, they sent a detachment of soldiers after me.

And we know what they found. No mention was made of my outburst in the square or the fact that the attendants had my bag the whole time I was near the temple. I was pictured as a penniless wayfarer, which, unfortunately, I was. My fame did little to offset this impression; even in those days, famous poets and storytellers were often penniless. The case was cut-and-dried. Open-and-shut.

I testified as to the truth, but what chance did I have against all those righteous priests? I had impugned Delphi before; denying the priests' story was like impugning the word of Apollo. I'm surprised the Oracle herself didn't come out to testify against me. Of course, I had been the one to send Pelaphus, my lone witness, away, and that was another act which now appeared somewhat imprudent. I had no character witnesses, since no one in the region knew me—though I could have had kings and gods speak on my behalf in other realms.

After a respectfully polite deliberation, the priests returned to their benches, and the eldest rose to speak. "Aesop, we find you guilty of blasphemy and temple thievery, the punishment for both of which is death. Sentence will be carried out tomorrow morning. Because you do not deserve the dignity of a funeral, you are to be cast alive from the cliff into the sea."

Into the rocks, was more like it, I thought glumly. "Am I allowed any final words or requests?" I asked.

"Final words, yes," said the priest. "Final requests, only if they are reasonable."

"My request is simple," I said. "If you have a temple or shrine to the Muses, I wish to visit it."

They could hardly deny me a religious request, and they didn't. "Very well," muttered the priest. "Now speak your words and be gone."

This lot was not about to escape a fable. "A frog and a mouse once struck up a friendship, and the mouse invited the frog to his house to eat. Wishing to prove himself just as generous, the frog invited the mouse to the pond and told him to dive in, that they would get their dinner at the bottom. When the mouse said he couldn't swim, the frog said it was easy, and he tied their legs together so that they might swim in unison. Of course, the frog reveled in the water, but the mouse only lived a few seconds before he drowned. With his lungs bursting, the mouse said to himself, 'I may be dead, but I'll repay this little trick.' Sure enough, when the mouse died, he floated to the top of the pond, dragging the frog with him. A hawk saw the mouse and grabbed it for his dinner; he was so delighted to find the frog attached, he ate them both."

The elder priest slammed the table and rose imperiously to his feet, his taffeta robes bristling. "Take him to the Shrine of the Muses, then lock him away until tomorrow."

I finally found something in Delphi I liked, the shrine to the Muses. Had I gone there first, I might have avoided much unpleasantness. The shrine was some distance out of town in a peaceful glade of flowering trees. Freshly painted white, the little wooden pagoda wouldn't have stood out in a community park in Illinois. At the center of the shrine was a statue of Mnemosyne, mother of the Muses. In this respect, it must have looked exactly like the shrine to the Muses I asked Croesus to build for me in Lydia. Though I left Lydia before its completion, I'd heard the shrine was quite a popular spot for the artistically inclined, and an amphitheater was even constructed nearby. Since it looked as if I would never again see that or any other shrine to the goddesses of the arts, I was very relieved to have discovered this tranquil oasis, if even for a few moments.

The soldiers, trusting me and trusting their ability to run down a hunchbacked dwarf, left me fairly alone in front of the white picket shrine. I bowed down on my knees; tears welled in my eyes, and my voice cracked, "Whatever wrongs and mistakes I may have committed in my life, they were worth it to experience freedom, both of voice and soul. I thank you so much, goddesses of free expression, for granting me the ability to have seen and done so much. The age of fifty is not such a terrible one to go beyond the veil, and I have had more than my share of adventures, romance, and friendship. Take word to Apollo that I don't hold him so much at fault as I hold my own arrogance and stupidity. Ah, yes, grant as many blessings as you might, dear Muses, you cannot erase man's foolish pettiness."

For a moment, through the haze of tears, I thought I saw nine lovely ladies dancing slowly in a circle in a field beyond the glen. Their feet were bare, and they wore the simplest peasant dresses of autumn colors such as brown and rust. Though the women danced with languid movements, their dance was sad and slow, and their long hair shrouded their faces and brushed against the weeds when they bent low. Holding hands, they circled once in each direction, then they stopped, lifted their hands to the sky, and vanished as the sky opened up with a sudden downpour. I wiped the tears and rain from my eyes and stumbled blindly after them, but the soldiers gripped me before I got more than a few steps. They carried me away like a pile of rags.

CHAPTER 23

Friends of Aesop

I dreamed that night that my winged men, the Babylonian boys and their swift eagles, swooped down to rescue me as I plummeted from the cliff. When I awoke, still in my dark clammy cell, reeking of earth and olives, I knew that the Babylonian boys were either back in Asia or on a ship somewhere in the Mediterranean. They were not likely to come swooping out of the sky tomorrow morning when I needed them.

As I blinked awake, I realized that it wasn't my pleasant dream that had awakened me, it was the unfamiliar sound of voices outside the heavy door. Shouting voices, angry voices, one or two of which I joyfully recognized. Pelaphus! Xanthus! They were arguing with the soldiers, obviously demanding to be allowed to see me. But some leather-lunged soldier was matching them shout for shout. Suddenly, an eerie female voice cut through the muffled din, and all the shouting stopped. The voice, which I also knew, laid it out in no uncertain terms: "You let us in to see Aesop, or I will turn you all into pigs!"

Netha!

In the dark of night, an argument such as this from a wild-eyed sorceress carries a certain amount of weight. The door suddenly opened, and I scrambled up the stairs, shrieking, "My friends! My friends!"

But it was a big soldier, who pounded me in the chest and knocked me halfway down the stairs. "You get back—they're comin' down! And they'll stay there 'til mornin'!"

When the guard got out of the way, Netha scampered down first. She looked more beautiful, simple, and frightening than ever, and I didn't think she had aged at all. I took her in my arms and wept for joy! Neither one of us could safely speak, so we just clung to each other.

As Pelaphus and Xanthus reached the staircase, the door was bolted loudly behind them. Luckily, Pelaphus was carrying a torch, or we would have been plunged into total darkness. Xanthus, who was thinner and more stooped than I remembered, warmly embraced me. "Aesop! Thank Zeus we're in time! Tell us what we can do to free you?"

"We can't fight our way out," scowled Pelaphus. "They took my sword, and they locked us in!"

"Is there another way out?" asked Netha.

"Oh, my friends, my friends!" I wept. "Let me just feast my eyes upon you before I relay the pathetic details." I took a deep breath. "The trial was yesterday, and I was convicted of blasphemy to Apollo, a charge I really can't deny. Come the dawn, I am to be thrown from that huge cliff where the temple sits. Don't tear your hair and gnash your teeth, I'm somewhat reconciled to the fact now."

"There must be a way to appeal!" Xanthus raved. "What kind of court?"

"A religious one," I shrugged. "There isn't any other kind around here. I've been caught in a trap, partly of my own making and partly of Apollo's."

"You're innocent!" growled Pelaphus. "Somebody's got to listen!"

"I'm innocent of stealing the cup," I agreed, "but I'm guilty of being arrogant and stupid."

"I'm more arrogant and stupid than you are," snapped Xanthus, "and I'm not being killed for it!"

I smiled at my friends and embraced each one in turn. They just clung to me, as the reality of the situation began to sink in. "Sit down, all of you," I said. "Permit me to tell you a story. They have kept me isolated for weeks, and you know how I like to have somebody to talk to."

Masking their emotions with uncertain smiles, my friends lowered themselves upon the cold ground of the earthen cell. Xanthus stared at me and wrung his frail hands, and I was shocked to think that nine years had elapsed since I had last seen him. Netha glared disconcertingly at me, and I wondered how I could get rid of Xanthus and Pelaphus to keep her alone for the night. Unfortunately, it didn't seem possible. Pelaphus just scowled and slammed a mighty heel on the earthen floor, digging a substantial hole in no time. Undoubtedly, he could have tunneled out of this cell in a matter of days. I, on the other hand, had spent my time thinking, just thinking, and I had invented a new fable which I wanted to tell my friends.

"In days past when animals spoke the same language as men, a lion was lying ill in his cave. He said to his best friend, the fox, 'If you want me to recover and live, use your honeyed tongue to get that buck deer who lives in the forest to come within reach of my claws. If I eat the brain and heart of that big buck, I'm certain to get well in no time.' The fox went off and found the buck frisking in the woods. He joined in his play, saying, 'I bring good news to you, Sir Buck. You know that our king, the lion, has taken ill and is near death. He has been considering which of the animals is to reign after him. The pig, he says, is senseless, the bear is lazy, the leopard bad-tempered, and the tiger's a braggart. The buck, he says, is the best animal to rule, because he is tall and long-lived, and his horns frighten the snakes. So, Sir Buck, he wishes to discuss with you the transfer of power and other matters of state. If you will listen to the advice of an old fox, I think you should come back with me and stay with him until he dies. That way, the other animals will know that you are the official successor.'

"The deer was so taken with conceit that he went to the

lion's cave without a whit of suspicion. As he poked his head into the entrance, the lion got anxious and pounced too soon; he only succeeded in tearing off a bit of the buck's ear. The deer beat a hasty retreat to the woods and hid deep in the thickets, while the fox moaned that he had wasted his time. 'Please try again,' begged the lion, 'I'll perish if you don't.' The fox, not having too many friends, decided to help the lion one more time. Following the drops of blood, he tracked the deer to the thickets, but the buck lowered his antlers upon seeing him and said, 'Foul liar, go back to your master, or I'll run you through!'

"Replied the fox, 'Are you are such a miserable coward that you won't even let the lion come close to you? The lion is short of breath and only wanted to whisper in your ear his last advice and instructions. But you could not even bear a scratch from the paw of a poor sick creature! And now he's angry at you and is thinking of making the wolf king! You don't want that scoundrel to be king, and neither do I. Return to the lion and don't be afraid. If you take a moment to study him, you'll see how sick he is. I swear by the holy crown of the forest, the lion and I only want to select a capable king.'

"Once again, the idea of being king of the forest was too much for the conceited buck, and he happily followed the fox back to the cave. The lion pretended to be deathly ill and unable to speak until the buck bent close to his mouth; as soon as he did, the lion pounced and made a meal of him, swallowing bones, marrow, entrails, and all. But the little fox made off with one tasty delicacy, the brain, and had gulped it down before the lion noticed it was missing. 'Where is the brain?' growled the lion.

"The fox replied sadly, 'In truth, the poor beast had no brain. How else could you explain his walking into the lion's den twice in one day?' "

Pelaphus, Xanthus, and Netha spent the entire night with me, and it was a memorable evening of camaraderie, nostalgia, and bravery. Xanthus and Netha told stories about my escapades on Samos, and Pelaphus described our descent into Hades and sojourn in Egypt. I filled in about Croesus and the trek from Lydia to Babylon. The Athenian guards took pity on us and slipped a wineskin through the door, and we had an even better time. My friends were still toasting me when the first light of dawn crept through the slats of the door, and we heard movement and voices outside.

"I can jump the guard," Pelaphus whispered, "and grab his sword. I'm sure we stand a chance if we can reach the shore and get a boat . . ."

"No," I said forcefully. "You'll not sacrifice your lives on my account. These Delphian priests are very efficient in their business, and their business is to keep the pilgrims and the money flowing in. You won't stand a chance fighting them, and I won't let you try."

"When you leap off the cliff," said Xanthus, "we can have a boat waiting for you . . ."

"You obviously haven't seen the cliff," I replied. "The rocks are like giant spear points. I'll be dead before I hit the water."

Only Netha grasped the reality of the situation. "Aesop's bag of tricks is empty," she admitted, "and we all know it. The best we can do is let him die with dignity and honor, as befitting a great orator."

I hugged her with gratitude, then turned to Pelaphus and Xanthus. "My good friends, don't you think I know how much you want to save my life? But the Delphians are even more intent upon taking it. I knew something was going to happen to me in Delphi, but I didn't know what. Now I know, and I've come to accept it. Maybe I'll finally find the freedom for which I've searched."

Punctuating the last syllable was the unlocking of the bolt, followed by the grating of rusty hinges. We looked up to see a soldier motioning to us from the open doorway, his form silhouetted in the silver glimmerings of a new day. "Aesop, you come up here first!"

I stepped up the stairs somehow knowing what they had in mind—I only hoped Pelaphus wouldn't be too mad. As soon as I was clear of the door, the soldier slammed it shut and bolted it before my companions had a chance to react. I could hear their muffled cries of outrage and the thudding of Pelaphus's shoulder against the heavy wood, but I was almost relieved not to have to endure the inevitable good-byes.

"We don't need any scenes, do we?" the captain winked.

"No, sir," I agreed. "But you are going to let them out after I . . . afterward?"

"Of course," nodded the captain. "Shall we go?" He pointed to the western horizon and the bluff which rose over the city, dominating it literally and figuratively. A new orange sun blazed between the twelve massive columns of Apollo's temple, and it looked imprisoned by them. Both the Sun and the Earth must spend half of their lives in darkness, I told myself, and why should a mortal's life be any different? Thinking back on my own uncomfortable tenure as commander of troops for both Croesus and Lycurgus, I began to have some sympathy for Apollo. I knew that a leader must perform acts for the good of the established order which he may personally find reprehensible. I thought of the way I had forbidden liberty to the Lydian troops for eight months of torturous marching, all the while making slaves carry me in a litter. Perhaps Apollo didn't personally want to kill me, but he couldn't ignore my public disobedience to his will.

I was very calm, considering I was walking to my death. Delphians lined the route, but they weren't jeering and taunting me as I expected. Most just stared, fascinated as always by the specter of death; others openly wept. I suppose in each man or woman is a love of liberty and justice which cannot be subjugated by injustice even when the injustice is to their benefit. In the faces that I passed, I saw sorrow, hatred, envy, resignation, and confusion. Our lives are always at the whim of mysterious forces, and nothing so reminds us of that fact as the sight of a clearly innocent man walking to his execution.

At the cliff, there was no sign of the priests who had condemned me, and I suppose they had their own penance to serve that day. As always, soldiers were given the unpleasant duty while the politicians hid. I was relieved that Pelaphus was locked safely away, for I knew that he could never observe my death without tossing a few of the soldiers over the side with me, and I had no desire to see either his life or theirs shortened.

It was entirely too beautiful a morning to die. The sun was shimmering in a golden carpet across the undulating blue of the sea, and not a wisp of a cloud obscured the view of the gods, should any of them have cared to watch. I heard the breakers groaning against the jagged rocks below, but I preferred to watch the sea at its endless horizon, a sight I had never beheld until my thirty-fifth year of life. Now, fifteen years later, the sea was to be my grave, and I found that fitting, having spent so much of my final years sailing from one end of it to another. The captain of the soldiers offered me a blindfold and also offered to have his men gently hurl me, but I declined both offers. Fifteen years ago as a mute slave in Phrygia, I would have welcomed death as just another injustice in an unjust world—now I had more for which to live but also more for which to die.

I leaped.

The wind was brisk and stirring against my face, and I must have been brave for leaping headfirst. I didn't feel brave, however, and kept my eyes screwed tightly shut. Therefore, I didn't see the winged companion flying close beside me until she gently wrapped her serpentine arm about my waist. I blinked my eyes and saw Alecto, the Fury, smiling at me with her aged weathered face. She whisked her wing over my head, and I never saw or felt the rocks.

AUTHOR'S NOTE

As with most ancient Greeks, not too much is really known about Aesop, although three points appear irrefutable. Aesop passed some time on the island of Samos, he traveled widely to places like Babylon and Egypt, and he was thrown off a cliff in a public execution at the city of Delphi. The probable year of his death was 540 B.C. So many Greek historians have written of these incidents that we have to believe them; Aesop's distinguished biographers include Herodotus, Aristophanes, Plutarch, Plato, Socrates, Babrius, Phaedrus, and Heraclides Ponticus. Some of my retelling is based upon an anonymous Egyptian version of Aesop's life written in the first century A.D.

RETURN TO AMBER...
THE ONE *REAL* WORLD, OF WHICH ALL OTHERS, INCLUDING EARTH, ARE BUT SHADOWS

ROGER ZELAZNY

The Triumphant conclusion of the Amber novels

PRINCE OF CHAOS   75502-5/$4.99 US/$5.99 Can

The Classic Amber Series

NINE PRINCES IN AMBER   01430-0/$4.50 US/$5.50 Can
THE GUNS OF AVALON   00083-0/$4.99 US/$5.99 Can
SIGN OF THE UNICORN   00031-9/$4.99 US/$5.99 Can
THE HAND OF OBERON   01664-8/$4.99 US/$5.99 Can
THE COURTS OF CHAOS   47175-2/$4.99 US/$5.99 Can
BLOOD OF AMBER   89636-2/$3.95 US/$4.95 Can
TRUMPS OF DOOM   89635-4/$3.95 US/$4.95 Can
SIGN OF CHAOS   89637-0/$3.95 US/$4.95 Can
KNIGHT OF SHADOWS   75501-7/$3.95 US/$4.95 Can